T0128565

The Chameleon's Bite

George Thomas Smith

AuthorHouse™
1663 Liberty Drive
Bloomington, IN 47403
www.authorhouse.com
Phone: 1-800-839-8640

First published by AuthorHouse   11/16/2011

ISBN: 9781467870245 (sc)
ISBN: 9781467870238 (e)

Library of Congress Control Number: 2011960708

Printed in the United States of America

Any people depicted in stock imagery provided by Thinkstock are models, and such images are being used for illustrative purposes only. Certain stock imagery © Thinkstock.

This book is printed on acid-free paper.

DEDICATION

This story is dedicated to all those who have felt their lives were ruined and totally lost. There is a way of salvation and transformation.

Contents

INTRODUCTION

The Chameleon's Bite is the story of misplaced patriotism, governmental deception, international intrigue, Special Forces combat, and the diabolical entrapment of a young American man who believed he could escape the bad environment of his youth and at the same time do something good for his country by joining the military. Because of his exceptional ability with languages and his skill as a marksman, Tomas Bernardo was recruited for Black Ops missions that took him to several countries to eliminate certain "targets."

What seemed to be legitimate military assignments morphed into a clandestine, off the books series of missions for an unofficial group that had connections with people in high government positions. Tomas Bernardo was too naïve to see through the deliberate deception until he discovered he was the pawn of a killer-for-hire organization.

When Tomas realized what he was involved with, his family and friends were threatened in order to assure his silence. Undeterred, he set about to uncover the workings of the shadow group that had deceived him and its association with what he believed to be a sleeper agent in the Whitehouse.

After being critically wounded on a mission to Afghanistan Tomas made attempts to change his life and escape the trap in which he found himself. This led Bernardo into a harrowing dash for freedom to a location where he put together what he knew of the illegal actions headed up by Colonel Tag Tagart. It became a fight for survival for Tomas.

The story begins with Tomas Bernardo on his first Black Ops mission in Afghanistan. His target is a leader of the Taliban.

CHAPTER ONE

TARGET ACQUIRED

A star-filled darkness draped itself over the barren, rocky surface of the Afghanistan moonscape. Nine thousand feet above the cold sands two black suited men plunged toward earth until it was time to open the equally dark, maneuverable chutes. Special Ops sniper Tomas Bernardo, who often went by the code name, Angel, and his spotter teammate, Troy Yeager, silently blended with the blackness of the desert as they dropped to a safe landing aided by their night vision equipment. The air was cold, but they took no notice. They had a job to do and the execution of that mission was foremost in their thinking.

There was no one more skilful with various means of rendering a target inoperable than Tomas Bernardo. His specialty was a sniper rifle. Strapped to the bodies of the two men was all the firepower they needed to accomplish their mission. Tomas and Troy unfastened the chutes and equipment, slipped out of the black jump suits, and buried everything except their weapons and emergency rations. They immediately cleared the area and hiked through the night to a position of safety where they could wait for the daylight and then reposition closer to the ultimate location the next night.

*   *   *

Three long days had passed since the two men arrived in theater. The daytime temperatures at the high mountain altitude were comfortable but the nights were cold. The two marines found hiding by day very boring, but necessary. Now, they were hunkered down in concealment behind several large rocks. Three hundred yards below and another five hundred yards southeast of their location was a series of one story earthen houses containing several Taliban fighters. Within that group of men were five terrorists; at least that is what Intelligence indicated. The Special Forces operatives were betting their lives that they could pick out their one target among the whole gathering, make the kill, and escape along a predetermined route to a zone where they would be extracted by helicopter.

Bernardo and Yeager were dressed as Afghanis, including beards and turbans. Two men who looked like they belonged and traveling light would draw much less attention than a whole squad of soldiers. Moving about only at night, they had managed to arrive at the edge of the target area. That is when the waiting game really began. At some point, they expected the VIP for whom they were looking would show himself in the open. Others had tried to take him out and failed. Unmanned drones came close to blasting him into oblivion, but Gunung Klabat, a name adopted from a volcanic mountain in Indonesia, had left the house ten minutes before the missile landed. The man's inclusion in the hierarchy of Al Qaeda clearly demonstrated the global connection of the terrorist organization with the Taliban.

The plan for the sniper team would be to make the kill, fire a couple of rocket grenades toward the compound to add confusion, followed by a covering air strike from a Predator drone, and then put as much distance between themselves and the Taliban as possible. If everything went as planned, they would be miles from the compound when the helicopter snatched them away from any enemy fire. There was always an "if" to such operations.

On the second morning of concealment, just as daylight broke over the arid scene and the sun peeked from behind the low brown foothills, a tall clean shaven man emerged from the central house along with three others who were each being very attentive to him.

"Is that the target?" Troy couldn't get a good look at the man's face.

Tomas answered, "According to the description I have, he must be the one."

"Are you sure?" The spotter again looked through his monocular.

Through the rifle scope, the sniper also took a long look. "If he would just give me a profile, I could verify."

Just then, the target turned to speak to one of the other terrorist.

He didn't hear the fatal shot. His head exploded and he dropped like the lifeless corpse he was. A moment later the sound caught up with the bullet and the Afghanis, who were stunned for only a few seconds, began to scurry about like ants, weapons in hand, and scouring the hillside for something at which to shoot.

From the cover of the rocks, Tomas and Troy fired two grenades for effect. Tomas plugged the barrel of the sniper rifle and dropped it as they made their escape down the back side of the high ground where they had been positioned.

"Tomas, you left the weapon!"

"Right! And the first guy who tries to fire it will eat shrapnel! I can't run with it and my M-16."

Keeping as low to the ground as they could, the two men put distance between themselves and those enraged Taliban who were in hot pursuit. "Jabba. Do you read?"

"I read you, Angel."

"Touchdown! You can spike the ball!"

Ten seconds later an air to ground missile arrived to complete the job and give more cover for the sniper team. They would have to make it to the predetermined extraction zone in six hours. It had been set far enough from the scene of destruction that roving Taliban might not interfere with the rescue. That meant doing all they could to be invisible in the daylight and then arrive at the zone at nineteen hundred hours. Survival until then depended on their training and their wits.

The day passed and twilight began to crawl across the land as the Americans found some concealment. They needed to rest before the final push to the zone.

"Jabba, this is Angel. Jabba, do you read me?"

"Angel, we read you. How goes it?"

"You hit a home run. I say again, home run, Over."

"See you later, Angel. Jabba out."

Troy had a question: "Tomas, why risk us on this job and still send a missile?"

"They needed verification and the best way was for us to eyeball the kill. The heavy stuff was just in case we missed."

"But what if our target hadn't been there?"

"There were enough bad guys to justify the action. I leave those decisions to the guys with brass on their hats. Let's find a place to get some cover!"

✳   ✳   ✳

Out of nowhere five Taliban converged on the sniper team. A rock tumbled down the slope from above their position to alert the Americans and they came up firing. A tumult erupted filling the air with the staccato sounds of the exchange of AK-47s and M-16s. Bullets whined off rocks and kicked up dirt. There was no place to go for a safer position. The Taliban fighter above Tomas and Troy took hits in the chest and rolled on down, landing between the two men. One down; four to go.

Another Taliban took a head shot that ruined his day. The other three Taliban chose to withdraw, but that left the Americans open to every other bad guy who might have heard the blasts of small arms.

"We've got to clear this area." Tomas motioned for Troy to move left in the opposite direction from the last position of the enemy. "There's bound to be a crowd around here in no time!"

"Jabba! Angel calling. Come in!"

"What's up Angel?"

"We've been spotted and are making tracks to Florida."

"We read you Angel. When you reach Miami give us an update."

"When we reach the beach then we'll go see Santa. Out!"

Troy surmised, "I'm guessing all that means we're moving south and then work our way back north."

"You know it, Troy. And fast!"

The Taliban were now between the Special Forces pair and the zone they needed to reach where they were to be extracted. After an hour of making a wide arcing swing southeast and then around to the southwest, Tomas and Troy had bypassed the blocking group. The enemy had no idea where the sniper team needed to go. It could be assumed that the Afghanis were scouring east of the skirmish area and were unaware that the Americans had circled back around to go north to the EZ.

The task at hand was for Tomas and Troy to hide out within a twenty minute fast march to the pick up zone. The very busy day was coming to an end. The two men found a cleft in a wall of solid rock and wedged themselves into it. They improvised some cover to disguise their presence. The time for moving on to be picked up could not arrive soon enough for them. It was a difficult and cramped place to wait it out.

4

Tomas began to think about what had led to his involvement with Special Forces and the missions to which he had been assigned. He had a strong desire to serve his country and had poured himself into the grueling training that eventually turned him into a man as hard as steel; not only physically, but mentally and emotionally. He had been a rather normal kid and teenager. He played many sports, but never pushed himself to be the best he could be in any of them. For him, sports were just a means of having fun. Others could take it seriously if they wanted to continue playing in college, but Tomas was from a family that couldn't afford to send him to college. His father was an Italian American who managed a grocery store and the young man's mother was a Puerto Rican immigrant who cleaned houses. Since the teenager wasn't totally committed to making a name for himself in sports, nor did he have the academic credentials, scholarships were not available.

Enlistment in the Marines seemed be to the only way Tomas Bernardo could find a little adventure and get three square meals a day without getting into the trouble like so many young men in his neighborhood had done. Their three squares, if they lived long enough, were provided by the penal system. Tomas was too young for service in Desert Storm but the attack on the twin towers in New York motivated him to want to see some action. He came up with the idea that he could be most valuable if he had some skills that were more unique than the men around him. In that way he would stand out from the crowd and be noticed.

Tomas had a knack for picking up languages. He could converse a little in several, but didn't know the nuances of the grammar of any. The young man determined to learn as much as he could independently and then listen well to how others spoke. That method gave him the street language and that was more valuable than correct grammar. Tomas wasn't planning on conversing with college professors or linguists.

The low ranking military superiors overlooked Tomas Bernardo because of his Puerto Rican ancestry. He had been accustomed to some prejudice in civilian life and it was no different in the military. He and his kinsmen often got the lesser assignments. Because he spoke English, Spanish and Italian and had ability for mimicking accents, Tomas decided that he would study as hard as he could to become fluent in languages that would be the most needed in the modern global political circumstances. The young man was a genius with grasping the hues and color of other people's speech. Between avidly studying language tapes and finding people who would work with him, he began to acquire Middle Eastern tongues.

Tomas was overheard by a Special Forces officer as he practiced aloud and that encounter began the change of direction for his military career. However, before Bernardo could even be considered for Special Forces training the military needed to find out how proficient he could become in speaking and understanding certain strategic languages.

✳   ✳   ✳

Shivering in the cold of the Afghanistan evening, Tomas' thoughts drifted back to his training days and Colonel Tag Tagart who had the final say on who would be deployed and where. He headed what seemed to be a special group that was separate from the other units. It was led by a hard nose, no nonsense, cigar chewing veteran officer. The Colonel wasn't sure how committed Tomas might be to the nasty work ahead of him and called him into his office to sound out what was going on in the young man's mind.

Tagart was an old war horse from Vietnam and Desert Storm. He had trained many Special Forces soldiers who fought in the Gulf War. The Colonel looked younger than his years and had the build of a pro football linebacker. No one could be in his presence without being very impressed and somewhat intimidated.

"At ease, marine. Take a seat."

Tomas dutifully followed orders and sat rigidly in a chair opposite the colonel's desk. "Thank you, Sir."

"You're doing very well. I get good reports about you. It seems you have a very special ability with languages, even to the accents. That's valuable for the work you'll be doing, but to this point you've only been shooting at non human targets. Do you think you can squeeze a round off at some poor slob who won't see it coming and end his life?"

"Sir, if he is a bad guy and my country deems it vital that he be neutralized, I can do it!"

"There's something else for you to think about before you become so confident! Son, don't count on a retirement plan. Are you ready to die if need be?"

Tomas squared his shoulders. "Sir, for my country, I'm ready!"

"Good answer, Sergeant Bernardo. By the time you're ready for out-of –the-country assignment you'll be wearing a gold bar on your collar. Just never forget, you can never disclose anything to anyone about your job. The lives of your fellow marines and soldiers are in your hands, as are your country's secrets."

"I realize that, Colonel, Sir."

"Sergeant, when we think you're ready, you and one other man will go to deal with a bad guy somewhere. When you're really good, we will infiltrate you on your own so you can put your chameleon attributes to good use."

Bernardo left the Colonel's office pumped up with a desire to make his new company commander proud of him. He was sure he had found his place in the military as one of the very best; at least he would be when he passed all of the ridged physical requirements. Tomas didn't want to let Colonel Tagart down, nor did he want anyone ever again to disregard him because of his background. There was a sensation of newly found pride. He wasn't a large person and that lack of size had allowed taller and heavier kids back in his old neighborhood to intimidate him.

✻   ✻   ✻

Tomas made friends with a marine who spoke Farsi and another who spoke Hebrew. Both languages were essential for anyone who might end up in the world's hottest hot spots. He was immersed in the process of acquiring the speech and the culture of people where he could be used in undercover operations. Tomas was housed with families that could help him perfect his speech and he progressed rapidly.

Two years of intense study of languages and cultures produced a valuable "tool" for the military, but the next step would prove to be far more difficult. The Marine Corp needed to turn Tomas into the "point of the spear" for special operations. At five feet ten inches and one hundred sixty pounds there were some disadvantages, but by the time his rigorous training was complete Tomas had bulked up to one hundred eighty-five pounds of useful solid muscle. He would be a force to reckon with in any form of combat. Bernardo was a finely tuned weapon.

Added to his physical and intellectual skills, Tomas was acquiring the essential status of an expert marksman; a skill required of an efficient killer who was also able to blend in like a chameleon anywhere he was needed. There were times when he would be traveling alone to infiltrate, hunt down, and terminate a prime target. It seemed that the young man needed the excitement and danger of the job. It made him feel more alive than at any other time. That's how he felt as he and his spotter waited in their hiding place for the right time to move out and on to the EZ.

Time seemed to pass so slowly as Tomas and Troy waited. Finally, it was time to crawl out of the hiding place and make a swift push toward the proper coordinates. Troy was first to emerge from the cleft in the rock and Tomas was right on his heels. The air suddenly exploded with automatic weapons fire. Troy staggered back from two rounds, dropped to his knees, and then rolled over on his right side. He was dead. A bullet ricocheted off the rock and grazed the left side of Tomas' head. He was down and unconscious.

Early on, the Americans had been seen by a separate group of Taliban, but they chose not to engage at that time and followed them to where the two men had taken concealment. The Taliban knew if they waited long enough, their job would be much easier. It was a fatal mistake by the sniper team to choose a place to wait that did not permit them the opportunity for observation and movement. Cover from the cool air had been elected instead of a more strategic position. Tomas was captured along with all of his gear.

When the surviving American regained consciousness, he found himself tied around his wrists and ankles and dangling from a hook attached to an overhead wood beam. His feet were just inches off the floor of a small, two room hut. The pain from his head wound was accompanied with the agony Tomas felt from the downward pull of his weight that compressed his lungs and made it hard to draw a full breath.

Noticing that the captive was becoming alert, the guard left the small room and brought back with him a heavily bearded man who, by his white hair, appeared to be in his late sixties. Mutafi Rafsanjani was a man of some importance among the Taliban, but he had an Iranian last name. He approached Tomas and studied his features for several moments. Rafsanjani was curious about this man hanging from the beam.

"I know you must be an American, but are you also Arab?" The man's English indicated he was probably educated in an American University.

Tomas said nothing.

"Your silence will only make things much harder for you. I guarantee to you that the pain you now have will seem like nothing. Now, once again, are you an Arab American? If you are, you are a traitor to all Arabs and all Muslims!"

Tomas mustered up enough energy to haltingly answer the Iranian in Farsi. "Wrong place; wrong time."

"What do you mean by that?"

Tomas made no further reply.

"Perhaps some persuasion will loosen your tongue while you still have one!"

The guard took delight in giving the helpless prisoner a hard hit to the gut. It forced a groan from Tomas, but nothing more. That began a period of beatings resulting in Bernardo lapsing into unconsciousness again. Each time he rallied there were more questions and more beatings. Lieutenant Bernardo revealed nothing. His heart and mind were steeled against all the abuse. He chose to keep silent even if it meant he would soon die.

Although the Iranian knew Tomas spoke Farsi, he was unaware that his prisoner also spoke Arabic and was able to understand the conversations around him. The American's physical appearance and the few words they could get out of him left his tormentors confused. Was this the man who had killed the terrorist leader a few days ago, or did they have some other agent? Who sent him, and what was the reason he was in the country?

Tomas Bernardo heard the interrogators speaking among themselves of an American called Saleem Karab. Rafsanjani referred to him as the "Secret One:" a person trained from early childhood in Madras schools and by a Muslim father in the ways of the faithful. This Secret One was known as "the American," but his heart was with Al Qaeda. He had earned his way to a most sensitive position in the United States as a *sleeper*. Rafsanjani bragged that one day this Saleem Karab, who had become revered by a great many Americans, would be used to bring down the Great Satan by creating an economic crisis with his ability to deceive the foolish Americans.

The bragging continued concerning the weakness of America. This moral weakness would be one way that the people would not be able to stand against the Secret One and his allies. The great crisis would soon arise and the people would turn to Saleem Karab as the one who has the answers to America's woes.

"How glorious it will be when the Great Satan surrenders to Islamic law. It will take time, but we are a patient people."

The Iranian went on to prophesy to his fellow terrorists that when the resisting part of the population tries to rise up against Saleem Karab it will be too late. The military will be divided in loyalties and after a series of bloody clashes, the forces loyal to the Secret One will prevail and the people will have no choice but to obey the great Saleem Karab.

"When the Great Satan is subdued all other western powers will have no choice but to surrender to the power of Allah!"

*   *   *

Because of his physical and mental condition, Tomas believed that what he was hearing was due to his delirium. His mind wandered back to his days of study and training and the people who helped him achieve his goals. There was Jamaal Conley who helped him with Farsi. Jamaal was a specialist dealing with intelligence gathering. His father was an Irishman and his mother Syrian. They met in college in England and fell in love, immigrated to Canada, and then later to the United States where Clay Conley became a manager of a joint venture electronics store. He later bought out his business partner. Clay's wife, Marisa Conley, converted to Christianity, but she taught English to Muslim girls and women in the Chicago area. She still wore the head scarf but dressed more like an American. Had they known of her conversion from Islam, they would not have studied with her, but Marisa answered whoever became curious about her religious beliefs by reminding the students that the class was for learning English, not religion. The people saw her as an Americanized Muslim.

Jamaal was born in Chicago and became thoroughly American in his thinking and loyalties. He was grateful for the country of his birth that had welcomed his parents and provided them opportunities to live a good life. Jamaal, a few friends, and some fellow marines played a role in equipping Tomas to be a chameleon and pass for many nationalities, but it was the Special Forces training that gave him the deadly bite of an efficient assassin. All that he had become was now needed for his survival in the extremity of his captivity.

✳   ✳   ✳

As Tomas hung from the beam, he used what concentration he could muster to slow his breathing to where it was imperceptible to superficial examination. He then relaxed his body and pushed the pain as far into the back of his mind as possible. Trained in self-hypnosis, Bernardo slipped into a state of mind that rendered him as near the appearance of being dead as he could be without passing the veil between this world and the next.

When the guard and Rafsanjani turned back toward Tomas they immediately noticed the face of a man who looked comatose. The guard gave a hard nudge to the prisoner's stomach, but there was no response. Tomas' head was drooped onto his chest and he showed no signs of breathing.

"Use your knife. See if a good jab wakes him."

The guard brought blood from Tomas' left leg, but there was still no response. "See, what did I say? These Americans are weaklings! Let him rot!"

After the days of abuse and lack of food and water, it wasn't too difficult for Bernardo to look dead. His face was swollen and caked with dried blood. In spite of everything that had been done to him, he managed to keep his life force viable. Tomas pulled back from the trans-like state of mind and took a quick glance down at his surroundings. He was alone. Slowly, and with every ounce of strength he could muster, the steel forged in him as a Special Forces soldier brought back the power to draw his legs up toward his chest and then to swing his entire body upward using the hook from which he was hanging as if it were a chin-up bar. With a surge of strength Tomas thrust his legs over his head. In one motion, his upper body followed and he hooked his legs over the wood bean. He then slipped his hands out of the hook.

Having accomplished a nearly impossible fete for a man in his condition, Bernardo used the hook to begin scraping at the dried mud and material that made up the composition of the house. There was no time to stop for a rest. If he was to escape, there was only time to keep digging until he had a hole wide enough for his body, or take a bullet in his back. Fortunately, there was little noise made from the effort and, as soon as he achieved the minimum amount of space, Tomas wrenched himself up and through to a flat roof.

It was dark. There was no moon and therefore no shadows. The only lights were the red glow of cigarettes being smoked by the guards. Soon, Tomas was free of his bonds. He used the hook that had been his problem to become part of the solution to get off the low roof. He embedded the end of the hook into the adobe-like material and held the other end as he slipped over the side and dropped the last three feet to the ground. Getting away and totally free was going to be a greater struggle. He was on his own with no means of contacting anyone for help.

Bernardo's best chance for survival was to come across an American or NATO scout patrol, or he just might stumble onto a base camp. But first, he had to discover exactly where he was in a vast and barren country and then recall the intelligence he had memorized about bases and troop deployments. A country with very few notable landmarks made the task doubly complicated. On the other hand, the darkness would help him in his escape. Time was short. He needed food and water. Tomas also needed to treat his wounds, especially the knife wound in his leg.

For the American to pull off the improbable, he would have to be seen by any Afghanis as a crippled old man. His original disguise had been taken from him. He needed native robes, a head wrapping, and then a crutch that would serve not only to aid his walking, but add to the appearance of an aged one. Tomas mused, "How in the world will I find the clothes I need and enough food and water to keep me going?"

It was a certainty that he had to leave the locale of his prison house, quickly. As soon as it was known he was missing, the area would be crawling with searchers and they probably would be willing to shoot anything that moved. Being barefoot only complicated matters. Footprints in the sand would be easy to detect in the beam of a flashlight. Tomas was counting on that. Stumbling over uneven ground, he took a direct line to what seemed to be a rocky rise outlined by the slightly darker cobalt blue sky. He reached the rocks and paused long enough to take the rope binding that had been around his ankles and wrists and began fraying the individual strands into something that resembled a crude brush.

Leaving the rocks at a right angle to his approach, Tomas brushed the frayed ends of the rope on the ground behind him to wipe away his footprints. He made sure he traveled in an irregular path out into the sand. In his mind, Bernardo reasoned that there would be more than one house where he had been held and he began to arc his direction so that it would lead him back to the general area from where he had just come.

Suddenly, noise and confusion broke the silence of the night. Shouts, anger, cursing, and a single pistol shot rang out. It could be assumed that the negligent guard had received his reward. Lights began to flash in one direction and then another. The search was on. Tomas reached a building on the far side of the cluster of houses. He slipped through a partially open door and came face to face with a man, a woman, and two small children. The eruption of sounds had awakened them from sleep. Surprise worked in the marine's favor and the man was dead from a broken neck before he could utter a word.

What was Tomas to do about the woman? If she began to scream it would mean his death. Instinctively the woman grabbed the children to shield them from danger and was not yet conscious of her man's plight. Tomas swung his arm in a wide semicircle and rendered a blow to the side of the woman's head. She dropped to the floor with the children still clinging tightly to her side. Killing the man was necessary, but the assassin could not bring himself to dispatch the woman and her children. She lay motionless with the little ones beside her.

Tomas quickly took the man's sandals, outer robe, and headgear. Without any hesitation he left, stopping only to put on the sandals and the robe. Lieutenant Bernardo continued in the direction he assumed to be southerly. He hoped that the terrorists were now following footprints in the opposite direction.

Putting distance between himself and the compound was uppermost in the marine's mind. Near the last house, Tomas stepped on a stick of wood. He retrieved it as something he could use. It was the nearest thing to a weapon he had, other than his hands. It also could help him walk. He was getting weaker. Finding help was becoming critical.

There was no time for rest as the marine tapped the stick against the ground like a blind man testing his surroundings. A fall against a rock or into a dip in the terrain could finish him. As long as he could stay on his feet and keep moving, Tomas had the chance, albeit a slim one, that he could escape anyone searching for him. For the first time since he was a child, the man prayed that he would be granted either rescue or a place to hide. Hiding wasn't really a good option. He needed to eat something soon and he would not find anything in the barren desert.

The sun was showing on the eastern horizon and it revealed just more and more flat and empty ground. The early light cast a long shadow of a hunched over figure plodding his way over the sand. Tomas truly resembled an ancient one. He sensed that he was moving away from an area where he might encounter a NATO base and that caused the weakening soldier to begin to lose hope.

As the sun reached toward ten o'clock, the cold had turned to oppressive heat and Tomas could go no farther. The waning strength of a hard-as-nails marine was slipping even more and he sank to his knees, slumped in a heap, and rolled over onto his side. Bernardo's eyes slowly closed.

*   *   *

Forty-five minutes later a mechanized column of advance scouts emerged out of the shimmering heat. Steadily, the column of vehicles drew closer until the lead vehicle halted thirty yards from a suspicious object. Sergeant Tanner called back along the line for a metal detector. "We have something up ahead and I want to make sure there isn't and IED."

Two soldiers came forward and slowly approached what looked like a body. "Sergeant, it's an Afghani and he looks like he's done for."

"Scan the corpse for metal and don't touch anything. I don't see any thing that looks like it could conceal an explosive, but don't chance it."

"Serge, I don't pick up any metal. It's clean. Wait a minute, this guy ain't dead yet!"

Sergeant Tanner dismounted and approached with caution. There was the flutter of eyelids as Tomas responded faintly to the sounds around him. "Take off the headgear and let's have a look at this guy."

With the exposure of more of Tomas' face and hair he emitted a low moan.

"Sergeant, do we shoot him or give him water?"

"You're not funny private! Check the body for identification and then we'll decide what to do with him. Hold on a minute! I have a hunch. Lift his arm and look on the inside of the upper arm. Do you see anything unusual?"

"Yeah! There's a tattoo. It looks like an eagle."

"That guy is one of us! Load him up and do what you can for him. I'm calling for a chopper to pick up what's left of this man. He looks like someone beat the liv'n stuff'n outa him."

Thirty minutes later, Tomas Bernardo was EVACed to the nearest field hospital. He had been hooked up intravenously by a medic in the scouting unit so that the re-hydration of his body could begin immediately. Additional attention was given to his wounds while aboard the aircraft. By the time he arrived at the base, signs of life were more pronounced. Had he not been so physically well conditioned, Tomas would never have survived his ordeal.

✳   ✳   ✳

Twenty four hours later Bernardo was en route to Germany. He spent a week at the military hospital and then walked to a plane for the next leg of his journey home. A Special Forces officer accompanied Tomas on the flight. He had been debriefed while at the hospital, but the officer handed Tomas a piece of paper. It was an official authorization for the soldier to tell the rest of the story.

"Bernardo, there are things you held back at the hospital. Let's get it all out. You were tortured. Could you have given up any sensitive information? If so, what was it?"

"Sir, I gave no information. I didn't even give my name."

"Are you dead sure?"

"Yes, sir; dead sure!"

"Okay; what did you hear that made any sense to you?"

"I was so woozy from being beaten and deprived that I'm not absolutely sure what I heard, except for some boasting."

"Give me as much as you can remember."

Tomas paused as he tried to recall what the lead Al Qaeda interrogator said. "It is a bit sketchy, but the head honcho was Iranian; I'm sure of it. He said something about Al Qaeda having a secret agent he called Saleem Karab high up in Washington politics and that this person had been planted in the U.S. since childhood."

"What was this Karab person supposed to do?"

"Something about helping Al Qaeda take down the Big Satan by fomenting an economic crisis."

"Sounds to me like the Iranian was just shooting off his mouth to impress his buddies. Anything else that you can recall?"

"No, sir; other than a lot of pain and I can't wait to give it back at those slimy….. Well, sir, you know what I'd like to do."

"Yes, marine, I know how you feel and after some R and R you'll get another chance."

"That won't come soon enough for me!"

∗   ∗   ∗

The flight to the United States was uneventful. Tomas tried to get his mind off of his experience, but his thoughts kept going back to the ambush and the death of his friend and spotter. Troy Yeager was not just a brother in arms. He was able to make Tomas come out of his shell and have fun from time to time. With Troy gone, Tomas would be even more into himself. He could not let anyone else get as close to him as Troy had.

While he was back at the hospital in Germany, Tomas had been given fluids and some good meals. The knife wound in his leg had been sterilized. Each day he grew stronger so that he was released for some State side recuperation. Bernardo knew he would enjoy getting back together with his brother Joaquin and Beverly Proctor, Tomas' friend. The relationship with Beverly was casual because of the nature of his job. Bernardo had few close friends. That meant there were fewer people to whom he might inadvertently say something that would reveal classified information. Never the less, the blue suits in Virginia were not comfortable with the possibility that Tomas' might mention something about the so called Secret One. It seemed to be a very sensitive issue.

Three days after Bernardo had gotten back home, a black government car pulled up in front of his apartment and two plain clothes personnel knocked on his door with an "invitation" to accompany them to another debriefing session. It seemed benign enough that Tomas did not suspect that there was anything sinister about the matter.

The two "suits" ushered the lieutenant into a gray block building in the center of Langley, Virginia. He did not recognize it as being connected to any of the official offices with which he had any previous experience. They took an elevator ride to the eleventh floor where they exited into a hallway that seemed to have no office doors. At the far right end of the corridor there was what looked like a utility room door, but it had no handle. One of the escorts slid a card through an electronic slot on the door post and the door opened to another, shorter corridor flanked by four office doors. Tomas was taken into the second room on the right and told to be seated.

"Do you gentlemen mind letting me in on why all the secrecy?"

"You'll know soon enough. Our job was just to fetch you."

"Hey, guys, I'm not a dog to be fetched. What gives?"

"Like my partner said. You'll soon find out from someone above our pay grade." With that, the two "suits" left.

Tomas looked around the rather bare room. There were no windows and just three hard chairs positioned around a small square table. It seemed obvious it wasn't a place where any work was being done. Bernardo concluded that it was for interrogations and nothing more. Fifteen minutes passed before the door opened and two men entered. One was in civilian clothes. The other man was an army major.

"Lieutenant Bernardo, thank you for coming so promptly." The man in the blue suit knew how to make coercion look like an invitation to a party. Tomas decided not to reply with what he was thinking. He would let the others do the talking until he found out exactly why he had been picked up and brought to a secret meeting.

Major Danford tried to ease the tension. "I'm sure you have many questions about this unusual situation, but what we need to discuss with you is a matter of national security. It relates to your captivity in Afghanistan."

Tomas interrupted. "Sir, I've been fully debriefed on this subject and I don't know of anything more I can tell you."

"Perhaps you don't, and perhaps you do. Sometimes things come to mind long after such a traumatic experience and we want to make sure all the bases are covered."

"I recall everything that happened and it is clear in my mind. I gave everything I know in two other inquiries."

"You say it was just two times that you have said anything to anyone about your captivity?"

"Absolutely, Sir!"

The civilian questioned, "Are you positive you didn't say anything to your brother? We believe you're very close to him and you might have let something slip and not meant to do it."

Bernardo was beginning to feel his blood pressure rising. The line of questioning indicated that there was doubt about his truthfulness and whether he had been faithful to his oath of secrecy. "Mister, I don't know who you represent or what stake you have in this. I'm neither untruthful, nor am I stupid. I would never put my brother in a position of danger by divulging classified matters to him!"

The Major interjected, "Easy Lieutenant! Keep your cool. No one, certainly not the army, is questioning your loyalty or your integrity."

Thomas replied, "Let me be direct. If this is about the Secret One, I've told the other debriefers all that I know. It could have been simply bragging on the part of the Iranian who had me tortured. If you're trying to get more information than I have given, then this is a dead end. I have mentioned this subject only to those who have asked me directly about it; namely my superiors in the government and the marines."

The civilian wasn't ready to drop the subject. "What about your girl friend, Beverly Proctor? Maybe there has been some pillow talk."

Tomas bristled with anger. "Mister, if it wouldn't land me in the brig, I'd stomp a mud hole in you and then I'd stomp it dry! Do you read me? Number one, Beverly is just a friend and I would not degrade her in the way you suggest. Number two, for the last time, I haven't spoken a word about the Secret One to a civilian, if he exists!"

Major Danford abruptly stood. "This is over! I'm satisfied. This ends it!"

The civilian, a man in his fifties with grey temples and a deep scar on the right cheek just below his eye, stared at the Major. The man wasn't ready to end the interrogation, but he could see any further questioning was futile.

Tomas had one more thing he wanted to say. "Up until today, I didn't put any real importance to the business of there being a mole for Al Qaeda in our government, but its obvious you do. Maybe you should concentrate on finding out if the claim is true and who it is, rather than wasting your time on me."

Nothing more was said. Bernardo was driven back to his apartment building and the black government car sped away, but the curiosity with which Tomas was left began to take hold of his mind. It would come up again and again during the time he waited for his next deployment.

CHAPTER TWO

ASSIGNMENT NEPAL

It was great to be home again, even if it was only for a month. There was more work ahead but, for the moment, Tomas Bernardo could enjoy the company of his brother, Joaquin. He could share things, as long as he wasn't compromising national security, with his younger brother that he couldn't tell anyone else, but he also cautioned Joaquin to keep to himself anything Tomas said to him about his trips out of the country. The secret life of an assassin was a very lonely existence. The brother was three years younger than Tomas. At age 24, he was taller than his older brother by three inches and slim of build. Tomas outweighed Joaquin by nearly thirty pounds; all of which was honed like steel. He would have made a formidable full back or linebacker.

At the end of the third week of Bernardo's furlough, orders came for him to report for an assignment. Duty came before anything else and Tomas said his goodbyes, but gave no explanation for where he was going or what he would be doing. "You know, my brother, I can't tell you about where the last mission was, or where the next one will be. In fact, until I'm briefed I have no details about what I'll be doing."

"The family keeps quizzing me about you, Tomas. They don't understand why you're so secretive and I can't clue them in because I'm also in the dark. You haven't made things clear to me. All I know is you are a marine."

"Joaquin, I wish I could share more with you, but you might not like to hear it. Just know that I'm serving our country. I'm afraid that there may be some people in very high places in our own government who are bad guys. I go abroad to help rid the world of terrorists, but I suspect we have some among us. I better not say anymore. I love you Joaquin. Pray for me and ask God to forgive me for what I have to do."

The brothers said goodbye and Tomas got into a taxi for a ride to the airport where he would catch a flight to Virginia. Joaquin stood and watched as the taxi drove away. He was confused by what Tomas had just said. What could his brother be involved with that he would ask that God would forgive him? And what person could it be in the government of the United States whom Tomas considered dangerous?

Tomas was soon in Virginia meeting with superiors and being briefed on his next mission. There was a Maoist communist leader in Nepal who was on the verge of getting various other leaders of rebel groups together to unite into a coalition to overthrow the government. Bernardo wondered aloud what would be so important in Nepal that an operation was needed there.

The answer came from Colonel John Kasparian. "Marine, there are bad guys everywhere who threaten our interests. Nepal is situated between India, a friend, and China, our enemy. India has nukes and to have a strong communist insurgency on her northern border feeding terrorists into India destabilizes the situation."

"Who's the target?"

"The Maoist leader is a guy named, Kamanai Damanda. He and his people have been shooting it out with the government troops for decades with a huge loss of life on both sides. It's a tough battle field because of the extremely high mountains and narrow valleys. You're going to have your hands full. This is one place where you'll not have the advantage of knowing the language. We know you're a quick study, but you only have four weeks to acclimate yourself to the geography and background of Nepal."

"So, what do we do about the language problem?"

"The military has an advisor who was raised in Nepal and he can help you with some of the basic phrases you can use in a tight situation, but your best help is going to be our contact in country. His name is Padam. He'll supply you with your weapons. He'll do the talking and you just act as his subordinate when you have contact with other people. If something happens to him, you'll have to wing it. I'm told you're good at that. By the way, son, you are now a member of Abishai. It makes you special and it is a term you are never to repeat to anyone and this is the only time you will hear it from me. It means you're the best we have. Now as to Nepal, Do you have a problem with this assignment?"

"No. Sir!"

"Good! Then go to room 302 and you're tutor will meet you there to get you started."

✻ ✻ ✻

Four intense weeks of preparation left Tomas well short of what he would have hoped to know, but he learned that the kingdom of Nepal was a killing zone. The Maoists pledged death to all their enemies. Some of the rebels were young girls. Bernardo learned that Nepal is the poorest nation in south Asia. The despotic King is determined to crush the Maoists and so the country functions in a state of emergency so that all personal rights and freedoms are subject to the interpretation of the government. Government troops who surrender to the Maoists are spared and recruited into the rebel forces.

It was a hard choice for the United States to decide to intervene and the Nepal government had no knowledge of the pending operation. The threat posed by the communists outweighed the disgust for the ruling regime. The degree of brutality on both sides was and is unthinkable. For Tomas, it would be like going into a hornets' nest and not knowing who might be his worst enemy.

The Maoist had succeeded in destroying the commerce which added to the nation's poverty. The poor were caught in the middle of the battles and the health of the countries' children remained deplorable. Hundreds of thousands of people had died in the fighting.

The tutor informed Bernardo that at a point in the history of the country the crown prince murdered the king and his wife, along with several siblings, and then took his own life. That tragedy left the power in the hands of the dead king's brother who declared himself king.

The tutor went on to say, "Maoists rebels create havoc almost everywhere in the country except in the Katmandu district and certain district capitals, but the countryside lives in terror. The communist rebel leader, Kamandai Damanda, has his main mountain hideaway north of Binayak." That's where Tomas was to go to eliminate the target.

Everyone involved in preparations for the operation knew that the death of Damanda would not be a permanent solution, but the absence of his strong leadership would throw the factions among the rebels into a struggle for a power grab. The confusion and distraction Damanda's death would create seemed worth the risk. Most of the risk, however, would be taken by Tomas.

"Okay, Lieutenant Bernardo, let's review what you need to know about Nepal. You probably know that the capital city is Katmandu. It's situated four thousand five hundred feet above sea level. The Himalayans reach above twenty eight thousand, but where you enter the country is more like the foothills. Your entry point is the border town of Neplagani."

"What's that place like?"

"I'll get into that later. The people you will encounter are dirt poor. Of the population, which is about twenty-seven million plus, six hundred ninety-five thousand live in the capital. The per capita income is two hundred twenty dollars. Nepal is approximately four hundred fifty miles long and about one hundred miles wide. The problem is the mountains and the lack of roads."

"So I'll be on foot most of the time."

"Correct. As I said; Nepal has very few roads: most are found in the eastern half and on the border with India. The only real road on the north border with China leads to the region of Mt. Everest, so you get the idea that it's rugged."

"What about the people groups?"

"There are several major ethnic factions and they're divided between eighty-six percent Hindu, less than ten percent Buddhist, and four percent Muslim. The official language is Nepali and then there are several local tongues."

Tomas was taking notes of the data being spilled out by his instructor, but this activity was interrupted. "Sorry, Lieutenant: no notes. You've got to retain this info in your head."

"So, what's next?"

"The terrain ranges from grasslands and forests in the southern lowlands to the Siwalik Mountains and deep valleys in the Central region. Of course, in the north is the main section of the Himalayans."

"What about rivers since there are few roads?"

"Well, the four main rivers are Ghaghara, Gandak, Kosi, and Karnali. You're going to get to know the Karnali first hand. With the wide variation of elevations you'll also find a variety of climates. The

Kingdom is divided between three regions: Bhadgaon in the west, Katmandu in the central, and Patan in the eastern part. Your mission is in the western part of the country."

"Tell me about the political situation."

"I've already mentioned the troubled history of the monarchy. In two thousand one, King Birendra, the queen, and six other members of his family were shot to death by his heir, Crown Prince Dipendra, who then killed himself. The first national constitution was adopted in nineteen fifty-nine. The elected parliament was dissolved the following year and replaced with a system of village councils. Mass protests began in nineteen-ninety and a new constitution was adopted to limit the power of the monarchy."

"So much for family unity! Do I need to know all of this?"

"You do if you're to understand the current conditions. There were nine government changes in ten years. The nineteen hundred-ninety Maoist Revolt resulted in three thousand five hundred deaths."

"Birendra's brother, Gyanendra became king. After a brief cease fire, the Maoist bloodshed continued and the Maoist insurrection caused the king to take direct control of the government and appoint a new cabinet in two thousand five."

"So, the country is pretty well an ongoing struggle between the Maoists and the government. But what good will it do to take out one rebel leader?"

"It's not *a* leader, it's *the* leader. Sure, his death won't solve the country's problems and we aren't trying to give the government a decisive edge, just trying to upset the rebels enough to limit their threat to our interests in India and Pakistan."

*　　　　　　*　　　　　　*

Tomas' genius for languages was astounding. Whoever he heard he could mimic perfectly and instantly, but understanding the grammar and variations in meaning was the second step in preparing him to pass as a national. There wasn't time to learn very much. In fact, it was even more important that he could understand what others were saying, since he had to rely on his contact man to carry any lengthy conversation.

During the in-country acclimating time Tomas would have to keep a low profile while in a town or village and then go about secretly scouting the outlying region to fix in his mind recognition of various kinds of terrain that he might have to use to make his way around the mountains and valleys. This assignment wouldn't be a quick insertion and extraction like Afghanistan was supposed to have been.

The typography of the country worked against a speedy mission. In forty-five days, Tomas would have to memorize his possible escape routes. He couldn't go into China. He had to go out the way he came in: back through India. If he made it to a predetermined mountain that rose above the southern plain, he could hang glide to the border.

Padam pre-positioned the apparatus with a "kicker" engine to keep it aloft. If anything went wrong, there would be no chance to use it, even if Tomas could find it. He would have to make his way to that location without being detected. The other option was to chance walking out through a rugged frontier while trying to avoid border security. Once Tomas "tapped" his target, there would be rebels throughout the mountains looking for the killer of the chief Maoist leader.

After his infiltration of Nepal through India, the circumstances predetermined that Tomas would be unable to receive any help from his superiors back in the United States. Everything was so secret that the mission was strictly on a need to know basis and tightly controlled through Colonel Tagart. To get into Nepal, Bernardo had to enter by way of the border town of Neplaganj and then secure himself in a designated hideaway along the border road and wait to be contacted by his guide. They would then make their way west to the Karnali River and follow the valley northward until they came parallel with the mountain village of Binayak. Along the way, Tomas and his contact would make a stop at Babiyachour to pick up supplies and find the sniper rifle Padam had hidden. It was a weapon that could be broken down to a concealable package.

✻   ✻   ✻

With the month of indoctrination finally over, Bernardo left the States and boarded a military transport as far as Riyadh, Saudi Arabia. While there, he received papers and an identity as an Italian businessman bound for Mumbai, India by way of a ship through the Persian Gulf out of Qatar. Bernardo's ship docked at the port known as the Gateway to India. The humidity was oppressive for someone not acclimated to it. Bernardo cleared customs and then went by taxi along P. D'mello Road to the causeway over the waterway called Thame Creek and into

New Mumbai. In the city, Tomas located his Indian contact at an open air market and began his long journey north through Andore and on to Kanpur.

Bernardo; now traveling as Antonio Rebaldi, successfully made the long trek via car and rail to Kanpur where he met a second contact who took him as far as the border town of Neplaganj. Tomas' papers were given a long look, but soon he was into Nepal with back pack, hiking clothes and shoes, and anxious to get to his hiding place where his next guide would take him to a more secluded area to begin the next phase of his preparation to take on, as much as possible, the appearance of someone who belonged in the country.

Getting into Nepal was only the beginning. The most difficult task would prove to be staying concealed while waiting for Padam to show himself and then move farther inland to Gutu. The plan formulated back in Virginia was to use Gutu for a temporary headquarters before moving higher into the mountains and closer to the area where the Maoist leader was located.

Tomas found a suitable place with enough foliage to camouflage himself from anyone who might pass by on the road. It was critical that he be alert in all daylight hours so that he would not miss Padam. The contact would be wearing a thin blue armband on the upper part of his left arm. The first day passed and there was no Padam. Another morning went by and it was long into the afternoon before Tomas saw a man about five feet tall coming from the north. As the Nepali drew closer, Bernardo could make out the blue armband, but was this the right man, or a decoy to flush Tomas out of hiding? He had learned to suspect everyone and everything. It was how he would stay alive.

If somehow the rebels had discovered what Padam was involved with, he might have been forced to reveal the plot. However, Padam wasn't supposed to know the entire plan until Tomas as in country. Only then would he be told who the target would be. Just the same, Tomas couldn't afford to trust anyone expect himself. Another means of verification was one that dated back to the invasion of Normandy in the Second World War. Paratroopers who dropped into France at night carried a little item that made a clicking sound when pressed.

As the man came in a direct line with Bernardo's hiding place, Tomas clicked twice and waited. The signal was heard, but the man did not turn his head. Instead, he stopped and sat down beside the road with his back to Tomas as if to rest. For five minutes there was no movement and thus no effort by the man to respond to the signal. Tomas was beginning to wonder if the plan had been compromised. It was then that the recognition response was given. Padam took off his hat and looked at the inside of it. He drew out a red bandana and tied it around his neck and then placed the hat back on his head. The response by the contact was given only after Padam was sure there was no one else in the area to see him and Tomas meeting on the side of the road.

The two men made slight bows toward each other and then Tomas spoke. "Have you had a long journey?"

"A journey begins with first step and ends with last step."

It was the proper verifying signal.

Another layer of verification was given. Tomas asked, "What bird is that in the sky?"

The man replied, "It is not a bird. It is an angel." Angel was Tomas' code name for the mission.

Tomas slung his backpack on his shoulder. "How long will it take to get to Gutu?"

"As long as it takes, Mister Angel. We first must stop for awhile in…" Tomas interrupted the man.

"Padam, we have to find another name for you to call me if I'm to fit into the scene."

"I will call you Binhab. Yes, Binhab will suit you well and will not draw attention when I call for you."

Tomas had gone by Rebaldi to get out of Qatar, through India and into Nepal. Unless he was forced to produce papers, he would continue to answer to Binhab. As per his orders, he would leave the talking to his guide and, if possible, avoid situations where he had to engage in conversation. The phrases he knew in Nepali might be enough to reply to yes or no type questions. Tomas would be able to pick up more of the language from Padam over the next several weeks.

The two men huddled under some tall bushes the first night on their trek. The second night, they found refuge from the cooling temperatures in an abandoned make-shift shelter that was barely large enough for both of them. The farther into the higher altitudes they traveled the drier the air and the colder the nights became.

*   *   *

At noon on the third day, Padam tapped Tomas on the shoulder and pointed ahead of them. "There, Mister Binhab, is the first sign that we are getting near Babiyachour." Two elderly women were scouring the sparse foliage beside the road for anything that could serve as fuel for a cooking fire. They would carry everything back to the town and sell part of their find and use the rest to cook their one meal for the day.

The region presented a scene that might have existed in the twelfth and thirteenth centuries. There were no electric lights. People lived by candlelight. They cooked their food in the open on fire pits or rocks. There was a type of feudal system, but instead of lords and vassals, it was the Maoists and the peasants. The Maoist had the guns and ruled the land. The peasants tried to eek out a living on the land, but the rebel lords took whatever they wanted for themselves. A reason for peasants joining the rebels was to have something to eat; as little as that might be in many circumstances.

The ill treatment over the years by the government only served to hand the rural population to the rebels. The people had a choice between two bad deals. Being outside of the district capitals meant the masses were left without protection and subject to exploitation by those who had the power. Power was in the barrel of a gun.

In many areas, the population left their houses in search of safer places and the Maoist moved into those abandoned structures. Villages, both those in which the peasants still lived and those taken over by the rebels, were often so isolated that the government troops could not get to them without suffering great losses. Helicopters were used to indiscriminately fire down upon them. In such instances non combatants were sometimes the victims of government attempts to kill rebels.

Padam and Tomas entered Babiyachour; a village within the territory held by the rebels. The men located the place of lodging which Padam had pre-arranged. They would rest for a day and a night before pushing farther upland. Padam left Tomas in the small hut situated on the back side of a larger stone structure facing the road. Tomas had to just sit and wait until Padam returned with the essential "bundle" and hope that when the door opened again it would be his guide with the sniper rifle and not a rebel with an M-16; a weapon preferred by the Maoist.

The American made assault rifle could be obtained around the world through arms dealers.

What Tomas needed was a rifle especially useful for his trade. It had to be hand made. Months before Tomas arrived; Padam had secured the "tool" and hidden it in a small cave outside of the village. Before Padam left the village he warned Tomas that it would be best to stay out of sight until he returned. If anyone suspected Bernardo was an American, it might not go well with him. He drew enough attention when he was with the guide.

    *   *   *

The structure used as a way station by the two men had one small window covered with plastic that was so dirty it was impossible to see anything other than a passing shadow. The single room had several large candles for illumination. On the floor were two grass mats for sleeping. Small creatures scurried in the darkness and Tomas hoped none were lethal.

Sleep came with difficulty the first night. The following day was used by Bernardo to disassemble and reassemble the rifle. He had to make sure every part was there and in fine working order. Fortunately, he could do it in the darkened room with ease. The cartridges that came with the weapon were hand loaded and steel jacketed. With this equipment Bernardo could bring down an elephant.

The second day found the two men outside people-watching as they sat next to the roadway on a crude stone bench. It was Tomas' idea. He didn't want to be cooped up in the little back room all day. Even the chickens that scratched the ground in search of whatever it is chickens hope to find were free to live out in the open. Tomas preferred to be in the upland air and taking in the atmosphere rather than being secluded.

Not only were Tomas and Padam observing people, who were just like the chickens going about their task of scratching out a living, but the men were being watched. All strangers were under suspicion by the locals. It wasn't so much a curiosity about Padam; he fit into the picture, but Tomas was different and anyone different drew a great deal of attention. The people tried not to make it obvious.

In a flat area of ground outside of the collection of huts that made up the village, a buffalo provided the muscle that pulled a wooden plow across very poor soil. In this primitive scene were people who seemed to have nothing at all to do, including the Maoists. These idle few were not timid about coercing tribute from anyone who might have some means to pay. It was a way of keeping the population subdued. Intimidation was a weapon they knew how to use.

The following day, Tomas stayed in the little room while Padam gathered the day's rations and something to carry along with them the next day. Tomas also made sure the rifle was well hidden just in case someone stopped around to inspect him and his little sanctuary. Padam returned in the early evening and the two men ate; mostly vegetables.

"Mister Binhab, a rebel officer asked about you today."

"What did he want to know?"

"He asked me if you were Indian or some other nationality."

"And….?"

"I told him you were an Italian businessman who wanted to do some hiking in the mountains."

"How did he react to that?"

"He grunted and walked away. I think he just doesn't like any foreigners, but I think he believed me."

Tomas was relieved that the soldier was apparently satisfied. Having eaten, the men were ready to get some sleep. Darkness had quickly descended over the narrow gap of land squeezed between mountain ridges and it was time to take stock of the day. It was Bernardo's habit to review each day before retiring. In so doing he could fix in his mind what he needed to remember and sleep on it. No sooner had Bernardo drifted off into a fitful slumber than he bolted upright at the sudden sound of shouting. He was ready for a fight.

"Mister Binhab, you can relax. I forgot to tell you that the rebels are having a rally this evening. The Maoists are trying to recruit young villagers to join the cause. There will be flaming torches, speeches, and the repetition of many slogans against their enemies; namely some ranting against the Nepal government and the American imperialists."

"What do the new recruits do during the day?"

"The young ones, both male and female, join the fighters and train to get into shape for whatever they might be called to do. The rest are indoctrinated in Maoist propaganda on how bad the government is and how it and the Americans are responsible for every bad thing the people endure. For all the plans the rebel leaders have, so far they have succeeded in nothing positive. The people are worse off than before the insurrection. Over ten thousand children die every year from intestinal diseases. But the answer to a failed economy and terrible conditions is to blame it on Katmandu or the United States."

"So, Americans become the scapegoat once again. I'll be glad to move on from here in the morning."

"Wherever you are going in this country, you will find the same efforts being made to control the population by threats and by forcing rebel beliefs upon the people. Keep in mind that we are in the heart of rebel territory."

"I guess they don't understand that it's this constant warring that has destroyed the economy."

"It is easy, Mister Binhab, to blame others for problems. No one wants to admit they are part of the problem. Communists can gain power only when the people are kept poor and are not free to think for themselves."

"Padam, how is it that you have escaped being pulled into the rebel fight against the government?"

"I have no love for the government, but I have less for the Maoists. Years ago, when I was living at home, rebels came to my village and demanded all of our animals and that my older brother and sister join the cause. My father resisted and his resistance was met with summary execution: he and my mother. I was wounded and left for dead."

"Is that why you limp?"

"Yes. My right leg was shattered and it did not heal properly. There is always a great amount of pain to remind me of why I hate the rebels."

"What happened to your brother and sister?"

"They were taken into the rebel army. I have not seen them since that day. They may be dead. I just don't know."

"Sorry about your losses. I'm curious about how you received an education."

"The local school teacher took me into his family. His wife nursed me back to health. The teacher taught me to read and write."

"How did you become an operative for the United States?"

"I really don't consider myself an operative. I became acquainted with a reporter who was writing articles about Nepal and its problems.

He interviewed the teacher and also asked me several questions. A year later he returned and that is when he asked me if I would be willing to be his guide and interpreter. As we got to know each other better, the man found out how I hated the Maoists. I didn't know at the time that he wasn't just a reporter."

"I understand. It all makes sense to me now."

✳   ✳   ✳

The travel day for Tomas and his guide began early while most of the people were still inside their huts. The air was cool and moist. Tomas knew that, as they continued toward higher ground through thin pine forests, the temperature would begin to fall. He also knew that the exertion required for hiking from four thousand feet to the seven thousand feet elevation would cause him to perspire in spite of the coolness that kissed his face. The two men left Babiyachour behind and moved an hour and forty-five minutes farther on to Gutu. The terrain began a faster rise from Gutu to Caukun which was situated at and overlooking the Karnali River.

As the two men were trudging up the steep trail they heard a strange sound. Tomas knew immediately what it was and grabbed Padam by his arm and held him tightly against the mountain wall. Swooping down through the gorge was a government helicopter. A burst of machinegun fire raked the trail beside them and then the copter kept moving south in search of targets.

"Well, Padam, it looks like things are going to get hot at Gutu."

"Yes, but the rebels are always on guard for such sudden attacks. It is hard to disguise the sound of a helicopter gunship."

The Karnali River bisected the mountains in its winding route in a northerly direction. It was wide at the lower level but as it got closer to its source in the high Himalayas it became progressively narrower. It was on the mountain high above the river that Tomas and Padam spent the night in the safety of monks.

In the following days, the men carried out the serious preparation required to accomplish the mission. They crossed the river, moved into the mountains on that side, and set up a headquarters in Turmakhad. It wasn't much of a place. Just a few scattered stone huts under the control of the Maoists; like the other mountain villages in the region. The rebel soldiers decked out in their camouflage fatigues used the place as a gathering point before moving out to cause more trouble.

It was known globally that the rebels would take children from their homes in order to add to their numbers. Strangely, this human rights issue was not being reported in western democracies. There was no such thing as individual rights of privacy or personal freedom in Nepal. What the Maoists wanted the Maoists took, whether property or people. If they could indoctrinate the people long enough, the people no longer would have minds of their own. Like sheep, they would follow their leader without questions.

✳   ✳   ✳

From the vantage point of the high location, the next several days and weeks would be used by Thomasl and Padam to scout the land between them and Binayak. There wasn't anything of consequence beyond Binayak except higher mountains. The rebel stronghold was where the mission would end if everything went as planned.

Finding the exact location of the Maoist leader's headquarters was the main goal, but knowing how to access a position to observe his movements and then to safely retreat once the job was done was equally essential. No doubt the leader would have his place remotely accessible and at an elevation that gave him a view of any approaching forces. However, it wasn't likely that any government troops were brave enough to enter the rebel stronghold.

Bernardo would have to find a position on the mountain higher than that of Kamandai Damanda's location. That also meant he would have to scout for a retreat over the mountain and away from the rebel headquarters. From Binayak there was a sharp rise to the higher Himalayans: an impregnable barrier that precluded any escape to the north.

There was only one way out of Nepal. Tomas had to traverse sixty miles back to India through narrow valleys wedged between mountains that required careful climbing and descending. He could be trapped in the river valleys and so he would have to risk the mountains with limited gear for climbing. That meant he would have to survey for the easiest possible routes.

If he could work his way west and skirt around the villages of Binayak, Kamal Bazar, and Turmakhad, Bernardo could get back to the river just west of Chaukun. At that point he would be far enough away from villages and low enough in altitude that he could go directly south to the east-west road. It would take him to Moradabad, India and less than a hundred miles from Delhi. It would take every skill Tomas had to make it to the border, but once he was there, he would be beyond the reach of the Maoists.

Tomas did not regard his work a suicide mission. In his mind, success also meant getting out of the country alive. It was just as important to him as hitting the target. On the long trek from Binayak to the border with India he would not have Padam to assist him in his escape. Knowing the best way to get out of the mountains was absolutely essential. Familiarity with the terrain would shorten the time needed to make decisions when unforeseen circumstances confronted Tomas.

Kamandai Damanda, the Maoist leader, was a shrewd man with an above average education. He had political experience as well as the ability to organize and command an army made up mostly of peasants who had no education. Many were just glad for a means of having a daily ration of food. Others joined the rebels out of fear. All were cannon fodder for the rebel cause. Life was cheap and getting cheaper and that was all the more reason for Tomas to eliminate the top man and a few of his henchmen in the process if it became necessary. Surprise and the ability to create confusion were in his arsenal of weapons.

The higher Padam led Tomas into the extremely rugged rock-faced mountains, the more he realized how next to impossible his assignment was. In fact, he began thinking he would have to do the impossible, not only for his country, but also for his own sense of worth. Failure was not an option, but in the back of his mind Tomas had thoughts that he tried his best to shake. Did his superiors know of the extreme circumstances of the mission they had given him? Did they really expect that he would make it back to India and then home again? Something about the entire situation didn't seem plausible.

Tomas Bernardo's mind drifted back to the interrogation he had endured concerning his information about a so called Secret One in the United States government and how he felt his loyalty was being questioned by the scar-faced man in the blue suit. The recollection of that heated encounter left its mark on Tomas. Certainly, the desire of the man in the suit to question him further couldn't be connected in any way with the assignment with which he was now faced. Tomas shook his head, as if he could physically stop the thoughts that were troubling him. He had to keep his mind focused on the task at hand.

      *   *   *

Weeks of scouting mountain trails gave Bernardo enough confidence to navigate the terrain alone and he came to the decision that it was time to take action. He and Padam had spotted the rebel leader's headquarters and a strategic place well above his house from which an expert marksman could take a kill shot. It was time for Padam to clear out of the area and protect himself from reprisal. Tomas accepted another layer of warm clothes and a poncho to wrap up in for the nights he might have to spend on the mountain while he waited for the optimum opportunity.

Two days and nights passed before there was an appearance of Kamandai Damanda. He stepped out onto a broad flat terrace composed of large flat rock cut to fit closely together. The leader was flanked by four men who guarded him. They smoked and laughed in a relaxed mood. Obviously, the Maoists felt very secure in their mountain retreat. From where Tomas was situated well above the group, it was going to be a clear head shot.

The problem the assassin had with the attempt to take out the target was the inability to have sighted in a rifle he had never used. Because of that handicap, Tomas had to prepare his little nest closer to Damanda than he would have preferred. It also meant that once he had made the hit his lead time for escape would be reduced by hundreds of yards. If the first shot missed, he would only have three seconds to reload and get off the second shot. After that, it was head for higher ground.

Just as Bernardo took aim, two more men appeared at the base of the terrace and shouted something to the group of five. Whatever it was, it caused the leader and two of the men to quickly go back inside. Tomas wondered if he had been spotted. He didn't dare move and if he stayed where he was, others might be moving up toward him. The choice was to sit it out and see what would happen.

A minute went by and then another. Tension was building for the sniper. If Damanda didn't reappear soon and Tomas didn't get off a kill shot, he might not get another chance and the mission would be a bust.

No one on the terrace acted as though they had seen him. No one looked up in his direction and that was reassuring.

Right as Tomas was guessing what might be happening, the leader and his men stepped back out onto the terrace. They had equipment and backpacks. They had someplace to go and Tomas had to make his shot immediately or wait days before he might get another chance. He couldn't do that. It had to be done now.

Through the scope Bernardo placed the crosshairs on the top of Kamandai Damanda's head and squeezed. The recoil was more than with the rifles he had used so many times in the past, but the result was the same. The man was down before anyone heard a sound. This time Tomas took the rifle with him. It was his only weapon, other than a hand gun provided by Padam, and he felt sure he would have to do some long range shooting before he got out of the region.

From where Tomas was, there were no trails directly up from the house. That fact would give him more time to put as much distance between himself and those who would soon be after him. The reverberating sound of the muffled shot confused the rebels. They looked in all directions for any sign of a shooter. Seeing no one, they all began firing aimlessly. A few bullets whined off rocks near Tomas and he decided he might as well make his move.

"There! Up There!" The words were Nepali but the meaning was clear. More shots rang out but Tomas was now out of range of the rebel's weapons. They knew the mountains and it was certain they would soon be on his trail and sending out word through the region. Bernardo had reason to believe that the anger of the rebels would be spent on anyone they thought might be the shooter. There would be no questions asked.

The rarified air made escape farther up the mountain very difficult, even for someone in the excellent condition of Tomas Bernardo, but there was no time to rest. His chasers were used to the high altitude climate. They might expect him to double back and head for the river valley, but Tomas had other plans. He stayed in the rugged highland terrain and moved away from the valley along trails he had scouted weeks prior to making the move on the rebel leader. He had to make time while there was still daylight. Not even the Nepalis would be able to find his trail in the dark. They would fan out in the hope of stumbling across Tomas. If they found him, some of them were sure to die before they could get close enough to return fire.

The heavy clothes Bernardo wore slowed him down, but they were an absolute necessity in order to survive in the cold, especially at night. It finally was becoming too dangerous to continue stumbling along the cliffs and uneven pathways in the rapidly fading light.

It was time to pick a place that could be approached only from one direction and hole up until first light. One wrong move in the twilight and the next step could be into thin air. The rebels wouldn't need to catch up to Bernardo if that happened. No one would ever know what the end of the story was for Tomas. He simply would never be heard of again. The thought came to him that perhaps that was the whole purpose behind the assignment. Bernardo mumbled, "Man, I've got to quit thinking like this. I've got to get the man with the suit out of my head and start trusting the people I work for."

✳   ✳   ✳

It was a long and very cold night. With the first inkling of light in the sky, Tomas stirred and stretched his aching body. There was only time to unwrap a power bar, stuff the paper in his pocket, and munch as he moved farther west. He had traveled for two hours without seeing or hearing anything that would pass for the living, whether man or animal. As Tomas rounded an outcropping he stopped to take a check on his compass. That's when he looked back the way he had come. A hundred yards east and fifty yards below him, the pursued saw two pursuers. Tomas froze in position.

It was clear that the two men had not seen their quarry yet. They were moving slowly and searching the mountain sides with their eyes. If Tomas was to act, he had to do so while he had the advantage. Slowly he shouldered the sniper rifle and took a careful bead on the lead man. No sooner had the projectile left the barrel that another round was being shoved into the chamber. The first rebel had just hit the ground on his back when the second man felt the impact that sent him tumbling down the side of the mountain. His body came to a stop a half mile below draped over a protruding boulder. If there were other rebels in the area, they would have heard the shots. It was time to move faster, but safely. Tomas didn't want to end up sprawled on a boulder like the rebel soldier.

Another cold night and another long day brought Tomas Bernardo well beyond any populated area. It was time to turn south. That meant the terrain would begin to be less rugged as he descended toward the foothills and then the grasslands. Two more days without detection and he would reach the east-west road and be on his way toward India. If Tomas came across people after one more day, they would be farmers and far enough out of the region where the rebels were more prevalent. He could discard the rifle and resume the identity with which he crossed the border from India.

As Tomas entered the low country he was surprised to see uniformed men in the distance. The rebels had expanded their search well beyond the mountains. It was time to change his appearance. A farmer's isolated hut provided the opportunity. Having learned enough Nepali to get by, Tomas approached a man feeding chickens and offered the extra clothes he had been wearing to ward off the cold in the mountains if the man would make a trade for the farmer's clothes. The attempt to barter was met with great hesitation. The strange request left the farmer not knowing what to say. He just shook his head and went on feeding his scrawny chickens, but when he was offered money and a handful of energy bars, the exchange was made.

Tomas calculated that he was about fifty miles due west of Chaukun and about thirty-five miles north of the main road leading out of the country. His pace of walking had to be slowed to fit his disguise as an elderly man. He had ditched his rifle as no longer useful and it certainly didn't fit his new profile. That left him with a handgun, a knife, and his lethal hands as protection. If anyone challenged him before he reached the border, it would mean engaging in close quarters and hand to hand combat. It never occurred to Tomas that he might want to pray that he wouldn't find that sort of fighting necessary. Then again, it had never occurred to him to pray very much.

*   *   *

In the grasslands, Bernardo increased his pace and, since he had not come across anyone who might be considered a threat to him, began making good time. However, he decided to halt for the night and rest to be ready for the effort he would expend the following day. The east-west road would make walking so much easier. He expected to take two more full days to reach India.

Tomas hoped for an open border, but it was likely there would be a customs house and guards if he stayed on the road. The next day went without incident. On the following day Tomas came across a band of six Maoist rebel soldiers approaching from the west. Four of them were girls. As he drew near the group, the soldiers divided and surrounded him.

Tomas felt the adrenalin begin to pump. He didn't want to kill girls, yet he knew they would not hesitate to take his life. He stopped in a hunched position in order to appear to be as an old man would stand and waited for someone to make a move. Under his outer garment, Tomas Bernardo clutched the revolver in one hand and a long bladed knife in the other. If he was going down, he would take as many rebels with him as he could.

A man who seemed to be the leader of the group spoke. It sounded like he wanted something. Tomas recognized the word for eat. They wanted something to eat. All he had was one energy bar, but they would wonder where a farmer would have come by such an item. In halting speech, Bernardo said he had nothing for them and he hoped they would not challenge his claim. The leader became more aggressive in his request and grabbed Bernardo by the arm. The rebel immediately realized he wasn't holding an ordinary person. There were hard-as-rock biceps under the clothes.

Special Ops training took over and the reaction was immediate. A flurry of deadly accurate shots rang out through the peasant garment. Three rebels were down before the others had time to respond to the surprise. As a rebel girl raised her rifle she took a round between the eyes. A fifth rebel behind Tomas tried to jam the butt of his weapon against Bernardo's head but was met with the thrust of a knife under the rib cage. The last rebel turned to run and was dropped with a well thrown blade sticking out of her upper back. There were two rounds left in the 9mm handgun and no more rebels in sight.

Tomas retrieved his knife and began dragging bodies off the road and into an area of low ground where he found some brush to place over the remains. He hoped that it would be enough to conceal the bodies for a day or so. There was no time to recover from the exertion of close combat. Bernardo had to pick up the pace if he was to get to the border before someone discovered the bodies.

*　　　　　　　　*　　　　　　　　*

Hours later Tomas neared the border with India. It was time for him to get rid of the peasant clothes and resume his identity as Antonio Rebaldi. He would keep his weapons until it was necessary to toss them into some bushes. He certainly did not want to be found with them on him as he went through the customs house.

Bernardo, as Rebaldi, presented his passport and other identification papers to the agent in charge and tried not to give any sign that he might be a little unsettled from his encounter with the rebel group and his long journey. Government soldiers watched him intently as the agent took plenty of time examining the documents. Finally, he stamped the passport and handed it back to a relieved Tomas who crossed over into India. The tension of the day was not yet over. There were a hundred miles between the border and Moradabad.

Tomas had walked fifteen miles when he spotted a bus coming from behind him. It was heavily loaded with people inside and many sitting on the top where there were metal bars normally used for luggage. Bernardo stepped to the center of the road and began waving for the bus to stop. At the last second, he leaped out of the path of the vehicle which then braked to a stop several yards down the road and he ran to catch up with the overloaded bus. In a country that was used to such inconveniences there was always room for one more. The body odors all mingled with Bernardo's so that no one had reason to be offended. He couldn't wait to get to a hotel for a long hot bath.

An overnight stay in Moradabad rested Tomas enough that he was ready to find transportation on to Delhi and then by train on south to Mumbai. When Tomas arrived in Delhi he began to feel nauseous and developed a fever. He decided to find a room to rent to rest for a few days, but on the way he began to feel much worse and passed out as he walked toward a hotel. It was in front of a leather shop. The proprietor and his daughter came out to assist him into their establishment and gave him water to drink.

Once again, as Tomas tried to stand, he collapsed and began to mumble. The owner of the shop became worried. "Ve haf to call an ambulance. Dis mon ees very seek."

Tomas rallied enough to protest being taken to a hospital. There would be too many questions. "No...hospital. Let me...lie down somewhere....I will be...all right. I...will pay...for you...to care for... me."

Daman Singh took advantage of the opportunity to fatten his money purse. He and his daughter Sari assisted Tomas to a back room where he rested on a cot. The girl, no more than sixteen, began to apply cold cloths to Tomas' forehead to try to bring down the temperature. The next week was spent in the back room of the leather shop as Bernardo alternated between fever and chills. Apparently, he either picked up an intestinal virus in Nepal or someone on the crowded bus to Moradabad was infected.

Bernardo was weak but able to continue his return trip to the United States once his intestines stabilized. Using a satellite phone, Tomas was able to get a message to Colonel Tagart which informed him that the mission in Nepal was complete and the delay in returning was caused by illness.

Bernardo took leave of his benefactors who themselves gained from a generous payment for the help they had given. Sari gave Tomas a strong hug and held on to the point that her father had to gently urge her to release the man she had nursed back to health. Tomas felt a little embarrassed by the undo attention, but gave the girl his expensive multifunctional watch as a token of affection and appreciation. She took the watch and held it tightly, but what she wanted to keep was waving good bye.

After having to spend the extra time in the city because of his illness Tomas was able to make contact again with the local agent he first met when he arrived in Mumbai from Qatar.

"Well, Angel, I'm really surprised to see you. It has been such a long time. I began to wonder if things had gone badly at the other end. As you no doubt have discovered, it's pretty messy up there."

"Yes, it's even worse than the wild west in America's early frontier days. I'll be glad to get back to the States."

Nothing more was said about the assignment in Nepal. It was classified top secret. Arrangements were made to start the trip home. From Qatar, Tomas returned to Riyadh. The next day he was on a military flight to J.F.K. and then to Virginia for a full debriefing. A week later Bernardo was back with his brother and Beverly. They were both very curious about his long absence and asked if there was anything he could tell them about what he had been doing.

"Remember guys, 'ask me no questions and I'll tell you no lies.' All I can say is that I am relieved and happy to be home again."

CHAPTER THREE

Three weeks of rest in the company of friends, his brother Joaquin, and other family members restored the energy that Tomas Bernardo had spent climbing through the mountains of Nepal. The one thing that disturbed his furlough was the recurring images in his mind of the six rebels he killed in order to complete his escape from the country. He had no problem justifying his hit on the Maoist leader and those chasing after him in the highlands, but the six young rebels may have been guilty of little more than being brainwashed into the Maoist cause.

The suddenness with which Tomas had dispatched them was, upon reflection, disturbing to him. He had become a killing machine. He acted without any real premeditation or conscience. It was all so instinctive. To preserve his own life he had summarily sent six souls to hell. Only now that he had time to reflect did the magnitude of his actions dawn on him. Was Tomas Bernardo losing his humanity? The fact that he had begun to think about it gave cause for hope, but he had a long way to go before he would really be concerned enough to consider a change from what he had become.

Tomas was rescued from his thoughts by a phone call. He had a new assignment. When he arrived for his briefing at Virginia, Tomas was summoned to the office of Colonel Tag Tagart where he was welcomed with a strong handshake after the customary salute.

"Lieutenant Bernardo, you have done an excellent job! Our inside man reports the Maoists are in confusion and rivalries have already begun to show for who is to become top dog."

"Yes Sir, that was the goal."

"Well now, son, you don't seem very pleased."

"Sir, I had to take out more people than the Maoist leader and it didn't make feel right."

"That's war, son! That's war! Things happen that we can't control, but you're here and that's success. We've got a job for you that will take your mind off what happened in Nepal."

"I hope it isn't a cold place with high mountains."

"As a matter of fact it's rather warm. Your assignment is Honduras. The target: Rafael Canales. The man is a former president who was deposed. Canales wants to take back his power and is plotting an overthrow of the current government. He is a leftist who has the backing of the Cuban and Nicaraguan governments. The man had joined the rebels in Nicaragua who have been inflicting great suffering on the Honduran people. Honduras is leaning toward cooperation with the United States and that makes President Cortador Martinez a target of the leftists."

"How do I get to my target?"

"You are to infiltrate, find Canales who is hiding just inside the Honduran border, and eliminate him as a threat by 'cutting off the head of the snake.' Intel has it that he's about ready to make his move. We don't have any time to waste."

"Pardon me, Sir, but can't the Honduran army flush him out and do the job themselves?"

"If they could have, it would have been done! There's so much corruption in the army that they can't find someone willing to sign off on the job. The loyalty of many officers is questionable."

"So, who can I trust?"

"Basically, no one, but we have our own people who can assist you once you're in the country. As usual, someone will have all the equipment you need to complete the transaction."

"You mean, kill the snake."

"Exactly! 'Transaction' just sounds better. You already speak the language, so that ought to be a plus for passing yourself off as a national."

Tomas replied to the Colonel's optimism, "Only if someone doesn't start quizzing me about the country."

"That shouldn't be a problem. You'll be spending most of your time dealing with semi-literates and not the intellectuals. Now, here's the picture: You fly to Belize. From Belize City you go by car down the coast road to Punta Gorda. That's where the road ends. From there, our people will take you by boat across the Bay of Honduras and along the coast to Iriona."

"I assume I'll meet someone who knows the plan."

"Of course! Our man will know what to do with you. You'll land at night. We'll have a man named Pedro Kattan meet you and get you situated for a few days. He will also deliver the goods you need for the job and be your guide. Pedro will take you by car a hundred seventy-five miles inland on the road that runs parallel along the Guayape River. At Cifuentes, Pedro will leave you and you will be met by a girl named Angelina Cordoza. She'll give you the current information on where you might find Rafael Canales. Our last fix on him was in the border town of Tablazo. This gal gets around and she'll be your best way of getting close to Canales."

"How is it that he can hole up inside Honduras?"

"Bribes and intimidation: it's an age old combination. There are local militia leaders and police who are protective of their benefactor."

"Sir, by what name will I be known?"

"Angel Valle."

*　　　　　*　　　　　*

The briefing was finished on Tuesday and on Wednesday Tomas was changing planes in Miami for a commercial flight to Belize City. He drew less attention by going commercial than if the government had chartered a plane to deposit their "point of the spear" in a Central American country. Bernardo hoped this would be his last job for a long time. Constantly living with the tension of one assignment after another began to wear on him and he was afraid it might affect his skill level. That could also mean making himself more vulnerable to getting caught. He hated to contemplate what that would mean to his longevity.

The airplane disgorged its passengers near the Belize City airport terminal and they walked the short distance to the building in search of some escape from the heat. Most of the passengers were tourists and there were a few businessmen. Bernardo tried his best to look like he belonged in the country, rather than among the people looking for a good time. The red and blue checkered neckerchief he used to wipe the perspiration from his forehead served as the identifying mark for his contact.

"Senior Angel Valle, my name is Roberto. I have a car waiting to take you to your hotel. In the morning we will begin our drive to Punta Gorda. We have a place there where you will spend two days before taking a boat to your jumping off place."

"Roberto, I hope you didn't mean that literally."

"No, Senior. We will be gentle."

The two men shared a laugh as the car pulled up in front of a nondescript, small hotel. It needed some paint, but Tomas really didn't care about the quality of the structure. He was used to places that looked even worse.

"Are you supposed to fill me in on the operation?"

"No, Senior Angel. I just provide logistics. When you get to Honduras your next contact will provide answers. I'm assuming this to be true, since I don't have a need to know what happens after I pass you off."

"I understand the necessity to compartmentalize information. The less each person knows about the others the better, just in case."

"We don't like to think about what 'just in case' means. When you are settled into your room, come down to the lobby and I will show you a good place to eat."

"Wherever it is, Roberto, I hope it's a place where I can watch my food being prepared. It's just a quirk I have. I don't like food surprises."

"Si, I understand."

             *   *   *

After the evening meal, Tomas went back to his room to get a good night's rest. He had a feeling he would be using a lot of his energy for what was ahead of him. He checked out the corners of the room for any unwanted creatures, did an inspection of the windows facing the balcony to make sure they were secure, and then propped a chair under the door knob before stripping down to his shorts and crawling under the sheet. The air hung very still and muggy. There was no need for any covering besides the sheet. Even that seemed to be a little more than he wanted. By the time Tomas drifted off to sleep he had already kicked off the cover. The berretta that Roberto had slipped him was beneath the pillow and primed for action. The chances were that he didn't need to think about having the gun so handy, but Tomas was not a man to leave anything to chance.

Bernardo slept the sleep of a man whose dreams were filled with ghosts. From time to time he twitched and made motions which were more aggressive than defensive. Six young Nepalese faces crept into his dreams and his movements became more exaggerated. Suddenly, Tomas sat up and yelled, "No, don't do that!"

Perspiration covered the face of a man haunted by the last souls from whom he had expertly snatched away their earthly existence. The sweat wasn't from the warm night as much as it was from the seeds of a moral struggle that had started a conflict within the man whose body had become a finely honed weapon. Tomas got out of bed and walked across the room to a table where there was a pitcher of room temperature water. He took a hand towel and poured the water on one end which he then used to wipe away the perspiration from his face and body. One thing he couldn't wipe away was a growing sense of dissatisfaction with what he had become, but it wasn't enough to cause him to give serious consideration to resigning his commission or leaving the military. For Tomas, it was still a matter of serving his country by neutralizing some very bad troublemakers who hated America.

The morning broke bright and hot. The eastern sunrise flooded Bernardo's hotel room with its early brightness. He stirred and swung his legs over the side of the bed. It had been a rough night. Just then there was a loud knock at the door. "Senior Angel! Are you up? It is time for us to go south!"

Tomas stumbled to the door and opened it. "Come on in Roberto. I should have been ready, but I didn't get much rest and I'm still a little foggy. Give me five minutes and I'll be ready to travel."

"I will wait for you at the car. I have something for you to eat as we drive. Is that all right, Senior?"

"Si, Amigo. That's fine."

Tomas tossed together his backpack, retrieved his berretta from beneath the pillow, grabbed his jacket, and hurried to meet Roberto at the car in front of the hotel. Soon they were headed south on the coast road and whatever destiny might have for him in Honduras. At Belmopan, Roberto stopped to top of the gas tank. He filled a spare can with an extra supply of fuel which he would need on his return trip from Punta Gorda. The total round trip would be about six hundred fifty miles and the only places he could expect to find gasoline was at Dangriga and Punta Gorda. He planned to top off the tank at both places. With the spare fuel in the can he was more than able to make the drive without problems.

Just south of the coastal town of Dangriga the rain began. At first the windshield wipers were able to handle the steady downpour, but is soon became a deluge. Roberto could not see through the monsoon-like rain and slowed down to barely fifteen miles per hour. Tomas tried to help the driver, but he could not see either. From time to time the tires would touch the edge of the pavement and Roberto turned the steering wheel enough to find the solid surface again. It was as if he was trying to use the edge as a guide. Finally, the rain's velocity lessened and the wipers were again able to clear enough of the water that Roberto felt he could safely accelerate.

∗   ∗   ∗

At Punta Gorda, where the road ended Tomas spent two nights in a run down house and then was handed off to three men with a speedboat. The thirty foot craft was carrying a number of gas cans with extra fuel for a long journey across the Gulf of Honduras and then down the coast a little over four hundred miles. Departure from Punta Gorda and arrival at Iriona was timed so that Tomas would be put ashore in darkness. If the weather permitted and there were no problems with coastal patrol boats, Tomas would make his appointment with Pedro Kattan.

Only light passing showers fell as the boat plowed through the gulf waters and approached the Honduran coastline. Tomas took the opportunity to catch some of the sleep he had missed the night before in Belize City. The shelter of the boat's cabin kept him dry. The other men wore rain gear and kept watch for any patrols. This was an unauthorized intrusion on Honduran territory and no one wanted to be forced to end up housed in one of the least desirable jail cells of a third world country; certainly not Tomas Bernardo.

Regular boat traffic along the coast consisted of fishing vessels and the ferry system that docked at major costal towns. Bernardo's guardians kept the boat out beyond the ferry boat's regular route. Ferry traffic ended at Iriona, and that was where Tomas was headed. The speedboat came to a stop three miles out from the town and the four men on board waited until three o'clock in the morning to make sure there would be a minimum number of people awake before moving toward the coast. At a mile out, the engine was set on idle and the drift of the current calculated for enough forward movement to make progress toward the coast.

Two miles north of town, Tomas was taken ashore in a two man rubber inflatable. As he crossed the beach and glanced back, the raft moved back out to meet up with the speedboat. For a little while Tomas would be alone. Twenty minutes passed as Bernardo waited at the edge of the sand where the grasses began. His ears picked up a slight sound inland from his position, but he remained stationary and listened for further movement. A prearranged bird call was answered by another. Pedro whispered, "Has God sent us an angel?"

Tomas answered, "Some people think He has sent a devil."

From thirty feet away a diminutive man approached, but Bernardo remained where he was until he could make out that Pedro was not carrying a weapon, at least not in his hands. "Welcome to Honduras." The little man spoke with authority. "Come with me. We will walk to where you will be staying for a few days while we go over plans for moving you closer to where you will take care of business."

"Gracias. I could use a walk after being cramped in the boat. How far is it?"

"A little more than a mile, Senior."

On the edge of town, Thomas was ushered to a single story house with a porch the full length of the front elevation. He and Pedro ascended the four steps, crossed the porch and entered a large room by way of a creaking screen door. Beyond what Tomas assumed was the living room or parlor was another room; a dining area, separated from the larger room by an archway. To the right of the second room was a small kitchen. A central hallway led to others rooms. That's where Pedro led Tomas. They stepped into a bedroom that was sparsely furnished with one bed, a chest of drawers, and a wardrobe instead of a closet.

"This will be your room, Senior Angel. The bathroom is down the hall to the left. I suggest that we both get rest for what is left of the night and we will go over what comes next in the morning."

"I like your thinking Pedro."

"There is a pitcher of water on the chest and a basin with a towel and soap. Good night, Senior."

"Good night to you Amigo. Many thanks for your hospitality."

✳   ✳   ✳

Thomas was up early and ready for what his contact had in store for him. He was eager to see the maps and learn all he could about the area where he might find Rafael Canales. He wanted to get the job done and out of the country as soon as possible. Pedro knocked on the room door and Tomas opened it to see his host for the first time in daylight. Pedro Kattan looked to be about five feet four inches and had the features of a Miskito Indian. His people had been forced out of Nicaragua by the Sandinistas. Many Miskitos fled because of the fighting between the Sandinistas and those who were opposed to them. There were refugee camps dotting the Honduran lowlands just in from the Mosquito Coast wetlands. Pedro felt he needed to give pay back to the Sandinistas. His wife and children had all died, either from gun fire or from disease. He blamed Rafael Canales for causing their deaths.

"Breakfast is ready Senior Angel." The little man showed Tomas the way back to the dining room where there was a plate on the table with scrambled eggs and some sort of meat. Tomas decided not to ask what it was.

"By the way, Pedro, I know it's polite of you to call me, Senior Angel, but I'd like it if you would just make it, Angel?"

"Si, Angel. I would like that too. Please, go ahead and eat. I have already had breakfast. I have some hot coffee for you on the stove." He left Tomas to eat his food and went outside and sat in a wicker chair on the front porch to smoke some tobacco.

When Tomas finished eating he joined Pedro on the porch and sat on the steps. For several minutes each man was absorbed in his own thoughts. Bernardo broke the silence. "Do you live here alone?"

"Si, except when a cousin comes by and needs a place to stay for a night."

"Are you expecting anyone soon?"

"No."

"Tell you what, Pedro, I'd like to get a look at a map of where we are headed and some idea of when that might be."

"Angel, you are just as anxious to go to work as I am. I am just sorry I won't be the one to take you all the way. I will have to leave you at Cifuentes."

"Yes, I was told that before leaving the States. Who is this Angelina Cordoza?"

"She is someone who sits in two houses. By that I mean she is one of the good people, but sometimes she has to be a bad person to get the information we need. If the Sandinistas suspected her, they would not hesitate to kill her, but first they would torture her just for the fun of it."

"Can I trust her?"

"Si. With your life."

*　　　　　　　*　　　　　　　*

The morning of the third day at Iriona Pedro and Tomas got into the car and headed in a southerly direction. Tomas had in his possession the forged papers that gave him "legal" status just in case there was a question about his identity. For the rest of the time in Honduras he would be known as Angel Valle from Guarita, Honduras. The hope was that no one would be acquainted enough with the little village near the border with El Salvador that there would be any way of checking the truth of his claim.

At Catacamas, a town in cattle country, Pedro pulled off the road near a cantina. "I'm thirsty, Angel. Let's get something to drink and a bite to eat."

"Suits me, but I don't drink anything with alcohol in it."

"Amigo, you got a real problem. If you are not used to the water in this country, you got to drink something else, or you be sorry."

"I guess I can have one drink. It won't kill me."

"Don't bet on it!" Pedro laughed at his own joke. "You know, Angel, you got to loosen up when you get to Tablazo, or those people will be suspicious of you. Everybody here drinks whatever kills the bugs. You know what I mean? From this point on we had better stick with Spanish."

Once inside the weather beaten wood structure, Pedro led Tomas to a table near the door. He always liked to be as close to an exit as he could get.

"Are you expecting to have to leave in a hurry?"

"You never know. This is a rough area and these people live hard lives. They also drink hard and that leads to arguments and that leads to fights, so I want to be close to the door."

"That sounds like a good idea to me."

Pedro ordered for both of the men and brought the tacos and drinks to the table. He and Tomas were almost finished with the last of the beverages when two men staggered into the place. Tomas whispered to Pedro, "Isn't it a little early in the day to be drunk?"

The taller of the two Hondurans turned around and faced Tomas. "You got something to say to me?" The man included a provocative word that seemed to question the legitimacy of Tomas' birth.

Pedro reached over and held Tomas' arm as the Special Forces marine started to get up from his chair. "Angel, let it go. We don't need trouble."

"Look, no man questions by heritage!"

The antagonist pressed his point. "You think you a big man? I am as big as you and I am better than you!"

Tomas was still seated when he added fuel to the fire. "Well, you donkey, you're also uglier than me and dumber than me."

As quickly as the drunk could, he lunged at Tomas, but it wasn't nearly quick enough. With one blurring move Tomas reached out and grabbed the man by his shirt and slammed his face into the table. That brought a reaction from the second man, but by the time he could move, Tomas had already gotten to his feet and flipped the drunk through the swing door and he landed face down in the dirt.

The taller of the two drunks recovered from his smashed face and came up behind Tomas. "Look out, Angel!"

Tomas whirled around with a leg kick against the side of the man's head that knocked him six feet across the room where he landed on the floor with his back against the bar. He had no more fight left in him. The other man got up from his dusty resting place and headed into the cantina, but was met by the door as it was sung outward. His day was also finished. Applause broke out from the other patrons as Pedro and Tomas laid some extra money on the table and walked across the road to the car.

"Angel, if you don't mind me saying so, you can be mean. But they had it coming. We need to get going before somebody else wants to see who is the toughest hombre in town."

"It's a spontaneous reaction. When I feel threatened I fall back on my training. It's instinctive. I'll try to keep better control the next time."

Dirt flew from beneath the tires as Pedro applied pressure to the gas pedal. In another seventy-five miles he would pass Tomas off to Angelina and then head back to Iriona after taking time for a siesta. He wasn't in a hurry to drive back through Catacamas.

*   *   *

The border town of Cifuentes consisted of mainly small run down houses and a couple of cantinas. Tomas decided to stay away from either of the establishments. He sat on the top of a short wall while pretending to not pay attention to the people walking by. Several women with small children were headed to a church at the end of a side street. There were very few men. He assumed that the men were out in the fields taking care of the tobacco plants. That seemed to be the main crop in the area.

From across the street, an attractive young woman stepped out of the cantina. She smoothed back her shiny long black hair and then let it cascade over her shoulders. That was the signal for which Tomas had been waiting. He slid off the wall and began to walk in the same direction an Angelina Cordoza, but on the opposite side of the street. She was also going toward the little church.

Tomas followed Angelina inside and copied her example of taking holy water and crossing himself. He then made a slight attempt to bow his head as he moved to the back row of several crude wooden benches and sat down. In spite of the fact that his mother was Puerto Rican and his father was Italian Tomas wasn't raised Catholic and was not familiar with all the customs, but he grew up among people who were practicing Catholics and knew some of the religious customs.

Women and children sat on one side of the church and the few men who came to pray were on the other side. When Angelina got up to leave, Tomas followed and engaged her in conversation in a side courtyard where they could be alone. "Senior, I am told you have a mission and I am to help you. I know the man you are after. I see him once a week."

"How is it that he let's you see him?"

"To my shame! And yet, I have my own reasons."

"Sounds very personal."

"And is not your reason also personal?"

"No. It's my job. I'm serving my country and I don't care anything about the local politics."

Angelina sat down on a bench beneath a large tree. "Senior, if you had my reasons, it would be very personal."

"If you and I are to work together, maybe you better tell me what's eating on you that has you in the position of 'sitting in two houses,' as Pedro said to me."

"That is a strange way of describing my problem, but it is accurate. This man, Canales, is behind the murder of my father and the rape of my mother. I was just a child when it happened. She later killed herself for the shame of it all."

"I'm so sorry. What happened to you after that?"

"My mother's sister took me in, but life was miserable for me because my aunt was always reminded when she looked at me of what she called my mother's unpardonable sin."

"Your mother wasn't responsible for being raped by the Canales' men."

"It wasn't that. It was taking her own life that so upset my aunt. She believed that God would not forgive my mother for what she did to herself."

"Angelina, you carry a very heavy burden. But how can you go to be with that man knowing all about what happened to your parents?"

"I go because I hate the man and I want my revenge, but I can't bring myself to kill him." The young woman began to sob and Tomas didn't know what to do. He started to touch her shoulder and then drew his hand back. He couldn't allow himself to be drawn into the woman's personal war. Their goals were similar, but their motives were quite different.

Angelina wiped her tears with a handkerchief she kept in the sleeve of her blouse. "I'm sorry, Senior. My anger and grief become all mixed up together and it is sometimes too hard to bear. But you, do you not hate the men you kill?"

"I don't know them. It's my duty to take out some very bad men who do things that threaten my country and the peace of the world. Does that sound strange to you?"

"Si, Senior. It does sound very strange to kill someone on purpose whom you have never met."

"Well, Angelina, there is a war going on in this world and it isn't like wars of the past. That's about all I can say about it. And, please, call me Angel, not Senior."

"Angel? Is that your real name?" Tomas hesitated to answer. Angelina continued her thought. "They send me an angel to kill a devil. You must be the Death Angel. Oh, forgive me, Senior. How do you cope with these things?"

"I keep this part of my life totally separate from the life I have with friends and family who don't know what my missions are."

"You can do that?"

"So far."

This man sitting next to Angelina intrigued her. She had never met anyone like him. And she bluntly asked, "Angel, do see me as attractive?"

"More than that. I see you as very beautiful. I love a woman who has dark hair and features as appealing as yours."

"Then, maybe, you could love me?"

"Look, Angelina, I have to focus on my job. If I don't concentrate on why I came here, it could get me killed. I value my own life even though I get a rush from the danger my work holds for me."

"You are different, Angel. Other men can't wait to pay attention to me. Do you have a woman in the United States?"

"I wouldn't call her my woman. She's a friend."

"Just a friend?"

"Yes, just a good friend and nothing more. The work I do is not something I'd be able to share with anyone. Such knowledge could put a sweetheart or a wife in danger. Therefore, I can't allow myself to get romantically involved."

"So, you are also noble. How can you be all these different people?"

"I have been living many different lives under many different names for so long that I sometimes begin to forget who I was before joining the military. Angelina, let's get off this subject. But there is one thing you could do for me that has nothing to do with my killing of Rafael Canales."

"What would that be?"

"When this is over, get out of this area as fast as you can. Go to where no one knows you. Find a good man and have a family."

Angelina stood up and turned her back on Tomas. "I don't think that would be possible. I have hated Rafael Canales for so long, that once he is dead I won't have anyone to hate any more. I just don't know if I can have a life of peace."

Tomas stood and walked over to Angelina. "I hope you will try."

"Senior Angel, we had better go over the plan. I don't know how many days Canales will be in Tablazo."

The plan involved having Angelina make one of her regular visits to Canales' hacienda. Tomas would make his way up into the bell tower of the little church near Rafael's compound and wait for an opportunity. Angelina would persuade the target to walk out into the courtyard with her to say good night. There would be enough background light from the house to outline Rafael. As soon as there was separation between him and Angelina, Tomas would drop him with a round from the sniper rifle which he carried broken down and warped in a serape.

Escape would be the next issue. Tomas would have to pull the rope for the bell up through the tower and use it to do a fast slide down to the roof and then to the ground at the rear of the church. From there, he would quickly make his way to the edge of town and retrieve a donkey Angelina promised to place there. On the donkey there would be clothes of a peasant. Underneath the blanket on the back of the donkey she would secure a machete, just in case Tomas had need of it. From that point on, he could expect no help.

Friday evening, Tomas slipped into Tablazo and made his way to the church. The adobe and block structure was unoccupied, but the door remained unlock just as Angelina said it would be. Bernardo made sure that the priest wasn't in any of the back rooms behind the altar and then quietly moved to where he gained access to the bell tower. There were no steps, just a very rickety wooden ladder. With his rifle still wrapped in a serape, Tomas ascended the ladder, pushed open the hatch in the floor of the bell tower, and eased his way up over the edge into the small square space. Directly beneath the bell was a hole in the floor. A rope from the bell rocker went through the hole and dangled just five feet above the concrete slab of the first floor.

Tomas slid over to one of the four windowless openings in the tower. The openings were two feet wide and four feet tall. The west side of the tower looked directly into the courtyard of Canales' hacienda. It provided an angle shot of fifty yards. Even in the dark, the kill shot was doable as long as Angelina could maneuver the man to a position where the light from the hacienda's windows would frame the target.

The hardest part of the operation was the fact Tomas had to spend a night and a day in the tower. Angelina would not be at the place until Saturday evening. Until then, the sniper had to stay out of sight and absolutely quiet. That had become an acquired skill that was essential for anyone stalking a prey or waiting in ambush.

The night was cool and moist because of the elevation. Tabalzo was a mountain town situated between ranges that rose to seven thousand feet on all sides. The Coco River came from mountain sources in western Nicaragua and flowed east to the Caribbean Sea at the border between Nicaragua and Honduras. The river passed the south edge of Tabalzo. The Poteca River was fed by a small lake on the boarder about half way between Cifuentes and Las Trojes, Honduras where it joined the Coco River at Tablazo.

The best way of escape had to be back toward Cifuentes because Tablazo was hemmed in on two sides with Rivers and the border of Nicaragua. On the east of the town was a range of high mountains, the Cordillera Entre Rios. Rather than a speedy escape, Tomas was faced with affecting a smart one. He had to be a good actor if anyone caught up with him before he cleared Las Trojes.

Saturday morning broke with the promise of a humid day in spite of the altitude. Tomas nursed his canteen of water to make it last as he continued to stay sprawled out of sight until dark. When the blackness gave him cover from the few guards who milled around on the edges of the hacienda he would take a position where he could see everything that was happening between the church and Rafael's place.

It was a little after ten o'clock when Angelina was ushered through the front gate and into the house where she was greeted by the man she hated more than anyone on earth. Her heart was thumping so hard in anticipation of a night of vengeance that she was worried that Canales would detect it. A few minutes later a light went on in an upstairs room. Tomas was glad he couldn't see into the house.

The next two hours seemed like an eternity and Tomas had to calm his anxiety. He wanted to get the job done and get gone. He also wanted this hit more than any of the others. It would be more than a job this time. It would be for Angelina. Two figures came out on the veranda and then down the steps to the middle of the courtyard. She was doing her part of the job well. There was a final embrace and a kiss.

Tomas thought that Angelina must have felt like she was kissing a snake. Rafael didn't want to let go of her and he was not gentle in the way he grabbed her arm and gave her a hard embrace. Tomas was getting more anxious, but he couldn't squeeze off the round until there was a clear separation. For a moment the couple moved away from the light streaming from the windows. As Angelina maneuvered Rafael back out of the darkness she pulled loose. It was all Tomas needed. The head of the snake was cut off; not literally, but the force of the projectile against the target's skull was just as effective. Angelina would have to play the roll of the grieving lover while Tomas made his way down from the bell tower.

There was no time to spare. In a moment the "ants" would be in a frenzy to find the killer of the king of the hill. Tomas dropped the rope through the tower window away from the side of the hacienda, wrapped cloth around his hands and did a fast slide for life to the roof. In spite of the makeshift protection, the friction from the rope was hard on his hands. He quickly ran to the back edge of the roof, slipped over the side and dropped to the ground.

Tomas heard the shouts and confusion. He even heard the wailing from Angelina, as if she had just lost her best friend. He hoped she would be safe, but the "snake" killer had to move with all haste to put distance between himself and the danger not far behind him. He found the donkey left for him and spurred the animal to move fast, but fast was like a snail's pace for a man wanting to save his life.

Bernardo would have to rely on deception. From the edge of town to the road between Tablazo and Cifuentes, He had to give his best impression of an illiterate peasant. Before he could get half way to Las Trojes, men in camouflage had him at gun point.

"Come down from the donkey!"

"Si, Senior."

Two soldiers held Tomas while the third patted him down for weapons. "Who are you and what are you doing out this late?"

"My name is Edgardo Alvares. I am out late because I don't live here and I want to go to Las Trojes where there is a stable I may use for the night."

"That story sounds very lame, Edgardo. Are you sure you don't have a better tale to tell?"

"Please, Senior, I do not lie."

"If you aren't from here, where are you from?"

"Guarita."

"Never heard of it."

"It is on the border with El Salvador."

"That is a long way from here, so why are you here?"

"Please, Senior, I came to see my dieing uncle; my mother's brother, but I arrived too late. He is buried in the cemetery back at the edge of Tablazo."

"If that is true, we will take you to the grave and if you are lying to us, we will plant you in the cemetery. What is your uncle's name?

"Pedro. Pedro Martinez"

When the soldiers brought Tomas back to the cemetery, he pointed to the fresh grave and the wooden marker. "See, I tell the truth."

"Don't try to tell me that you brought this donkey all the way from Guarita. Do you take me for a fool?"

"No, Senior. This stupid animal is my inheritance. The old man always talked like he was rich. Him and his big stories! But he was poorer than me."

"Go on, get out of my sight! You are too stupid to be the man we are looking for. Get moving and don't stop anywhere if you have to walk or ride that donkey all night! If I see you again, I'll shoot you where you stand!"

With that order, the soldier doing all the talking slapped Tomas hard on the back of his head and he fell against the donkey. For an instant, he was ready to wreck havoc against the three soldiers, but steeled himself, said nothing, and led the animal away without looking back. As dark as the roadway was, Tomas chose to take the advice of the soldier and kept moving through the night, He carefully picked his way along until he reached Cifuentes. He found the courtyard of the church where he had first talked with Angelina. Tomas stretched out on the bench, pulled the serape around his chest, and soon drifted off to sleep. In two hours it would be daylight and time to find a way to complete his escape.

*　　　　　*　　　　　*

Exhaustion made Tomas sleep longer than he had intended. It was nearly nine o'clock and the sun was bright. He started to sit up when he heard a familiar voice. "Senior Angel, don't you think you should take your donkey and leave this place before soldiers decide to look in Cifuentes for the killer of their benefactor?"

Tomas stood to his feet quickly. "Angelina, how did you get here? Hadn't you better go somewhere that's safer?"

"The guards were so angry and excited that they scattered to look for the Angel of Death and that gave me the chance to get away. I ran until I could go no farther and then I hid in a tobacco field. When I rested, I ran some more. I just got here when you began to awaken."

Tomas took the woman by her shoulders, "Come go with me! I'll find a way for you to get to the States and you can begin a new life."

"No, Senior. This is my world. I don't fit in anywhere but here. These are my people. Perhaps I can find someone else to hate since that is all I have known from the time I saw my parents killed."

"There has to be something better. Like I told you the other day, go far away from here and find a good man and start a family!"

"Do you have a good woman and a family? No you don't. So why don't you take your own advise?"

"Maybe I will someday. If you aren't coming with me, then we had better not be seen together. It wouldn't be safe for either one of us. I think even those clowns who were working for Rafael might add things up and decide we were in this together."

With that bit of wisdom the two began to leave the courtyard by different ways, but Angelina ran back and kissed Tomas on the check. "Thank you, my angel." She turned quickly as tears began to roll down her cheeks."

Tomas just stood for a moment and then led the donkey out into the street and onto the road to Danli. It was early evening before he decided to stop for the night. He tied the donkey to some bushes, wrapped himself up in the serape and spent the night several feet off the roadside. The braying of the donkey awakened Tomas before sunrise and he chose to start off for Danli which he expected to reach before noon.

The sound of a motor caused Bernardo to lead the animal off to the side of the road as the sound grew louder. He was able to determine that there were two motors. They sounded like motorbikes. Two soldiers came upon Tomas and pulled to a stop next to him. "Hey, hombre, we want to talk with you! We found your girlfriend, Angelina. It took some serious persuasion, but she confessed to helping the Angel of Death kill our former president. Is that angel you, Senior?"

Tomas leaned against the donkey and felt under the blanket for the machete. He clutched the handle and waited for the right moment. "You must be mistaken. I am no killer. I'm just a poor peasant."

"Don't try to deny it. Before she died a slow and very painful death, she said the killer was on this road. That has to be you." One soldier dismounted and walked toward Tomas.

Like the strike of a cobra, the machete was withdrawn from its hiding place and in one deadly swipe severed the neck of the soldier. The next move was just as sudden as Tomas spun around twice, ending up next to the startled second cyclist who's pistol dropped to the ground as he tumbled from his sitting position covered with his own blood.

In an eerie duplication of his escape from Nepal, Tomas pulled the bodies off the road, dumped one of the cycles into a ditch and mounted the other for his transportation to Danli. At a cantina, Bernardo sold the cycle to a man for enough money to get a bus ticket to the capital. In Tegucigalpa, he made contact with Colonel Tagart who arranged for a flight back to the States. Another mission accomplished, but a lot more blood on Tomas' hands.

*   *   *

Tomas Bernardo went through the all too familiar process of being taken to Tag Tagart's office to begin his report. There was the usual salute and then a handshake, but there was something about Tagart's demeanor that bothered Tomas. He didn't know what it was, but the man was more sober than the last time they were together.

"Well, son, you're a hard man to kill."

That wasn't the greeting Tomas expected. "It certainly is not because several people haven't tried."

The Colonel sat back down behind his desk and motioned for Tomas to take a chair. "How was your vacation?"

"If you want to compare this mission with Nepal, it was a little easier, but certainly not a vacation."

"Just a little humor Bernardo. I know it had to be very rough, but you did your job and you did it well. Take a month. We'll talk when you're fully rested. I'll have a much better assignment next time.

Chapter Four

Lieutenant Tomas Bernardo found that a period of rest and fellowship with his brother Joaquin, friend Beverly, and others was just what he needed to temporarily mask some of the bad memories of Honduras, even though the current pleasant times were only momentary mental diversions. It was at night, when everything became quiet and there were no friends around to help fill his thoughts with trivial distractions that Tomas had flashbacks to Angelina.

Once Tomas went to his apartment at night and was alone, the horrible images began to flood back and engulf his thoughts. He especially found a great sadness swept over him when he thought of Angelina's fate. Her satisfaction of having revenge over the man who had murdered her parents so brutally had only a momentary sweetness. It lasted less than twenty-four hours. Her torture and death nagged at Tomas' heart, although he was not present when it happened. He began to despise the nighttime: too many faces and too many moments of regret. He had not had such feelings until the killing of the six youthful rebels in Nepal and now more, because of Angelina. Was it time to quit? Could he quit?

The call he dreaded came four weeks after escaping Honduras. It was Tagart again. "Come see me tomorrow at ten o'clock. I've got that easy assignment I mentioned to you when you first got back. No sniper this time. No running around in the mountains."

"I suppose I have to wait 'til I see you to get the punch line?"

"That's right. See you in the morning."

The morning came too soon to suit Tomas, but he was curious about where he would be going next. At the receptionist's desk, Tomas was told to go to a room other than Tagart's office. He stepped through the doorway and was greeted by the Colonel and two other men. Both were in blue suits.

"Come on in Bernardo. Meet Samuel and Alfred. You don't need last names. These gentlemen are experts on the country where you're going in about two weeks."

"And where would that be?"

"Keep your shirt on, son. We're giving you a chance to meet an old 'friend.' You met him in Afghanistan."

"Mutafi Rafsanjani!"

"Right the first time. He's heading up a cell of Al Qaeda in Indonesia. You see, the guy you popped in Afghanistan was a big cheese there and this Mutafi guy is taking his place to establish a training base. You will be using Angel Michael as your name."

"So what's my cover?"

"You're a Puerto Rican travel writer doing a piece on various resorts throughout the islands. We want you to establish yourself in the Celebes Island in the city of Ujung Pandang. After you're known and people learn what you're supposed to be doing, then you can start charting your target's movement and see if he has any patterns of behavior that will help you find the right time to get your revenge. You better be convincing. You have to look and act like you're no threat to anyone."

"This Mutafi, is he staying in Pandang?"

"Part of the time. There's a resort of sorts he uses. The rest of his time is spent in the interior of the island doing his Al Qaeda thing."

"How soon can I get there?"

"Woe! Slow down. You're too anxious. If you rush things, he's going to detect something and maybe look at you too closely. The work you do is like a high wire walker performing without a net. One slip and it's your funeral, except there won't be anyone there to mourn your loss."

"He would never in a million years peg me as the Special Ops he abused."

"Just the same, go slow: do it right. These two gentlemen will familiarize you with the location and coach you on your cover story. When they think you're ready we'll arrange for you to get there and you'll have map plans to get you out when the job is done. Tomas, this one is going to be close up and very personal."

"I wouldn't have it any other way. I want to see his eyes when it happens."

Tagart smirked. "What happened to the dispassionate professional?"

Tomas stared directly at the Colonel. "I'm still professional, but the last two assignments have gotten me right in the faces of the people who blocked my path. It wasn't hundreds of yards away from the target like in Afghanistan, but hand to hand. You can't be dispassionate when it's kill or be killed."

"Well, son, good luck on this one." Tagart left the room and Tomas began his orientation with the tutors. On the two huge monitors attached to one wall of the room were maps of Indonesia and a close up of the Celebes Island. Geography and language were the subjects for the day and each day following.

Several days later Tomas learned the street map of Pandang, even to the back allies. Satellite pictures made it seems as though he was right there with a bird's eye view of the city. Alternate plans for getting away after the hit were essential. Tomas had to have a number of possibilities for escape. These had to be fixed in mind. Since he would not know where he might find his opportunity to take out Mutafi, those escape routes would have to be recalled instantly.

With the preparations complete, it was time to make a phone call to Joaquin. There was no way of knowing how many weeks or months Tomas might be out of the country. He wanted to make sure his brother would check on the apartment and keep the utilities and rent payments up to date. Bernardo hated to leave things like that in the hands of others. He had always planned to make all his monthly bills automatic withdrawals from his bank, but just never seemed to have gotten around to it.

"Well, my brother, I'll be away for awhile. I can't tell you when I'll get back. They have given me another mission and I have no idea how long before I'll be able to communicate with you."

Joaquin was disappointed. He had hoped that Tomas would be able to spend more time with him and his wife and child. He and Tomas had a passion for auto racing and there were some big NASCAR events coming up soon. "Where are you now?"

"Can't say. You know the routine. No questions. I can't say when

I'm leaving, where I'm going, and I have no idea how long it will be before I get back home. Take care of yourself, Joaquin. Give my love to Mavis." There was nothing more to say to each other, except make their goodbyes.

The first leg of Tomas' flight was to Los Angeles. He had to lay over a day before taking a non stop to Sidney, Australia. After two days in Sidney to refresh himself and go over the plans for his assignment, Bernardo boarded a flight to Jakarta. It was important for Bernardo to act like a reporter and have enough people in the tourist industry take note of him just in case someone might check later where he had been since landing in Indonesia. He spent a two weeks being seen in and out of hotels and restaurants.

Tomas was often seen in public places tapping away on a lap top computer. He frequented the docks where tour boats and ferry boats tied up and made a show of taking notes as he interviewed locals and asked many questions that one might need to know if a tourist would be looking for some place in the Pacific to spend a vacation.

When Tomas had spent what he thought was sufficient time in Jakarta, he took a ferry boat to Banjarmasin, Borneo and repeated the same activities he had performed in Jakarta. A week later, he traveled to Ujung Pandang by ferry. Tomas went from the docks to an inexpensive hotel where he had a reservation for a room overlooking the main street. It provided him an observation post to see who was coming and going from the large and more expensive hotel two blocks closer to the center of town. Mutafi was known to frequent the establishment when he was not at the Al Qaeda camp.

Once Tomas was settled into his hotel, he went daily to the coffee shop in Mutafi's hotel to try to get a look at his target. He was beginning to think the man would never show, but one morning Mutafi came down from his room for breakfast. The man made no effort to disguise who he was. There was no need for that. He was in friendly territory, except for one very interested fake travel reporter.

The most obvious thing on the Celebes Island to be observed and felt was the temperature and humidity. With consistent eighty plus degrees and the February rainfall of around nine inches, Tomas needed to acclimate to the environment in order to function effectively when it came to the time for him to make his exodus from the Island. Rain and humidity could sap his energy and affect his efforts to avoid detection. The plan to have a motorboat stashed on the east side of the docks required some arrangements with a local who only cared about money and not from whom it came.

The cover story for obtaining the boat was that Tomas wanted to be able to scout the coast line of the Celebes whenever it was convenient for him. Therefore, the boat had to be ready at all times. To try to take a direct route out of the island from the docks' regular ferry service might provide easy detection by anyone who would be looking for him after he did the job.

The sixth morning in the hotel coffee shop was eventful, but had nothing to do with Tomas' mission. He was noticed by a tall, pleasingly thin, blond woman who appeared to be in her early twenties. When she saw him seated alone and recognized him to be someone other than an Indonesian national, the young woman approached the table and introduced herself as Anna Forman, an American graduate student doing research on how the minority Christian sects in Indonesia are dealing with the violence aimed at them by militant Muslims.

Tomas tried to play it cool but the young lady seemed to be attracted to his manliness. Being wary was part of Tomas' makeup. Since he had to live a lie he was always on guard for others who might be doing the same thing. He gave Anna his cover story that he was a Puerto Rican travel writer doing a piece on various resorts throughout the islands. Anna was not accustomed to directly approaching a man who was a stranger to her, but her prolonged time in the islands found her bereft of the type of companionship she felt suitable. This loneliness caused her to go against her normal protective aloofness.

Because Ms. Forman was a dedicated Christian and Tomas was a devoted assassin there was no real possibility that either of them could find anything mutual in their meeting than to share conversation and a cup of hot coffee. Yet, over the next several days, the two people seemed drawn to regular meetings during the morning routine. Anna noticed that, in spite of Tomas' friendliness, he was constantly observing what was going on around him rather than focusing on her as she talked.

"Mister Michael, are you expecting to meet someone?"

"No, why?"

"It's just that you frequently scan the room and the hallway while we talk."

"I'm terribly sorry. I don't mean to be rude. I'm interested in what is happening around me. It's part of being a writer, I suppose. I'll try to pay better attention." Bernardo thought it best that he redirect the conversation to something about the young woman. "Did you tell me the other day that you're a graduate student doing a study of something?"

"Yes I did. I'm working on a Master of Arts in Church History and I'm trying to discover how Indonesian churches are surviving in a country that is almost totally Muslim."

"Don't you think that's a little risky?"

"I'm careful around authorities. I usually work through Christian leaders who are willing to give me the information I need for my research. Our meetings are casual and in places where we would not be suspected of plotting any trouble."

"Like here?"

"Yes, just like I meet with you. I hope I'm not being a boor."

"By no means could you ever be a boor. I find what you are doing with your life is very interesting, just as I find that you are. By the way, please use my first name. Being called Mister Michael makes me sound like an old man."

"I suppose we've known each other long enough to use first names. Angel, were your parents Christians?"

"I guess they were. I really don't know. They both worked so hard to provide for the family there didn't seem to be time for church. Why do you ask?"

"Because of your name."

"I assure you, my parents did not think I was an angel. Probably it was more than likely they would have considered me a little devil when I was a kid."

At first, Tomas believed there would be an advantage for him being seen with a woman known in the town as a graduate student doing research. The six years between their ages made no difference in their friendship and soon the relationship began to take on a more serious nature but, fortunately, there wasn't enough time for things to develop to the point it could get in the way of the mission.

The end of the grant for Anna's research project was nearing and she had to return to the States. She and Tomas, whom she only knew as Angel Michael, were both sorry for the necessity of their parting. Tomas took Anna's phone number and address and promised to contact her when he was able to work a visit Stateside into his plans. She made him promise he would keep his word as they said their goodbyes. With Anna out of the picture Bernardo could get his mind back on his mission.

*   *   *

Mutafi came back to town after two weeks in the boonies and Tomas again was able to observe the habits of the man. He always had two short, dark-skinned goons with him. In order to make the hit, Bernardo either had to be able to take all three out at one time, or find a way to isolate Mutafi. Tomas made the situation more difficult by his personal desire to somehow let the man know who he was during the fatal moment. It was part of the payback for the treatment Tomas had received during his capture in Afghanistan and it wasn't going to be just another professional hit.

Part of Mutafi's routine was to take a daily stint in the hot tub in the facility at the end of the long hall behind the restaurant. His two guards sat outside of the room so that their master could have his privacy. There was no other access to the room, but if somehow Tomas could get the guards away from the door, he would have his tormentor all to himself. How could he draw them away, or should he eliminate them all together? That seemed to be the better choice, but to approach them without alarming them was the big problem. Mutafi spent the better part of an hour in the hot tub each morning. That would be plenty of time for the Chameleon to do his work and make his exist.

Another week went by and Tomas was getting anxious to take action. The opportunity finally presented itself one morning when Bernardo sat at breakfast. Mutafi and his guards got out of the elevator and walked down the long hall to the room containing the hot tub. There were only a few people having breakfast and that made for fewer eyes to see Tomas make his move. The target went into the room and his men stationed themselves for the long wait.

Tomas was prepared. He had obtained a servant's white coat and several towels. These were placed in concealment on a shelf around a corner from the hallway where the men were seated. Tomas quickly put on the coat, picked up the towels, and purposefully strode down the hall. As he approached the two men, they stood up to intercept him.

"Please, Sirs, more towels are needed for the hot tub."

"You can't go in!"

"Then, please sirs, would you take these to the gentleman?" Tomas reached forward to hand the towels to the first man who was not expecting to receive them. It was enough distraction that it enabled Tomas to thrust the knife he had concealed beneath the towels into the exact spot for a quick kill. The second man was taken totally by surprise and the power of Tomas' kick against the guard's head was hard enough that it left him with no defense against a thrust from the already bloody knife blade. In just seconds, without any confusion or undue noise, the guards gave up their lives for their leader.

The silence of the attacks alerted no one to what had happened. Tomas quietly eased open the door and slipped into the room. Mutafi had his eyes closed but was awake.

"I do not want to be disturbed! Stay in the hallway and keep watch!"

Before the Al Qaeda leader could say another word Tomas was upon him with a towel to muffle the man's cry. A knife thrust, but only to disable, not to kill, and Tomas had his man. "I just want you to know that the man you had tortured in Afghanistan is here to give you what you deserve. What do you think your great Secret One in the Whitehouse can do for you now? How does it feel to know you're going to die and miss out on Saleem Karab's glorious day of victory over the Great Satan?"

Mutafi's eyes widened as he realized who his killer was. Another plunge of the blade and a twist was all that was needed. That part of the assignment was complete. The next thing was to leave undetected and put distance between him and the hotel before the bodies were discovered. It took only a minute to drag the dead guards into the room with Mutafi, take off the coat that was no longer white, and use it to wipe the blade. Tomas then draped the coat over Mutafi's sightless eyes.

Quickly, but with not too much haste, Tomas closed the door, walked back down the hallway, and left the hotel by a back door. He made his way through allies and side streets to the docks. His gear was waiting for him on the boat. The destination was in the opposite direction from the main docks of Pangdang. Anyone looking for a killer might assume he would go for the ferry boat to leave the island.

Doing what would not be a normal move to escape, and the probability that no one would be looking for a travel writer as a suspect, gave Tomas the temporary advantage in his attempt to avoid detection and put out to sea from the east coast of the island. The logical way for a killer to escape an island would be by boat and that meant Bernardo only had a limited amount of time before the police would be searching dockage besides the ferry boat.

Eventually, the authorities would find out that someone had taken a craft from the place where he set sail. Tomas hurried to where his boat was tied and quickly made preparations to board the craft. People in the vicinity of the remote dock paid little attention to him as they went about their own business.

The boat was fueled and ready when Tomas Bernardo arrived. All he had to do was cast off and put distance between himself and Pangdang. With several hours of daylight available to him, Tomas made his way around the tip of the island and then east across the Teluk Bone Bay. There were numerous small boats around which he maneuvered his craft. Some were anchored. Others were on their way out to do a day of fishing to bring to market enough catch to make a little profit.

Once Tomas crossed the bay there were straights to navigate between several smaller islands where he would put in and replace the fuel spent getting around and away from the city at the tip of the island. He would then swing north along the Tenggara mountainous coast with its many volcanoes. Indonesia's many islands have more that two hundred volcanoes. Tomas knew he would have to refuel again somewhere up the east coast. As he checked his maps it looked like the only place was Mondeodo. He would have to take on all the fuel the tanks and cans could hold to make it all the way around the northern Tengah peninsula. If he could get all the way to the very tip of the peninsula, he might be able to top off his tanks one last time at Maliku.

Tomas' destination was Teluk Tomini Bay and the town of Toboli where he planned to ditch the boat. From there he would cross over the narrow finger of land to Palu on the west coast of the Celebes. This swing around the Celebes, rather than going in a straight line to another of the many islands that make up Indonesia, might be enough of a surprise to whoever would be after Tomas that he could get away without detection. It was a long end run and a great many miles of water that no one in their right mind, except an assassin on the run, would dream of attempting to cover as quickly as he needed to do it.

From Palu it would be a short ferry ride to Balikpapan, Borneo and then by vehicle down to Benjarmasin where Tomas could take another ferry back to Jakarta and then book a flight to Australia before returning to the United States. At least, that was the plan.

Four hours out from Pangdang, Bernardo heard the sound of a larger, more powerful boat coming his way from the south. Unknown to him the man who supplied Tomas' boat was persuaded to tell the authorities about a foreigner who bought his craft days before the killings. That was all the information that was needed to send a patrol launch to try to catch up with the foreigner and detain him for questioning.

Tomas was not about to be taken captive again. It was escape or die trying. He was nearing the Island of Kabaena and, according to the charts, the water around the island contained reefs. His boat might make it across a reef and into a cove, but the larger craft could not venture inside the reef. It was nearly four o'clock and there were still a few hours of daylight.

If the patrol boat did not spot him before he got inside the reef, Tomas planned to ease back to save fuel and snake his away along the coast and through the straights until he arrived on the east coast of Tenggara. At that point he would need to turn north and hit top speed to the next refueling location.

Idling to reduce the sound of his engine, Tomas swung toward shore. He tested the depth of the water and stayed outside of the surf. He didn't want a wave to beach him. That would be a disaster. The larger boat's motor covered the sound of Bernardo's engine. The smaller craft sat low in the water and the swells added some cover from detection. Shadows cast by the island's high mountains, as the sun began dropping in the west, made it harder to spot a small craft near shore. His confidence was beginning to increase as the shadows lengthened and the ability to see his location became more difficult.

To Tomas' surprise, the patrol boat gunned its motor, turned back west and out into Teluk Bone Bay. He reasoned that either they decided to go up the other side of the bay to find his boat, or it was a decoy to make him show himself. Tomas played it safe and continued his slow progress through the straights while avoiding bottoming out on the reefs. Three hours later he docked at Mondeodo, took fuel, and immediately continued northward along a shoreline protected from rough water and thus less chance of being pushed by waves into trouble.

By the time Tomas reached the Tengah peninsula and the off shore islands it was dark, but a full moon provided just enough illumination that he could make out the shapes of the mountains and the shoreline. To be really sure that he would not ground the boat, Bernardo navigated in the deeper water of the channel. There were a few nighttime fishermen with their kerosene lanterns hanging off the bow of their boats. Having others around actually gave Tomas a sense of comfort. He wasn't alone in the watery blackness and these were not people who had any interest in him. They might, however, wonder why he had no running lights, so he clicked on the small lights fore and aft and kept his distance from the fishing boats.

✳   ✳   ✳

After what seemed to be an unending night, the sun began to show first light as Tomas finally reached Maliku at the tip of the Tengah peninsula and began a westward direction. He estimated that by noon he would be close enough to Toboli to pick a place on the coast to leave the boat. The sky was clear and the sun in full bore as Tomas crossed the open bay. His water supply was nearly exhausted and the rays of the sun over the past two days had had its burning effect on his skin. In short, Bernardo was feeling miserably.

At long last the boat neared the shoreline south of the town and Tomas prepared to slide over the side into the water. He set the bow in an eastward direction away from shore, let the motor run at an idle, and then got into the water and swam the short distance to the beach. His hope was that the craft would beach itself some distance from where Tomas contacted land. By the time he walked from the landing point to Toboli, the sun had dried his clothes.

Re-supplied with water and some food, the fugitive made his way across the land along the road that connected Toboli with Palu where Tomas made inquiry about any boat sailing to Balikpapan. The first two people he spoke with either did not understand what he wanted or just refused to have anything to do with him. He approached two men who were facing away from him and asked again about a boat. When they turned to face Bernardo he realized what a terrible mistake he had made. They were policemen. Every town on the coastline of the Celebes had been alerted to be on the watch for a man trying to find a way off the island.

"May we see your papers, please?" Tomas retrieved the documents from a waterproof pouch and handed them to the ranking officer who looked at them carefully. "Do you always protect your documents in this manner, Mister Michael?"

"As a matter of fact, I do. The humidity has its effect as you know."

"This seems to be a rather remote place for a foreigner traveling alone. Can you explain what you are doing here?"

"Why, yes, of course. I write for a travel magazine and I'm doing a series of articles on island getaways around the world."

As Tomas and the man holding his papers talked, the other officer made his way around behind him. Tomas sensed that the second man had taken his pistol from its holster. He also sensed that, in spite of all the fighting skills Bernardo possessed, if he tried anything he would be shot in the back. This was a situation where he would have to go along with what was about to happen and bide his time for a better opportunity to escape.

"Mister Angel Michael, I am placing you under arrest for suspicion of three counts of murder."

"Three murders? Sir, this is one huge mistake! I couldn't have killed anyone! I'm a journalist!"

Tomas protested loudly, thinking that the harder he claimed his innocence the more the two officers might be inclined to go easy and provide that moment when he might regain his freedom.

"Mister Michael, be very still while I remove the large knife you carry from its sheath. Why do you carry such a weapon?"

"Sir, I don't think of it as a weapon. It's a tool: an essential item for someone who might wish to…."

"To do what, Mister Michael? Were you about to say 'take a boat out to sea?' Where is your boat?"

"I don't have a boat."

"No, you certainly do not, but you do have a large and very sharp knife; an efficient killing instrument."

           ✳   ✳   ✳

There was no roadway down the west side of the island until beyond the high mountains. The road down the east coast was long and tedious, so the decision was made to take the next ferry back to Pangdang. It left just before noon and would arrive sometime after ten o'clock. Tomas' wrists were secured but his feet were left free as the arresting officers escorted their captive to the boat. It was their hope that a reward for their alertness might be offered when they arrived at the regional office of the Indonesian Security Forces.

Without a separate and secure cabin in which to place Tomas, he was held on the upper deck between the two policemen. The ferry pulled away from the dock at Palu and out into the Makasar Straight as a tramp freighter appeared plowing its way through the sea from the south. Its course took it within fifty yards of the ferry. Bernardo began rapidly calculating the speed of both ships and at what distance between the two would be the opportune point at which a swimmer could leave one boat and, at a fast swim, intercept the other boat without being left stranded in the water.

All eyes seemed to be on the freighter as it approached. It was a rusty looking bucket of a ship, belching black smoke from its stack as it labored along in a northerly direction. At the critical moment, Tomas swung his arms back and smashed his elbows into the faces of the officers. While they were recovering from the blows and the surprise of the attack, Tomas raced to the railing and did a perfect swan dive into the sea. While holding his breath, the fugitive reached down and retrieved a short knife from a sheath strapped to his right ankle. Turning the blade around, while he kept himself from sinking farther by rotating his legs in the water, Tomas was able to cut through the plastic shackle. He then began stroking as fast as he could while still under water before coming up to grab more air.

Tomas heard the shouts from the ferry boat and the strange sound of bullets striking the water and being deflected. When he felt he had to risk the exposure, he surfaced and began swimming with all his might. His body sliced through the surface on a course to intercept the freighter that had to be carrying a full load of cargo, judging by how low in the water it ran. That was fortunate for Tomas, because the anchors also hung almost to the water. It would take all the strength he had left to thrust himself up and out of the water to snag the starboard side anchor. As he took hold of the anchor, the barnacles and rust dug into his flesh. It was painful, but the adrenalin was pumping so hard Tomas barely noticed. Because the surface was so rough, he was able to maintain his grip.

By the time crewmen from the tramp freighter were able to throw Bernardo a rope and haul him on board there wasn't anything the police could do except wave their arms and shout words that could not be heard above the chugging engine of the freighter. They were moving south on the ferry and Tomas was moving north toward the Philippines.

"Why did you jump from the ferry boat and who are you?"

"Captain, I would like to speak to you alone please, and then I'll answer your questions."

The ship's captain took Tomas to his cabin and posted two seamen outside the door. The explanation was heavily loaded with fabricated information about an innocent man being unlawfully detained. Out of fear for his life and total desperation the escape attempt had to be taken. In addition to the lies, which the captain was not prone to regard very highly, Tomas offered something else. He lifted his shirt and opened the pouch wrapped around his waste. The amount Bernardo was willing to provide the captain for safe passage to the next port of call was three times the amount the man could make in two months as captain of the rusted tub he called a ship.

From a sea soaked fugitive, Bernardo suddenly became a welcome guest of captain Stavos Apadopoulus. Tomas exchanged his wet clothes for comfortable and dry seaman's denims. The captain was pleased to have Tomas on board. It gave him a welcome distraction from the routine of a long sea voyage. The two men exchanged lies and laughter and shared a potently sweet dessert the Captain brought with in from Greece. It had the texture of soft butter, but was as strong in taste as it was sweet. A dip of the finger into the container was enough supply for one indulgence.

"Captian, I have never tasted anything so sweet. A little goes a long way for me."

Apadopoulos laughed loudly at Tomas. "You must have more to get the full flavor. My ancient mother makes this for me and sends it with me so that I will never forget my homeland."

Tomas declined another dip of the finger into the gooey substance. "Thank you, captain, but if I eat any more of your mother's sweetness, I too will never forget your homeland."

Stavos did not quite understand the comment, but joined Tomas for a hearty laugh anyway.

✳   ✳   ✳

The city of Davao in the Gulf of Davao at the southern tip of the Philippine island of Mindanao was the next port of call. From there, Tomas was able to travel by bus to the north coast and by ferry boat to Cebu where he got a flight to Manila. Bernardo had his alternate identification documents in the same pouch where he secured his currency. Bernardo assumed yet another identity. The papers had all the necessary, but fake, customs stamps.

He was now Antonio Valdez and had no problem booking a flight to Australia as an intermediate stop before returning to Los Angeles where he decided to rest up for four days before reporting back to Colonel Tagart in Virginia. Since no one knew when he would return from his mission, or even if he would return, Bernardo chose to sleep for twenty-four hours and then make some notes for the debriefing that was to eventually follow.

Tomas had funds wired to Los Angeles from his account at a Virginia bank where his payment for services was regularly deposited. Because of the nature of his business, Tomas was paid handsomely for each mission, as well as his regular military pay. That arrangement should have caused him to question what sort of employment he had. Part of Tomas' personality was to trust his superiors. He believed Colonel Tagart when the man called the compensation "hazard pay."

Personal expenses were very low for Bernardo who was a frugal man. The result of that was he had managed to save most of the money he received and it was amounting to a very substantial sum. It occurred to Tomas early in his career as a chief assassin to spread the deposits to other banks. The bank in Virginia, one in Miami, Florida, and another in North Lauderdale, Florida were the main depositories.

In addition to his missions in Afghanistan, Nepal, Honduras, and Indonesia, there had been lesser forays into Kenya, Romania, and Mexico where the job was to meet and eliminate obscure individuals whom Tagart declared to be threats to American interests in those countries. Bernardo, the loyal, naïve, and obedient soldier, did not question those assignments. It was his duty. It wasn't until Nepal and Honduras that he began to question whether what he was doing had any real affect on keeping America safe. Instead, his efforts were being interpreted by world governments as America showing its ugly side. How world leaders were able to connect his missions with the United States confused him. These were supposed to be secret, clandestine, and unofficial actions, but the dots were being connected and they lead to Washington.

At the same time as the black ops missions were being interpreted as America's effort to destabilize other governments, the United States was suffering from an economic collapse. There was a growing dissatisfaction of the people with the direction the administration's policies were taking the country. People were becoming fearful of the future and making noises about a new revolution to take back the country from the Socialist Progressive Agenda that was tearing the country apart and polarizing public opinion. It seemed to Tomas, who was not an economist, nor was he politically savvy, that there was a deliberate element to what was happening to the country.

✳   ✳   ✳

It was time to file his report for his handler and face the boss. As the non stop flight took off from Los Angeles, Tomas settled back in his seat and began to reflect on the past several weeks. Somehow he had survived another close one. He thought, *How many times can I beat the odds and come home?* He had been captured in Afghanistan and tortured, chased by Maoist rebels in Nepal, barely slipped away with his skin still intact in Honduras, and then almost miraculously spared from drowning off the coast of the Celebes Island in Indonesia. Those were just the most outstanding close calls.

How many more narrow escapes did he have left before the inevitable happened and he would simply vanish? No one would know what happened to him. Even if the government knew, it would be kept a secret. Tomas began to wonder if he could keep on spinning the wheel and coming up a winner, or was it time to get out? Maybe he needed to present the matter to Colonel Tagart.

Back on the ground on the east coast of the United States, Tomas

Bernardo took a cab to the headquarters building and found a comfortable chair outside of Tag Tagart's office.

"Colonel, Sir, Lieutenant Bernardo is waiting in the outer office."

"Amazing! That man is amazing! Send him in!"

Tomas entered the office, saluted, and announced he was reporting. "The job is done, Sir. The beast who tortured me is no more."

"Son, have a seat. Are you satisfied now that you got him?"

"I'm glad he's gone, but there was something different this time. I was too busy saving my neck again to think about the other two men that got in my way. It was too easy and there wasn't much feeling. It's all in my report, except this personal matter I'm wrestling with."

"I'm anxious to read your report, but I'd like to get the assessment directly from you."

"Sir, do you mind if I stand?"

"Not at all. I can tell you have something heavy on your mind."

"Yes. I've been thinking about it ever since I arrived back on U.S. soil. With every mission I have come right up to the door of being left dead in some forsaken part of the globe and no one, including my family, would ever know what happened to me. I'm thinking it's about time for me to find some other way to serve my country."

"Bernardo, each of us who have been doing this kind of work have come to a point where we think about what you just said, but son, you're too good at this to quit now. There aren't many men who have the mental and physical skills you have. That's why you keep coming home. Just think of the bad guys you have stopped from doing a lot of terrible things to good people."

"I realize all of that, but I liked what I did to Mutafi. I enjoyed taunting him about his great Saleem Karab. That's who he bragged would take over in America one day. I saw in his eyes that his dream of seeing that day was about to die with him."

Colonel Tagart stiffened and his jaw jutted forward. There was a flash of anger in his eyes, "I thought we had put this issue of a mole in the Whitehouse to bed and were done with it!"

"Sir, it was not my intention of resurrect the problem. I'm just reporting the details of what happened in Indonesia and how I feel about it."

"Just strike that part out of your report and hand it back in tomorrow.

When you have done that, take a month and cool your heels somewhere and let me know where that is so I can reach you if I need to do that."

The men saluted each other and Tomas turned on his heels and left the office. As he passed through the waiting room he saw a man in a civilian blue suit. It was the same fellow who, after the Afghanistan mission, wanted to take the interrogation of Tomas deeper than he was permitted. The two men faced each other without a word. The animosity hung heavy between them. If the man in the suit was aware of what a killing machine Tomas was, he didn't appear to let it bother him. Bernardo brushed by the man and stepped out into the hallway. He never had much in the way of personal feelings for the really bad guys he had taken out, whether as a sniper or hand to hand, except for Mutafi whom he really hated, but the joker in the blue suit also got under his skin. Tomas thought that he wouldn't mind having him as a target.

Right there in the hallway, Bernardo suddenly realized that he was becoming something other than an authorized black ops soldier. He was starting to like killing the people he hated. A sensation of disgust swarmed over him and he felt sick to his stomach. Tomas rushed out of the building and went down an alley where he emptied himself. Behind the façade of an unemotional, rock hard soldier was a man who hadn't yet lost all of his humanity.

Back at his apartment, Tomas took a hot shower and then phoned his brother Joaquin to let him know he was home again, but there was no answer. He tried again later in the evening, but there was still no answer. *Certainly Joaquin will get my message and call back as soon as he gets home,* Tomas thought. Finally, he got tired of waiting and called his aunt Maria.

"Maria, this is Tomas. I've been trying to reach Joaquin…."

Angrily, Maria interrupted, "Where on earth have you been! Everyone has been trying to get in touch with you! Joaquin is dead!" The hurt in her voice projected right through the telephone.

"Dead! Joaquin is dead?! It can't be! When did it happen and how?"

"He was killed on the Ohio Turnpike west of Cleveland three weeks ago. We buried him that same week. No one knew where you were. What is so secretive that you can't tell anyone where we can reach you?"

"It's government business and it's secret. That's all I can tell you."

"Your family doesn't care about government secrets! You should have been here!"

"I'm sorry. How did it happen?"

"A large delivery truck crossed the median and struck Joaquin's car. It was a horrible thing. He died at the scene and the truck driver was never found. The newspaper said that the truck was a rental and the driver's identification was fraudulent."

That bit of information brought a flashback in Bernardo's mind to the day he was being questioned by the man in the blue suit. The man asked specifically if Tomas had let anything slip to his brother about the allegation that there was a mole in the Whitehouse. He also asked the same thing about Beverly. A feeling of panic came over Tomas and he excused himself to his aunt and said he would call her back the next day to talk more about the strange circumstances surrounding Joaquin's death.

Tomas touched the keys for Beverly's number which rang several times before she answered. "Bev. It's me, Tomas...."

"Tomas, I can't talk right now! Meet me in half an hour where we used to watch the stars." With that terse message, the connection was broken. Tomas quickly dressed and got his car from the rented garage a block from his apartment.

The Observatory building was closed, but Beverly was waiting in the shadows on a stone bench. She didn't get up until Tomas joined her in the darkness and then she embraced him and began to sob.

"Hey, what's the issue?"

"I'm terribly scared! Do you know about Joaquin?"

"Yes. I talked to Aunt Maria."

Beverly whispered, "They threatened me."

"Who threatened you? Why?"

"I don't know who they were. It was two men in business suits. They asked if I knew anything about your military service and I told them I knew nothing about what you did. They said I had better stay away from you."

"You took a chance meeting me. I guess you're place is bugged?"

"I think it must be. That's why I didn't want to talk on the phone."

"Bev, do you have anyone out-of-state you can go visit for awhile? I need to look into this and I want you safe."

"I have a cousin in Montana who has been asking me to visit her."

"Good! That ought to be far enough from here. Just go out there as soon as you can arrange it and don't try to contact me. Make your calls away from your apartment. I'm too toxic. I'm sorry things have to end this way, but it's best for you."

The couple went separate ways and the next morning Tomas made a visit to Colonel Tagart's office. The list of offices next to the elevators was stripped clean of any names. He took the elevator to the floor where he had always reported but the offices were empty. There wasn't even a piece of furniture.

✳   ✳   ✳

Tomas Bernardo sat around his apartment for two days while trying to decide what his next move should be, but could not think of who he ought to approach about an operation that wasn't even supposed to exist. On the third day, a knock came to his door. When he opened the door he found two marines officers standing there.

"Lieutenant Tomas Bernardo, we have your orders to report for duty two days from today. You have been imbedded with a special operations group for an assignment in the Afghanistan theatre of operations."

"What do you mean imbedded?"

"Your unit is made up of combat Marines, CIA agents, and a sniper team. That's where you come in."

"But I just got back from a mission. I haven't had any rest and I'm already assigned to Special Duty Ops "

"We don't know anything about that outfit. You are a marine and you have your new duty. Where and when you assemble is in this envelope."

The door was shut and Tomas felt like someone had just kicked him in his gut. His first instinctive thought was to just disappear, but that would be desertion. He had no choice. He had to report as ordered.

Chapter Five

DEATH IN THE TRIBAL REGION

One hundred miles west of the Helmand River that stretches north and south through Helmand Province in Afghanistan, and just south of the King Road that runs east and west, are the main bases of the British and American camps. The American troops received reinforcements whose task was to kill as many Taliban as possible and drive out the rest from the province. The marines stationed there welcomed back some experienced troops for their second and third tours of duty. Among the many newly arrived marines were several first timers. With this mixed assemblage were Lieutenant Tomas Bernardo and a squad of handpicked marines. Attached to them were a few C.I.A. agents. This special contingency was separated from the regulars and trucked to the far south end of the American camp where they dismounted and began to occupy isolated quarters. There was a concerted attempt to maintain a separation of Tomas and his companions from the main body of troops.

"Listen up, men!" barked a tough looking Major Bo Hinds. "You have ten minutes to stow your personals and meet me outside."

There were no questions. The order was obeyed and the group of eleven assembled in front of the barracks. "At ease, troops! Huddle up around me and listen close. I'm not going to be shouting."

A tight circle of men formed around Major Hinds. "You are all here for a special operation. The Central Intelligence agents are calling the tactical shots on this one. All I can do is explain to you the overall objective. They will lead the charge. South of here, about two hundred kilometers, is a place called Marja. It is a cluster of villages where the Taliban has reconstituted itself after being driven out earlier. We aren't here to take on the whole rats' nest. That's the job of the rest of the marines. We have a job to do within the overall operation. There's a Taliban leader in Marja who needs to be taken down. When the big push begins there's a chance he will slip away and we need to prevent that. We're going to move in there as quietly as we can and take a position. If they detect our presence, the game is over and we regroup to fight another day. Agent Barstow will tell you what the specific target is."

"Thanks, Major. Intel informs us that in one of the dried mud houses there is a top Taliban leader. Snatching him out of there is too tough a nut to crack, so we have to isolate him and cover our sniper team while they take care of business. When the target is taken down the Taliban fighters are going to come for us like fire ants from the nest."

One of the marines questioned why there were so few troops and he was told it was in an effort to make as small a footprint in the area as possible. "You've got to know that these people have been run out of Marja in the past, but they keep coming back after things settle. So, they are pretty confident about their ability to meet force with force. We go in quietly, sit, and wait."

"What if the force they put onto us is enough to smother our small group?"

"Lance Corporal, we have that covered. We're going to station backup troops within quick striking distance of your position. There will also be air cover ten minutes out from if you need it."

"What about the sniper team, Sir?"

"Lieutenant Bernardo, you and your spotter will advance ahead of the support group on your own and take a position that will be determined by aerial snoopers. Once you've been given coordinates and are in position, it will be on your say when to fire and then make your exit under the covering fire of your unit."

"When does this happen, Sir?"

"You will be told when there is a need to know and then we move. Until then, make sure your weapons are clean. This sand is brutal on weapons."

Tomas asked for more information about the target. "How will I determine which man of many is mine?"

"We have our own Afghani in there. He will be wearing a yellow checked neck scarf. Keep your eye on him. When he approaches the target, gives a slight bow, and then hands the target something that's your go sign. Just make sure you don't take out our man."

"Sir, I only hit what I aim at."

"And that's why you're here, Bernardo."

Another marine asked an obvious question. "Why not use a drone and lay an egg right on top of the place?"

Major Hinds took that question. "Collateral damage. The new rules of engagement call for precision and if we can't be precise, we stay back and wait for a better day. This is all the more reason we need to do this Taliban leader quickly. He could be gone somewhere else within days. At least that's what our people believe will happen."

Another marine added his thought. "Whoever the inside man is, he sure has a lot of guts."

"He has a special reason for putting his life on the line. The guy we're after wiped out his entire family five years ago. His parents and siblings were all pro government. The only reason our man was missed was because he was in a field nearby playing soccer with some other teenagers. He watched the massacre of his family and vowed then he would have his revenge."

The briefing ended and the marines moved into their barracks. The C.I.A. group separated themselves to their own quarters. Waiting for something to happen is always the hardest thing to deal with. Marines are men of action. How many times can you disassemble and reassemble a weapon?

Bernardo and his spotter busied themselves with checking their special equipment. Tomas had never worked with this marine, but he was sure they would coordinate well. Small talk led to some questions.

"Where did you go to college, Lieutenant?"

"Gunny, I never went to college. If you're asking how I got commissioned, it was a special needs promotion. I speak several languages and have had Special Forces training. Somebody thought that deserved a commission as a Second Lieutenant. I don't make a lot of it. As a team, I think we ought to forget the rank and use names, How about it, Dristol?"

"That suits me. My first name is Doug."

"And mine is Tomas."

"Tomas, where have you served?"

"That's where I can't go. It's all classified."

The last remark by Tomas cut off any further questioning and both men resumed their weapons checks. Bernardo had a problem with sharing much of himself with anyone. His brother, Joaquin was the exception and even then he had to draw a line concerning his deployments. Now, his brother was gone: killed under strange circumstances and Tomas couldn't keep from dwelling on his loss.

There were so many unanswered questions in Bernardo's mind. The sudden closing of the office where Tomas made his reports to Colonel Tagart and the threatening of Beverly planted many doubts in his mind about everything he had been told. He even questioned the legitimacy of his missions. He felt used and angry. If all of his missions were tainted in some way, then there was a cloud over his kills and the value of his life and service.

Lance corporal T. D. Drew introduced himself to Tomas and was curious about the sniper rifle. He noticed how careful the Lieutenant was to keep it close to him and how he handled it. "Sir, you act like that thing is your baby. What is the make?"

"It is my baby and it's special issue with some modifications I've had made, so it's the most valuable possession I have. I've had others that I had to leave behind, but the only way I let go of this baby is when they take it from my dead hand."

"What's it like to deliberately go out to get some guy when he has no idea anyone is looking for him?"

Tomas considered his answer for several seconds. "I don't think about that. It's a job and it takes a whole lot of work to know how to adjust for temperature, wind-drift, gravity, and distance. That's what I think about, not the end result. You can't allow yourself to think about what happens a second after you squeeze off a round. Like I said, it's a job."

"How many kills?"

"Don't ask!"

Drew shook his head and went back to his bunk.

Dristol came across the room right after Drew left Tomas. "Either that guy thinks you're the coolest dude he's ever seen, or he thinks you're a nut case."

"There's nothing cool about what we do. As far as being nuts, well…." Bernardo didn't finish the sentence. Dristol laughed and went back to cleaning his own weapon.

Tomas had the feeling that one day he might be called into account for his part in the assassinations if they were not authorized from the top. Bernardo shook his head to try to get the thought out of his mind. After all, every target was a really bad guy. That's what he had been told. He had to reason that way to justify what he had done. Now, he was called to stalk another man. He was sure this mission was righteous. After all, he was surrounded by marines. The Central Intelligence Agency was part of the operation, so it had to be authorized. It contrasted with the tight knit secrecy of the other assignments he had been given when he went to remote places alone to take out some person he considered second rate bad.

In the beginning he did not question his assignments, but the last two missions began to raise questions in his mind. This time he was part of a large team and that made Bernardo feel comfortable with what he had to do. At this point in is life he hadn't considered that there was a higher authority who would ultimately judge his deeds.

*   *   *

Two days after arriving in theater, Tomas and his unit made their way through the countryside to take up positions near a cluster of dried mud houses. Everyone was glad to be on the move. Sitting and doing nothing, except daily exercising, only made them more anxious to get on with the job. Tomas and his spotter moved ahead of the others to a position with cover and waited for instructions. When the coordinates came down the sniper team didn't have to relocate. They were situated right where they needed to be. Hours passed and the time for making the strike was getting short.

Around five o'clock the shadows began to make it hard for the spotter to distinguish colors. Ten minutes after five the man with the scarf was seen following a taller man from the nearest house, but there was no clear shot while the target moved away from the house toward a pickup truck. Mister Yellow Scarf stood in the way and the opportunity was lost.

"Angel to Foxy. It's an abort. No prize today. The wolf has escaped the cage."

"Okay, Angel. Come home. The eagle will follow the prey."

Before Tomas and his spotter, Doug, could pull back from their position two men who were patrolling the perimeter of the housing compound noticed them and began to fire. Tomas swung his sniper rifle around to his left and took the first man off his feet with a through and through shot. The second Taliban soldier hesitated a second too long. Dristol dropped him with a burst from his M-16.

The brief fire fight alerted the "ant nest" and dozens of Taliban rushed out to join in the skirmish. By that time, the support team ran forward and engaged the enemy. Choppers were heard in the distance and closing rapidly. The Taliban also became aware of the danger from the sky and retreated into the compound for cover.

Fortunately, the Americans suffered no injuries and all withdrew under the protection of the deadly fire from the Cobras. The lead C.I.A. agent radioed the status of the team and transport choppers soon arrived to whisk the marines back to base.

Major Bo Hinds gathered the men to get a first hand account of what took place. "Bernardo, I understand you didn't take a shot. What happened?"

"That's right, Sir. I had no clean shot. The guy with the yellow scarf kept himself between me and the target. He stuck to him like glue."

"He must have had a reason for it. At least we'll give him the benefit of the doubt."

Sergeant Dristol asked the next logical question. "Major, what about the Taliban leader? When do we get another try?"

"Can't answer that, yet. He's being tracked from a Predator. There are four pickup trucks in a convoy, but we can't tell which of the four contains our objective. Until we're sure, we can't drop ordinance and if we did, there's the possibility that we wouldn't get the man we want."

"So, why can't we take out all four vehicles?"

"Bernardo, if it was my decisions, I'd say blow them all to kingdom come and let God sort out the mess. I just take my orders and live with them. It looks like they are heading east for Kandahar Province and then to the Pakistan border. My hunch is they will move north after crossing the border and end up in the high mountains of the Tribal Region."

"So, we've lost him?"

The lead C.I.A. agent interrupted. "We don't give up that quickly. If we don't lose contact, we'll know where they stop and that means,

Bernardo, you'll get another chance. Our man put a tracking devise on one of the vehicles. We will go wherever the vehicle goes."

"Into Pakistan?" Driscol asked.

"I said, we don't give up. Do you have a problem with that?"

"No sir. I never have before and this is no different."

"You all have been to the mountain fighting training grounds out west in the state of Utah. This will be an opportunity to put your training to the test. You will be issued mountain uniforms and in six hours the team will be lifted north and be pre-positioned on the Afghanistan side of the border until we are sure where Abdul Safar holes up."

           *   *   *

The marines and the Central Intelligence agents were helicoptered to the airfield at the capital city of Kabul and then transferred to high altitude choppers that took them to a suitable location in the region of Badakshhan. From the landing zone where the troops were deposited it required some hard marching in rarified air to reach a location near Pakistan and directly over the mountains from Chrital.

Three days on the mountain in bitter cold temperatures tested the team. The waiting was almost as difficult as the weather. There was no time between Helmand Province and the mountains to acclimate. The transfer was abrupt and the terrain extremely demanding.

On the fourth day a satellite message confirmed the initial information. Abdul Safar and a contingent of approximately thirty Taliban with five Al Qaeda guests arrived to occupy a series of caves in the mountainside above Chrital. Satellite observations produced photos. The inside man with the yellow scarf was still among the Taliban.

It was time to move up and over the mountain and then down to a position two hundred yards south of the caves. The hope of the brass hats at headquarters was that Safar would be meeting with the Al Qaeda types to plot some strategy against coming elections. They also felt that there would be an effort against the central government in Kabul. If the Al Qaeda men happened to be collateral damage, that would be a bonus. Tactical restrictions that applied to action in Afghanistan did not apply in the Tribal Region.

It took a full day to reach the pass between mountain peaks and then move over the border. The attacking force finally achieved the designated location. A rear guard was positioned higher on the mountain to protect a withdrawal while Tomas with his spotter, Dristol, made their way to a point above the caves to wait for a repetition of the signal from "Yellow Scarf."

"Lieutenant, how's Ol' Yellow Scarf going to know we're up here?"

"He can't know for sure, but he's got to believe we would stay on the hunt. We would expect him to do a repeat of the signal he was supposed to give us down in Marja."

In spite of trying to put a positive face on all they had to go through to be in position, Tomas was beginning to have doubts about the reliability of the inside man. Would he actually try to put the finger on Abdul Safar, or have they wasted four days? Tomas had hoped he would never have to pull an assignment in high, cold mountains after surviving his ordeal in Nepal.

Thinking about Nepal brought back to Bernardo's mind the sudden manner in which he was reassigned to Afghanistan without any word from Colonel Tagart. Being summarily dumped from his independent missions and put in with several other marines with no explanation was still eating on him. And why were Tagart's offices suddenly empty?

*　　　　　*　　　　　*

It was mid afternoon when some movement was detected in front of a cave opening. A group of seven men came outside and stood in a circle. Through the scopes Tomas and Doug could see that the men were rather animated in their discussion. Five of the men shook hands with one of the remaining two and waved as they began to proceed down the mountain to the village. One of the two men still standing outside of the cave wore a yellow scarf. That had to mean the other man was Abdul Safar.

"Come on Yellow Scarf, do your thing." Tomas wanted to get on with the job and get away. He had a strange feeling that something wasn't just right about the entire operation. He couldn't understand why he had a sixth sense that hunting Safar wasn't going to end well.

The man with the Yellow Scarf couldn't have known the assassination team was in the area, but neither could he know if they were not. The C.I.A.'s man in the Taliban camp could only play out his role and see what happened. As the sniper team watched what was happening below them, their man dipped his head and reached out to touch Safar's shoulder. Tomas squeezed off the fatal shot and Abdul dropped like a sack of cement. Yellow scarf gave a shout to alarm the men in the caves. He had done his job and now he had to cover himself from suspicion.

Bernardo and Dristol grabbed their weapons and began moving back toward the team when the air was filled with whining bullets. The marines returned fire as did the C.I.A. agents. The sniper duo had to drop behind some rocks to keep from being hit in the cross fire. A swarm of Taliban spilled out of the caves firing as they climbed toward the marines. Rocket propelled grenades flew in both directions and Taliban fighters began dropping due to the disadvantage of fighting uphill.

Tomas and his spotter hugged the ground. Standing would have been suicide. A hard object rattled off the rocks and landed next to Dristol. Tomas was aware that the object came from up on the mountain. The rocket grenade exploded with a deafening roar. Dristol took the full force of the explosion and shrapnel tore through him and into Tomas. The world went black and there was no sound as far as Bernardo was concerned; not even the sound of the furious fire fight going on around him. He became numb and began losing consciousness.

Captain Shaeffer ordered Lance Corporal Romaine down the hill to check on the sniper team. He found Dristol, or what was left of him, dead. Bernardo was hanging on to life, but his lower abdomen was ripped badly and he was losing a lot of blood. "Sir, Dristol is gone and the Lieutenant is in really bad shape. He's fading fast."

One of the CIA agents said that they had to leave Tomas because his wounds were fatal and there is no way of getting him out of the mountains in time without getting the whole unit killed. But the marines refused. "We don't leave a wounded man on the field!"

Shaeffer ordered, "Get Dristol's tags. Do what you can for Bernardo. I'm sending down help to haul him out of there."

The marine detachment's suppressing fire drove the Taliban back into the caves while Tomas was retrieved, hooked up with plasma and carried up the mountain. The unit took turns transporting him as rapidly as they could and then down to a pick up site where a high altitude chopper flew in to take Tomas, along with the medic, to the nearest field hospital. The rest of the unit was lifted out later.

Bernardo wasn't totally out of it. He couldn't move, but he could think and sense some of what was happening to him. He needed more plasma and he felt a strange sensation in his body. It wasn't exactly a tingling, but more like a moving "presence;" not of a person or anything outside of his body. It was inside him and it moved upward through his chest and into his head. When it reached that point, everything went totally black again and there were no more sensations or thoughts.

On the operating table at the field hospital paddles were applied to Tomas' chest and a charge made his body convulse. No results! Another charge and still no results. A doctor said to give it one more try and if that didn't do it, that would be it for Lieutenant Tomas Bernardo. The power was increased and a third jolt raised the body from the table. That's when a flicker of life pulsed. And another. And a stronger, irregular one. A nurse gave Tomas an injection and moments later the heart began to beat slow and steady.

"What's his pressure?"

"One ten over fifty."

"I think we have him back, but barely. Let's try to keep him."

Surgical teams went to work to try to stabilize Bernardo. They did reconstructive surgery to reconnect severed blood vessels, and removed part of the colon, along with several metal fragments. It was all too much for a field hospital. The surgeons commented between themselves that they did not understand what was keeping Tomas alive. One remarked, "I've seen fewer holes in Swiss cheese."

The next step for the Lieutenant was a non stop flight to the same military hospital in Germany where he had been taken following his previous assignment in Afghanistan. There he went through more extensive surgeries over the following six days. The prognosis was not good for his survival. Nerve damage to his lower spine and groin made it extremely doubtful that he would ever walk again.

Doctors were able to stabilize Tomas, but he was very critical. Blood vessels had to be tied off and several more fragments of metal and rock removed from his torso as well as his extremities. There were some large fragments that had torn through the abdomen and lodged against the spine. It was necessary to keep Tomas in Germany for several weeks. During that time he was heavily sedated and artificially maintained. He was vaguely aware of his surroundings from time to time. He did not know whether it was day or night. There was no sensation of the passing of time. Sometimes Tomas sensed he was receiving medical attention from a nurse, but most of the hours came and went without him being awake enough to care.

After three weeks Bernardo was more alert for longer periods of time but still drifting in and out and having episodes of being in a semi conscious condition. One day he opened his eyes and saw a blurry vision of two dark forms. The subdued light of the recovery unit was behind the forms, but he knew there were two men at the foot of his bed. They spoke in low voices. He heard his name mentioned. Tomas also realized that these were not doctors and they did not appear to be military. He also heard the statement, "We failed again. He's a hard man to kill." Tomas drifted off to sleep and the next time he opened his eyes there was no one around, except a nurse checking his vital signs.

Had he really seen men in his room talking about him, or was it the effect of the medications? In the next several weeks, the memory of that experience faded and he was more concerned with surviving his wounds and making a recovery that would give him back his normal functions.

CHAPTER SIX

REHABILITATION AND DECISION

From the hospital in Germany to Walter Reed Hospital in the States, Lieutenant Tomas Bernardo's flight was completed without him being aware of his surroundings. He was sedated for the long trip to Washington and there was only a vague and fleeting sensation of being airborne. He had no awareness of day or night and hadn't since he suffered his horrible wounds. Occasionally he felt the presence of someone when a medic or nurse checked his vital signs. With the breathing tube down his throat he could not have spoken had he been conscious enough to verbalize. It was like being in a twilight zone: he was neither dead nor fully alive.

As the huge military aircraft winged its way toward the United States, the attending medical personnel heard Tomas mumbling incoherently about someone named, Saleem. There was also the name, Mutafi. He mumbled about situations that were out of context with anything related to how he was wounded. The word, mole, was often repeated in Bernardo's delirium. One of the people on the plane who overheard Tomas' ramblings was with him on the mountain. He was a C.I.A. agent and was very curious about what the Lieutenant was saying. The agent jotted down a few notes and stuck them in his pocket.

Dr. Hughes expressed his deep concern for Tomas' survivability. "I hope we can get him to Walter Reed in time to deal with the blood clots. His heart rate is forty-five and erratic. His pulse is one ten over fifty-two. Keep a close watch in case he begins to go into cardiac arrest." Captain Hughes cautioned the nurse to be very vigilant.

"Doctor, how did he get his wounds?"

"I heard it was friendly fire, but don't quote me. There will be an investigation, but the details of the incident are cloudy. It was in the heat of a Special Ops mission, but no one will say exactly where."

"When will someone tell him about his paralysis?"

"That will up to the team at Walter Reed."

✳   ✳   ✳

The ten hours of flight time droned on until finally there was touchdown on U. S. territory and a rush by air ambulance to the emergency room where another evaluation of Tomas' condition took place. From there he was transferred to a critical care unit. Bernardo was as weak as a rag doll and dead weight for those who had to move him from the gurney to his bed, but at least he was on home soil.

Two surgeons ordered more x-rays and CT scans. Later, it was determined that an MRI was necessary. The evaluation was made concerning the next steps to save Tomas. Doctors Burris and Agnew looked long at the evidence before speaking. Burris, a tall man in his early forties was the first to break the silence. "This young man is going to be handicapped in several ways. First, there is the paralysis. He may never walk again. Secondly, the nerves to his lower abdomen are damaged beyond repair. Some of the damaged nerves are essential to his reproductive capabilities."

Doctor Agnew, a man in his fifties and short of stature, concurred. "Yes, and that means, even if he does learn to walk and function reasonably well, he's going to have to make a big adjustment socially and psychologically. I really feel for this guy. What a physical specimen he must have been before this happened to him. His records indicate he is Special Forces. Those guys have to be in the best shape to just make it through the training."

"Well, Doctor Agnew, we will have to leave to the psychiatrists how he is able to cope with his inabilities. We have our hands full just piecing him together and giving him a long shot at being ambulatory."

✳   ✳   ✳

The medical team did its work over the next weeks and the results, medically speaking, were better than anyone expected. By the time the first surgeries were complete and Tomas was awake enough to understand what the doctors had to tell him, it was time to break the news about the prospects of him walking again.

Dr. Burris took the responsibility to present some hard facts to Bernardo. "Lieutenant, you're a bit of a miracle. I hope you realize that." Tomas just listened. He knew there had to be a lot more to what being a miracle meant. "We have taken a lot of metal fragments out of you and did some reworking of your organs and they all are expected to function well with time. I don't think you will have any complications in that regard."

Tomas opened his eyes wide. He knew there was more to the report and he had a very good idea what it was. "You don't have to be easy, doctor. Come out with it. Give it to me straight."

"Lieutenant, there has been a great deal of nerve damage. Some of the nerves may regenerate and some will not. You may not be able to walk again."

Bernardo gave no indication that he had been given bad news. He waited for what was to come next. He expected the doctor to tell him what the treatment would be. In his mind there was no question that he would be able to walk again and resume his military career. He was an overcomer; not a defeatist. He had some matters to get straightened out with Colonel Tagart and he also had some mysteries to dig into.

A reoccurring thought kept invading his mind: *Who is Saleem Karab?* Somehow Bernardo was determined to find out if there really was such a person, or was that a code name? To find the answers to his question he had to first get into fighting trim. Walking was a necessary first step.

"Son, do you understand what I just told you?"

"Yes sir. I've been aware I have a problem. I've tried to move my toes."

"Have you been able to move them?"

"No. Not yet, but I will!"

"Well, at least you have the right attitude. You'll need as much positive thinking as you can muster."

"Doctor, I assume you will prescribe a lot of physical therapy?"

"Of Course. Some of it will start while you're still confined to your bed. The physical therapist will move your legs for you in order to help retrain those nerves that have been damaged in your lower back."

"Just make sure she's pretty!"

"It might not be a she."

"That's the worst news you've given me today!"

"Keep thinking good thoughts, Lieutenant. You might get what you want."

As doctor Burris stepped out into the hallway, Doctor Agnew suggested that he not be told of his other injuries until the psychiatric team had a chance to work with him. "It's too soon to bring that to his attention. Let's get him over this first hurdle before we lay another burden on his shoulders."

After sixteen days the colostomy and catheter were removed. Three months in the hospital and another three months of out patient rehabilitation, plus the determined work that Tomas did by himself, brought exceptional progress. Tomas Bernardo's tremendous will power and his dedication to therapy paid off. He did his first solo walk twenty feet down a hospital hallway and back with the aid of a cane and then progressed to using a treadmill just two months later. The prognosis for his mental and social rehabilitation was not as promising.

When Bernardo was finally given the news that the nerves essential for him to function as a normal male had been permanently damaged the information hit him hard. He had always dreamed that one day he would have a son to follow in his footsteps; not in the military, but just in being a man with a love for his country: a child for whom he could provide the love and care his father had given him.

Tomas became withdrawn and unwilling to talk with the psychologist in charge of his case. He could put his life on the line to go into extreme situations to take down a bad guy and he could grit his teeth to do the next-to-impossible accomplishment in rehabbing, but when it came to dealing with something over which he had no control, Tomas became frustrated and depressed.

Nine months from the time he arrived back in the States Bernardo was given a medical discharge from the military. His career was over. Tomas gave up his expensive apartment and found a one bedroom rental in a part of town he did not prefer to have as his address even though he could afford something better. He wanted to reserve his wealth for the personal mission he was planning. He knew it could become costly. It was quite a come down from when he was getting his "hazard pay" and bonuses. That financial arrangement alone should have caused him to realize that something about his "special duty" wasn't according to regulation, but he had swallowed the line fed to him by the Colonel and he liked coming home to a high end apartment in the better part of town.

The stubbornness that had kept Bernardo alive drove him to workout five hours a day. He was obsessed with regaining as much of his fighting form as he could, which would still make him better than most men his age and equal to men he had bested prior to his injuries.

Tomas' motivation was to be man enough to confront Tagart, or whatever his name really was, and also to take pleasure is tearing the "blue suit" guy to pieces. But first he had to find them. He blamed them for his wounds and even wondered if he had become their target after he reported the things he overheard concerning a mole in the Whitehouse. Maybe Tagart wanted Tomas out of the way. Sending him on assignments where there was a great probability he wouldn't come back was better than a straight forward termination. If Tomas' body was left in some remote part of the globe, there would be no questions and he could still be used as a scapegoat to further the aims of Tagart's organization.

One thing Tomas was not ready to do, and probably never would be willing to do, was to begin any kind of relationships with a young woman that might eventually lead to marriage and intimacy. He had it in his mind that that part of his life was over. He assumed he could never find a woman who would love him as a person regardless of his inabilities. A burning hatred for the Colonel was getting hotter while Tomas continued to regain strength in his legs and arms.

✳   ✳   ✳

Located in a nondescript two story building in the outskirts of Washington, D.C. two men sat opposite one another at a table. There was a pot of hot coffee between them and they consumed several cups as they discussed a scene that had taken place several months before. It was when Tomas was still in the hospital. The two men were Tag Tagart and the nameless blue suited special agent. Their problem was a marine lieutenant who somehow had survived every attempt to get rid of him while trying to make it look like a mission that had gone sour.

They shared a piece of paper with notations detailing the things Tomas Bernardo had said in his sedated fog while being flown from Germany. They had been at the hospital to get a first hand appraisal of their "problem." Unknown to the two men, Tomas, although only barely conscious of his surroundings, had overheard them as they stood near his bed talking about him. They were aware that Bernardo was clinging tenaciously to life and both men hoped his wounds would finish what had been perpetrated in the mountains of the Tribal Region.

By all medical indications he had been at death's door from loss of blood and a host of complications including blood clots. It would later become clear to Bernardo that the men must have been Tagart and his associate. The "blue suit" had said, "This guy is hard to kill but I think this time he's done for. We won't hear any more talk from him about Saleem Karab."

The other shadowy figure had conjectured, "Finally, we can say things are moving in our direction. We'll achieve our goals. When the time is right we'll reveal the assassinations were carried out by the U.S. military and blame them on an anonymous right wing element. That will cause nations around the world to call for the U. N. to condemn the United States. Even if the U. N. doesn't take strong action, the effect will be that America will be viewed as the eight hundred pound gorilla in the room. Bernardo will take the most heat whether he survives his wounds or not." Having a fall guy who was a military officer and unable to fight back and refute the charges was a huge plus. His involvement would shock the nation.

✳   ✳   ✳

That day in the hospital room was in the past. Since then Tagart had learned of Tomas' recovery. He put down his coffee cup and came to a conclusion. "Bernardo's survival is not in our best interest. Some news agency might want to publish his story. Few people will believe him if he is able to tell it, but it might raise doubts and cause some to ask too many questions. We don't want to take a chance. He has to go and then we'll make sure the documentation of the murders he's committed will surface. We're in the clear. No one knows our connection with the administration. If he should speak of us, we are phantoms and we have cover from the top."

Tagart and the "blue suit" were not officially part of the government. The entire black ops project was fabricated. They had taken advantage of a patriotic kid from the barrio who wanted nothing more than to serve his country and they turned him into an efficient assassin. They operated on the philosophy that the end justifies the means. So what if it meant killing a few of their own people around the world. Sacrificing a few leftists and Jihadists in remote places as pawns for the greater good was no different than persuading suicide bombers to give up their lives.

When the Al Qaeda master plan eventually came together the "fifth column" in the Whitehouse would activate and grab a greater concentration of power in the top executive; a puppet of the Jihad. Such was the convoluted thinking of the home grown Al Qaeda extremists.

The assumption was that Americans are too decadent and too materialistic to be aware of their own doom until it overtakes them. Peppered throughout the military and the government were "sleepers" who would become active at the proper moment. Even if it should come to an armed struggle between factions in the United States, that would work to the advantage of the Jihadists.

The goal of the master plan was to cause mass confusion in the people's minds and lead the Congress into unwitting decisions that would bring about an economic crash. An out of control economy falling into bankruptcy and the decline of the dollar would destroy individual savings and security. It would also make people willing to follow whoever would claim they had the solution.

✳   ✳   ✳

Sitting alone in his small rental unit, Tomas mulled over his future. His career in the military was finished. He felt a growing disgust for everything he had done and had a desire to bring down those who had led him into committing so many killings, but he didn't know where Tagart and the others could be found. He was equally sure that if he didn't keep up his guard, they might find him first.

Tomas believed it was to his advantage to just disappear until he could sort out his own thought processes and find a new direction for his life. But where could he go that he didn't need to be thinking about who might be around the next corner? He knew too much and he was concerned that Tagart was planning to throw him to the wolves as a cover for the long term plans. They would soon begin to have all their operatives looking for Tomas

There were several reasons why Bernardo felt compelled to escape the life he had been living and get away from the clutches of his handlers.

He struggled with great guilt over pulling the trigger on people just because he was under orders. Tomas lost respect for himself and the notion that he had been doing something patriotic didn't ring true any more. He had been used and it angered him.

Another reason for dropping out of sight was because the people who had been moving him around from country to country like a pawn on a chessboard wouldn't want him to reveal what he knew about the mole. He realized the day was coming when the hounds would be let loose to track him down and try to do to him what he had done to others. He needed a place where he could compile and document what he knew about Tagart and the whole operation. Even if the main stream news organizations might consider him a crack pot, the tabloid press might be willing to listen and run with the allegations.

In the meantime, Bernardo was no longer willing to risk being a sitting target. The attempt on his life in Afghanistan hadn't done the job. A more direct assault might be immanent. Tomas wanted to hit back at the people responsible for his brother's death, but he didn't know how to go about it. He knew how to kill. That wasn't the issue. How to do it and be able to go on with his life was the problem. Bernardo was not suicidal. He loved life. He had seen how cheaply others viewed the life of anyone who needed to be crossed off the list of expendables.

Tomas Bernardo looked for a remote location in the West Virginia mountains where he could hole up while he tried to figure out what to do next. He felt he was being watched even if it wasn't a fact. In order to make his escape he had to lay several false trails. Booking flights to four separate cities would help cover his movements. He flew to one of those cities and then took another flight. On the third leg of his movements he checked into a hotel and then immediately took a taxi to the airport. At the airport he switched taxis after entering the terminal. He then went to another concourse. From that location, Bernardo picked up a prearranged rental car. The paranoia would have been justified if there was truly an active contract on his life.

The "rabbit" then tried to avoid the "hounds' by driving back roads to an out-of-the-way parking lot in Canton, Ohio. At the parking lot of a supermarket, Tomas changed to a four wheel SUV placed there by a former Special Ops soldier whom he knew he could trust. He didn't tell why he wanted the vehicle at that location. The man just had to trust

"Angel" in the way he had when their lives were on the line during a mission. After making the switch to the SUV, Tomas was West Virginia bound. If everything went as planned, whoever might be tailing him would be chasing in circles while he was going down Interstate 77.

The miles clicked off rapidly. From Canton, Ohio to Charleston, West Virginia it was smooth sailing. Tomas drove a few miles an hour under the speed limit. That assured him that everyone would be passing him. If someone laid back and kept pace with him, he would know it. And if someone who had used that tactic changed and went around, Tomas would watch to see whether the same vehicle dropped in behind him at a later time. He didn't need to worry. His false leads had hidden his destination well. Bernardo was free and it felt very strange. The next step was for finding a safe house in a secluded location. He had already designed a cover story for a new identity and had enough cash with him to take care of his limited needs for several months.

✳ ✳ ✳

From Charleston, Tomas navigated the twists and turns along Route 60 up through the mountains to Rainelle, West Virginia where he made contact with a realtor about finding a remote house. There was one available seven miles south at McRoss. The solitary life in McRoss, a dot on the map, afforded him privacy. He found the hundred year old house well off the main highway which he rented. Access to it meant he had to drive across a small stream by way of a wooden bridge and then up a gravel road that snaked around the side of a mountain.

The house was so situated that no one could see it until they were practically on top of it. The single story house consisted of a small living room, two small bedrooms and an eat-in kitchen. There were porches on the front and rear of the house. The only out building was a woodshed. The only cook stove was ancient looking and was heated by either wood or coal. Parallel to the entry road, which dead ended at the next house, was a railroad track that was no longer in use. It once had been used for carrying logs off the mountain.

Once Tomas was settled into his hide-away he began thinking seriously about his plans. What would be so opposite from what he had been doing for the past years? It had to be a profession: something so different that Tagart and his men would never suspect he might be engaged in it. He pondered the question for days and then decided it had to as a minister. He laughed at himself for coming up with the idea. It did not occur to him how hypocritical it was. At the time, it didn't matter. Tomas was just trying to be the chameleon he was once called.

If he was going to pass himself off as a religious person, he had to know a whole lot more than he did. His religious training was extremely limited and his knowledge of the Bible was even less. He decided that the best place to start was to familiarize himself with the Scriptures. He would also purchase a book on theology to learn the jargon of the church before trying to visit one, or he would never pass inspection.

✳   ✳   ✳

For three months Bernardo spent several hours a day pouring over the pages of the Bible and outlining the doctrines that he found enumerated and discussed in a book on Christian theology. Companion to those books were his studies in a set of commentaries on the New Testament Scriptures. He became fascinated by the life of Jesus and especially what he read in the Gospel of John. The more he read, the more convinced Tomas became of his sin and unbelief. This led him to the conviction that He needed to become a participant in a local church so that he could claim a denominational allegiance. What followed those efforts was still a work being processed. He had some knowledge, but his heart was as unmoved as ever. Conviction had not led to confession.

In the little Baptist church of McRoss, he found people willing to befriend him and provide him the social life he had been missing for so many years. Still, he was cautious not to let anyone get too close to him. The simple, uncomplicated preaching of Reverend Thadius Gwinn pulled at Tomas' heart and he began to sense that God was not only real, but that God loved this man who had killed so many people, even as God loved Saul of Tarsus before he became the Apostle Paul.

Through many nights, when Bernardo was all alone in the darkness of his little house, he paced back and forth and argued with God that He had no reason to love such a horrible sinner. One evening before turning out the lights Thomas opened his Bible again to John chapter three and verse sixteen, where he read for the seventh time in the last few weeks that God did love him so much that God was willing to allow His son, the Lord Jesus Christ, to go to a Roman cross to pay the sin debt for all you will believe.

"God, I believe you mean it. I want freedom from my guilt for the

101

things I have done. I ask you to give me peace in my heart. I am so unworthy and I need your help. I need you so very much." It came close to repentance, but not quite. There were still reservations. Did he really want to surrender his life to God? Not fully and not yet.

The tears began to moisten Tomas' cheeks and he struggled to get out from beneath the conviction he felt. He had a desire to escape his sin, but had not come to a place of full commitment to Jesus as Lord of his life. He had yet to cry out for forgiveness. Bernardo slumped to his knees in front of the couch. "Oh, dear God in heaven, I have been so programmed to be what I have been and to do the things I have done. It's so much a part of me, I don't know if I can make the change the Bible asks of me. I'm so afraid the old hatreds and habits will overwhelm me again. Please, God, be merciful to me!" Minutes later, Tomas got up from the floor and went to bed. For the first time in many weeks he slept a full eight hours. When the dawn came, the old feeling of estrangement from God resumed.

✳   ✳   ✳

Tomas assumed the name and identity of Mitchell Harrington and, in his convoluted state of mind, reasoned that once his trail was ice cold he would emerge into the world again and pursue the religious life with his new persona. He thought it might atone for his past and gain some reason for living. It would be as far removed from his former work as anything could be and it would be a shield against his enemies, as well as former friends and associates. He had no idea what a religious life might involve, but decided the first step would be to go to a theological school. With his new identity and falsified academic credentials he was accepted in a Midwest seminary. His change of mind and heart was not complete and the old habits of deception and the sin of creating his own truth continued. He truly was a chameleon.

Tomas, as Mitchell Harrington, sent his documents, along with a recommendation from Reverend Thadius Gwinn, to a theological seminary near Chicago and was accepted as a student in the fall semester. The time rolled around to leave McRoss and the mountain seclusion for the big city of Chicago. He placed the few belongings he had into the back of his SUV and then went throughout the house to make sure he hadn't left any clues to his real identity. Satisfied that there would be nothing remaining to give evidence that he had been there,

Tomas Bernardo drove the crooked unpaved road around the side of the mountain, crossed over the stream by way of the wooden bridge, and turned left on to the asphalt road leading back to Rainelle.

On the north side of the town, Bernardo turned onto route 60 to follow the mountain road to the Capital city where he picked up route 64 going west to Huntington and then he crossed over into Ohio on routes leading to Columbus. On the south side of Columbus, Tomas connected with Interstate 70 which took him through Ohio, Indiana and into Illinois. At the junction with I-65 he turned north to Chicago and what he hoped would be a new life.

✳   ✳   ✳

The first year at the school was difficult but promising. Tomas caught on slowly to the new terms and religious phrases that were more familiar to the other students. Once he became more at ease with theological terms and issues he began to progress rapidly. In the second and third years, Bernardo excelled in church history and biblical languages.

Whereas Tomas did very well academically, he kept to himself and did not socialize with the other students. Many of the other theological students had extensive church backgrounds. Some had been Christian from childhood and very active in the life of their home churches. Bernardo was at a disadvantage when it came to discussing church related topics and so he chose to avoid those times when he felt vulnerable and not able to easily explain why he wanted to study for the ministry.

Most of the students were younger than Bernardo and their life experiences were decidedly different than his. What he could talk about he dared not mention. How could he speak of all the countries to which he had been without provoking questions of why he was there? If he confessed he had been in the military, people would want to know what he did in the service of his country. Of course, he could never say that he was an assassin.

Anyone who began to probe into his life received a cold response and soon learned that Mitchell Harrington was a very private person. There was little in the way of truth that he could share with anyone. Tomas was like a fish out of water, yet he persevered with his education and adjusted to his new identity.

The Greek and Hebrew languages were easy for him and he was often asked by other students for help in understanding the proper translations. His professors took note of his ability and urged him to consider going on to higher degrees and becoming a professor of biblical languages. The entire idea of achieving a doctorate and being a teacher of others was way beyond his plans. For the foreseeable future Tomas was content to be out of circulation and unknown. He immersed himself in his books and tried to suppress the memories of his past.

*   *   *

Three years went by quickly: too quickly to suit Tomas Bernardo. He had lived a lie for the entire time of his studies and he graduated with a degree in church administration and community relations. That qualified him for a position in a large church where there would be multiple ministers with specific responsibilities and he soon gained employment with a mega church in the west suburbs of Chicago.

The memories of the people he had killed as a professional assassin, and the thought of his brother being killed the way he was, haunted Tomas. His new identity and life didn't fully satisfy him, but he knew of no other thing he could do. His social skills were only at a professional level. Because of the complications of his wound, and because of his flash backs and nightmares, he chose to not get involved with anyone on a personal level. He kept relationships superficial. Tomas Bernardo, now Mitchell Harrington, avoided commitments and this frustrated any woman who became interested in him. What few relationships he did develop were temporary. The tension in his life grew as did his nightmares and the dual natures of his life clashed. There was a war within him and it became evident to some of the people in the church that he was different in some way.

The one young woman with whom he was able to maintain an ongoing friendship was someone he met at an open air concert near the Chicago lake front. Sandra Early liked classical music and, in spite of Bernardo's background, he also enjoyed listening to Chopin, Liszt, and other composers' music being played by a large orchestra. His favorite pianist was the late Vladimir Horowitz. Listening to the music had the effect of drawing Tomas away from the past and his concerns about the future. As the music played he found himself living only for the moment. It was like medicine to soothe his emotions.

An occasional dinner, a concert, and a visit to one of many museums in the area were the loose ties that kept Tomas and Sandra seeing each other. She was not interested in what his profession was, because she was not religiously inclined, but never-the-less she was a pleasant and moral woman. That suited him just fine. He was happy to share some time and to enjoy mutual pleasantries while avoiding anything deeper. Tomas was sure if any one dug below the first layer of his skin to find who he was, they would be repulsed, even as he was of himself.

He lived with a fear of discovery; not by his enemies, but by the new people in his life. There were so many skeletons in his closet there wasn't room for anymore. At least, he hoped there would not be anymore. Bernardo had pushed to the back of his mind the passion to get revenge on Colonel Tagart, but little things triggered feelings of hatred for the man and that would last until he became preoccupied with his work or became involved with a new acquaintance. It was at night when old feelings and old wounds came alive and he had to battle them all over again.

       ✳   ✳   ✳

Chapter Seven

A year into his ministry among youth and young adults at the suburban church, Mitchell Harrington, a.k.a. Tomas Bernardo, was feeling a relaxation of tension he had never known before. He was more at ease with others, partly because he felt safe from personal involvements. His relationships were primarily related to his duties and he did not allow any personal feelings he might have to mix with his responsibilities.

Life was beginning to be better than ever. He had even dated a couple of young woman he met at the training club where he worked out twice a week. Most people could not detect that he had been so severely injured. His movements were steady and sure. The loss of muscle tone he had experienced during the years in seminary when he was devoted to his studies was being regained and he appeared younger than his years. His healthy appearance and youthfulness was not lost on some of the young ladies at the church. Even some older teen girls had crushes on him, but he either was not aware of it, or considered their admiration to be childish and not serious.

What Tomas failed to notice, others did, especially the parents of the teenage girls. A conflict soon reared its ugly head when certain members began to question whether it was proper for a single man of thirty-four to be too closely involved, from their perspective, with older teenage girls in the church social programs. Questions became rumors and rumors became nasty accusations. All of this was done without Tomas being aware of the depth of the feelings of certain girls or their parents.

The rumors finally made their way to the pastor and, in an attempt to head off a serious rift in the congregation, Pastor Stephner asked Tomas to come into his office for a discussion concerning his duties. The real reason was to probe into Tomas' thoughts with regard to the brewing controversy. It led to a frank discussion of his supposed behavior.

The office was quite large: three times as long as it was wide. At one end was a leather couch. At the other end was a large mahogany desk. Tomas was invited to take a seat on the couch while the pastor positioned himself comfortably behind his desk. That left about fifteen feet between the two men. It certainly was not a setting for a discussion between two people on the same staff. Tomas had the feeling similar to what he had known in grade school when he was called into the principal's office.

"Mitchell, please have a seat. First, I want to commend you for the work you've been doing in coordinating our social programs with the community and cooperating other churches. You're doing a fine job."

"Thank you, Pastor, but I sense that there is a caveat coming."

"You are a very perceptive young man. There has been some talk.... What I mean is, there are some folks who are concerned that you might be getting too close to some of the young ladies and...."

Tomas stood up. "I don't mean to rudely interrupt you, but I can't do my ministry if these kids are kept at a distance. It's essential that I build trust with them so they will open up and tell me what their conflicts and needs are. My effectiveness in my part of this church's ministry depends upon everyone being open and honest. If someone believes there is a problem with my conduct, I would hope that they would come directly to me for the facts."

"True. True. You're right. However, perception too often becomes fact in people's minds."

"And, sir, I have to tell you I'm stunned by this. What are those perceived facts?"

"Mitchell, I don't really know the truth. I just thought you should be aware of what is being said. Of course, I don't believe any of it."

Mitchell walked to the window. He stared off at nothing in particular for a moment. Should he confide in Pastor Stephner things he had not spoken of to anyone, or leave the doubts about him hanging in the air and let the rumors continue that he might have improper thoughts and actions toward any of the girls?

Mitchell sat down again and leaned forward. "Pastor, you need to know some things about me that should put your mind at ease. I probably should have told you this when you interviewed me for this position,"

"I hope you're not going to tell me you…well, I hesitate to say it… don't like girls!"

"First, let me share something with you and then I'll answer that concern. I have confided in you that I once served in the military and have been in battle a number of times. For personal reasons I asked that the exact nature of my military service be kept private. On one of those missions I was severely wounded. I received shrapnel when a rocket propelled grenade exploded close to me. It tore through my lower abdomen and severed intestines and some vital nerves. I barely survived and it took months before I was able to walk again, but some important nerves were permanently destroyed."

"My word, son, but you look the prime example of health!"

"Pastor, the damage done doesn't show on the surface, thankfully."

The man the pastor knew as Mitchell Harrington paused as though he wasn't sure he wanted to share the rest of his story. Stephner waited with some anticipation for him to continue.

"Allow me be blunt. I am not a threat, sexually, to anyone because of my battle wounds. That's why at thirty-four I'm still single and that's why I would never, under any circumstances, be romantically involved with any woman my own age, let alone teenagers. Yes, I have had dinner dates with women outside of the membership of this church, but that's as far as anything ever goes. I have no desire for anything but casual friendships. And for some gossip to interfere with my ministry among the kids because of a too fertile imagination makes my blood boil."

"Well, I see!" The pastor sat back in his office chair to consider what he had just heard. "You must have times when you experience a great deal of frustration."

"As a matter of fact, my physical condition does not frustrate me. What frustrates me are wrong-headed people who suppose and assume and then talk when they have nothing on which to base their conclusions. Oh, yes, to answer your question. I do like girls. I like them as a Christian man ought to and want to protect them from foolish mistakes. I've been out there in that foul and ugly world and I want to spare as many kids as I can the suffering and the consequences that follow bad decisions."

"Mitchell, I'm sorry that you had to reveal your personal secrets and yet it gives me the insights I need, but now we have to figure out how to stop these rumors before it affects the young people and spreads through the congregation."

"Well sir, I suggest that we assemble all the youth and their parents, along with the deacons and elders, and let me set the record straight once and for all."

"Oh, I don't know about that! It could make matters worse if everyone knew! Don and Celeste Anderson have told me that their daughter, Emily, has a crush on you and that you have encouraged it."

"That is utter foolishness! She is only fifteen and that's what some fifteen year olds do. It will pass! How am I supposed to go on with the way things are and have people thinking I could have unrighteous designs? If the parents are wondering about me, the kids will soon be asking questions among themselves. I've noticed some glances from some of the mothers, but I couldn't put it together until now. If I can't deal with this head on, then all the ugly rumors remain and will still be a problem for the young people after I'm gone."

"Are you saying that you might resign?"

"If I'm not allowed to deal directly with this issue, then people will still believe that I'm the problem and I can't live that way! Thank you for your time, Pastor. I'm asking for two weeks away from everything to consider what I should do. Of course, it's your prerogative to dismiss me right now if you wish."

"No. No, I... I think the decision should be yours. Take two weeks and we'll talk again. That's when a resolution has to be made."

Bernardo got up and shook hands with the pastor who did not offer to pray with his staff member. It seemed obvious to Tomas that Stephner just wanted to wash his hands of the situation and make it go away. Tomas left the office, gathered his brief case from his own office, and exited the church. He decided to go to the regional mall on the edge of the city where the chances were he would not meet anyone he knew. He would just walk the stores and try to get his mind off what he had just experienced.

He didn't know if having told Pastor Stephner about the result of his battle wounds was the best thing to do, but Mitchell Harington; that is, Tomas Bernardo, didn't know what else to do. At least he hadn't confessed that he had been a trained assassin, although he thought that the news might have been accepted better than the possibility that he was being too familiar with the opposite sex.

Tomas began to wonder if the decision to take on his new life as a minister in to order run away from his former employment as an expert sniper was the best decision. He hadn't really thought it through when he left the mountains to begin seminary. It seemed like a good escape. He had no idea of the interpersonal relationships and responsibilities a minister could be involved with. It was a purely selfish decision.

The effort to fake a religious life was turning out to be a terrible mistake. He had no background for it and no calling from God. It was just another deception which Tomas continued to carry forth every day of his life. He was a fraud. His superficial religious experience at the little McRoss church was a spiritual abortion.

It seemed clear that the present situation could not continue. There had to be some other way to avoid Colonel Tagart's radar and still have a life, but what could it be? Maybe he should just run back to the hills and stay there. No, that wasn't the answer. He was used to an urban life. Being buried alive in some remote corner of the Appalachians wasn't something he could endure indefinitely.

There was another unresolved issue. Tomas wanted to expose Tagart and his assassination program and uncover the mole in the Whitehouse. He had done some horrible things that were supposedly in the name of his country and he was compelled to try to make amends for those deeds by publishing what he knew, but that would take time and he had found sufficient time to put it all together yet. While Tomas walked around the mall without any real purpose in mind, he was recognized by a former associate and was approached by the man who called him Angel, his former code name. Tomas tried to deny who he was.

"Friend, you have mistaken me for someone else. That seems to happen to me a lot. I guess I have a universal face."

"Look Angel, or whatever you want to be called, I know you. I heard you were discharged from the Corps and dropped out of sight a few years ago."

"Again, I tell you that I'm a minister on the staff of a local congregation and not the person you suppose me to be."

"Okay. Have it your way. You must have a pretty good reason for denying who you are, but you can't escape the truth."

With that remark the former associate walked away. He looked back twice before disappearing into the crowd. Cold shivers went up Bernardo's back. All his efforts to start a new life may have been blown by a chance meeting of someone who knew who he really was. That potential disaster, on top of the trouble at the church, was causing his world to come apart at the seams. What should he do? What could he do? The confidence that Tomas had developed over the past four years began to erode and he needed someone he could trust to help him sort through his dilemma.

Unknown to Tomas, the man who stumbled across him in the mall doubled back and began shadowing him as Bernardo left the mall and went to his car. He sat behind the wheel of the vehicle and prayed for guidance. It was a prayer of desperation rather than a prayer of faith. Several minutes passed before Tomas started the engine and drove away. He went directly to the church with the intention of clearing out his office, but decided he would leave everything where it was. He wouldn't need the books and equipment any longer. Instead he knocked on the pastor's office door. When he heard Stephner say for him to come in, Tomas entered.

"Mitchell, I wasn't expecting you so soon!"

"Pastor, I have decided I need to speak to a counselor; someone who doesn't know me, and get some help to sort things out. Can you recommend someone?"

"Splendid idea! Yes, I have a man to whom I have referred people. Here is one of his cards."

Mitchell thanked Stephner and quickly turned and left without saying another word."

       *   *   *

Tomas' former associate in the assassination business took note of the name of the church and watched as Bernardo left. He followed Tomas to his apartment. As the man sat in his car down the block, he punched numbers on his cell phone. "Colonel, this is Mike Cromer."

"Cromer, it's been weeks since I've heard from you."

"Yeah. It's been awhile. Guess who I ran into a little over an hour ago?"

"I don't have time for games."

"Okay. Well, it's your old buddy, Angel."

"I can't believe it!"

"No, I'm not kiddin'. I found him in Chicago."

"We lost track of him in Virginia. Do you know how to get in touch with him?"

"Yeah, I have his address, but you'd never guess what he's doin'. He's a minister on the staff of a Community Church."

"That sure takes the cake! Send me what you have."

"Okay, I'll text to you all I have. See you, Colonel."

Tagart sat back in his chair and smiled. "Yes sir, Angel, I've got some unfinished business with you."

∗   ∗   ∗

Tomas Bernardo was completely unaware that he was back in the crosshairs of his former boss, but he had an uneasy feeling that troubled his mind. He began thinking a series of what ifs. What if Cromer told someone that Tomas was still in circulation and living in the Chicago area? Just that much information would be a starting point for Tagart's men to begin tracking him. What if the information got out to his new friends about his past? What if Tagart decided to let him live and just throw him under the bus to federal investigators?

While still contemplating what Tagart might do, the phone rang. "Angel, is that you?"

There was no mistake about the voice. "How did you get this number?"

"Is that a way to greet an old friend?"

"You closed up shop and kind of left me hanging, didn't you?"

"That's just the way things work out sometimes, but we have a new location. I could come and see you, but it might be better for you to come here."

"What makes you think I want to have anything to do with you?"

"Look, Bernardo, it is to our mutual advantage to sit down and talk."

Tomas retorted, "I've been under the impression that you would like to eliminate me."

"Tomas, that's just a misunderstanding. We need each other." The Colonel's voice dripped with sarcasm. "You have information I would just as soon others didn't know, and I could let it be known that you did some pretty naughty things in various countries. So let's scratch each other's back."

Tomas gave a laugh, "Said the spider to the fly!"

"Let's play nice. There is no contract on you. Frankly, a situation has come up and your skills are needed."

"I'm out of the business. Don't you remember? I have a new life."

"Something tells me your new life is getting a little complicated and could get a whole lot more complicated if you want to play it that way. Come on, son, let's just talk. This mission could set you on easy street. It's worth a hundred grand plus expenses. I'm sending a car for you and a private jet. By the way, there are a couple of my people camped outside your place to protect you."

"Protect me from whom?"

"From yourself, Tomas. Yourself!"

Against his better judgment, Bernardo agreed to meet with Tagart, if for no other reason than to have it out with him. If things weren't settled one way or another, Tomas would be looking over his shoulder and running from one place to another for the rest of his life. He packed a carry-on bag, locked up the apartment, and went outside into the hands of two of Tagart's men who placed him in a black SUV that pulled away and headed for an airport.

An hour later Bernardo was in a private jet and on his way to a meeting with the man who had him in a squeeze play. It had to end. Two hours of flight time brought Tomas to Virginia and then a short drive to the door of Colonel Tag Tagart.

The man who answered the door patted Tomas down for a weapon, even though he had been thoroughly searched by the men who were sent to fetch him. Tagart stepped forward and extended his hand to Tomas who refused to take it. The Colonel smiled riley and motioned to a chair opposite the couch upon which Tagart chose to be seated.

"Let me be blunt, Angel. One job and you're done. No strings, no ifs, ands, or buts."

"And if I say no?"

"Well that creates a really serious problem. You see, we have your old girl friend, Beverly."

"How did you…."

"Oh, it wasn't easy, but all things come to him who searches. I changed the saying a little, but it's still true. Never mind the details. Would you like to verify that we have her?"

"Yes!"

Tagart punched in some numbers and spoke to someone and then handed the phone to Tomas. "Bev. Is that you?"

"Yes, Tomas. I…."

"That's enough!" Tagart took the phone from Bernardo and turned it off. "You see, I have an idea that you don't really want any more of your friends to pay for your mistakes, so you had better listen to what I have to say."

Tomas kept quiet and listened as the Colonel explained that a certain individual in his organization had gone rouge and was a potential problem. His independent actions were making things hard for the leadership and, since this individual knew almost everything about the group's plans and personnel, he had to be stopped.

"You expect me to take out one of your own? That sounds strange to me."

"This guy knows everyone we could send who has any chance of doing the job. We need you and, clearly, you need us. At least Beverly needs somebody."

"I've given up killing people. I promised God I was finished with it."

"Tell that to your God when you're the one responsible for Beverly's early demise. No, son, you're not through! There is still one more. Is it going to be my enemy, or your friend?"

It was either take a mission and save Beverly or lose her and have his sins revealed to all those who had grown to trust Tomas in his Mitchell Harrington persona. Beyond that, he could be exposed to federal authorities in the Justice Department who take a very dim view of actions like those conducted by Tomas in the past. They would be eager to prosecute former black ops personnel. Some of the liberals on the Hill would fall all over themselves to get their faces in front of a camera and play god.

"Who's the target?"

"He is known as Ishmael Omar."

"And where is he?"

"Yemen."

Tomas sat up straight. "Yemen! You expect miracles?"

"I know you, Angel. And, yes, I expect you will pull off a miracle for your friend and your freedom." Tomas was subdued by the situation and hesitated to make the commitment, but there wasn't any way out. "Come on, son. I hold all the cards and you know it."

Tomas agreed to one operation with one condition. "Not that I don't trust you, Colonel, but make it two hundred thousand with half up front and the balance when I get back. After all, I'll be unemployed and probably unemployable after this is over."

"You drive a hard bargain, Angel. I'll wire your account."

"When I see it's in the account, I'll take on the assignment."

He realized the very thing he hoped would never happen had come true. A person can change his name, his profession, and his appearance, but unless there is a dynamic internal transformation nothing really changes. The past once again jumped up and smacked him right in the face. Living the lie wasn't working.

Somehow Tomas had to find a way to get Beverly's release so that he could renege on the mission. He just didn't know how. The thought came to him that he ought to pray, but he doubted that God would hear him because of the horrible things he had done and was about to do again. There was no use for Tomas to try to go public with what he knew because of the threats against family and friends. He was convinced Tagart and his goons were responsible for Joaquin's death. There was also little doubt that the so called friendly fire that wounded him was not an accident.

Unless Bernardo could anonymously reveal the dirty inner working of Al Qaeda within the U. S. government, all he could do was bide his time. The first priority was the safety of the people for whom he cared. After that, Tomas really didn't care what his enemies might do to him. He wished he could just disappear rather than be sucked back into the quagmire, but there didn't seem to be any other choice than to take the mission and hope he survived to give Tagart what was due him. He had read the Scriptures where Jesus said to love your enemies, but Tomas wasn't Jesus and Tomas was not a mature believer. Revenge was still on his mind, but saving Beverly came first.

Bernardo checked his bank account two days after his meeting with Tagart and found the hundred thousand dollars had been deposited. He immediately transferred the same amount to a bank in Miami which he had under another name and different Social Security number. Tomas had absolutely no trust in the Colonel and assumed he might find some way to take back the funds.

If Tomas survived the trip to Yemen, he would need to disappear again and all the money he had stashed in various safe deposit boxes in different places would enable him to make his escape and provide the resources he needed to start a new life. He believed strongly that he might have to leave the United States and would need to quickly access those accounts.

Before he had to leave the country and begin what he hoped was his last job, Tomas decided he would pay a visit to the psychologist Pastor Stephner recommended. He had to try to talk with someone and get some things out in the open so that an unbiased person could react to his story.

✳   ✳   ✳

Tagart had already set his own plan in motion. Bernardo was being watched night and day. Every move he made was filmed and sent to the Colonel. Every person Tomas spoke to was photographed and, where possible, the conversations were recorded. It was clear that when Tomas returned from Yemen he and anyone Tagart suspected would not be long for this world.

An undercover agent paid a visit to the Community Church and was able to speak with Pastor Stephner. The agent, dressed in an army officer's uniform, gave a fabricated story to try to get more information of people Tomas, as Mitchell Harrington, may have spoken with in the past two weeks. It was a matter of "national security."

"Reverend, I know this is an unusual request, but you are aware that your staff member, Mitchell Harrington, was in the Marines before becoming a minister."

"Yes, I am aware of that."

"What you do not know is Lieutenant Harrington has a high, top secret security clearance and has in his mind information that is vital to our country's security."

"Well, I am certainly impressed. Mitchell never mentioned anything about his service except that he was severely wounded."

"Yes, Reverend, that is true. Harrington is a hero. The reason it is so urgent to contact him is because some of the data he has provided us is missing. We cannot retrieve it from our computers. The Lieutenant could help us restore the data, but we cannot locate him. Can you assist us with his whereabouts?"

"I wish I could, but he has left our employment."

"This is unfortunate. Do you have any idea if he might go to someone looking for new employment?"

"Employment, no, but he might want to speak to a counselor I suggested. I shouldn't even tell you about this, but Mitchell said he had some decisions to make before he left us and I gave him a referral to a Doctor Peterson. Since this is of such national importance I suppose I can give you the doctor's business card."

The agent accepted the card with a broad smile and the feeling that he had pulled one over on the naïve minister.

CHAPTER EIGHT

CONFIDENTIALITY

The conflict within Tomas Bernardo was being compounded by recent events, including the problem at the church and the danger posed to Beverly Proctor. He was sure he was finished with the church. There was no going back to that situation, but Beverly was constantly on his mind. If the woman had been more than a friend, the tension that had a strangle hold on Tomas would have been even harder to bear. He felt compelled to seek a private counselor who would listen to his story; someone who would not divulge any information Tomas might find it necessary to reveal to him. He felt pulled in so many directions and hoped to get some personal issues settled before leaving for Yemen. Whatever he decided to do, someone was going to be hurt. Worse yet, someone would die.

Tomas made an appointment with Dr. Peterson. In order to shake from his trail anyone who might be following him, as well as to protect the psychologist, he drove around for an hour and then pulled into a public parking garage where he left his car and walked five blocks away to a group of stores. Tomas used reflections in windows to keep an eye on people behind him. He stopped repeatedly to window shop before going into stores where he spent several minutes pretending to look at items.

Each time Bernardo stepped back onto the sidewalk he did a scan both ways to check out people on foot. He then carefully observed the traffic for any vehicle that he thought might be used by Tagart's goons. This cat and mouse game went on for another hour until Tomas decided to step into a small diner where he sat at the counter and ordered a cup of coffee. By facing the mirror behind the counter he could see anyone passing on the sidewalk. Satisfied that he wasn't being followed Tomas took one more precaution just in case he had missed something. He slipped out the back door and hailed a taxi that took him to his appointment with Dr. Marvin Peterson.

The receptionist, a tall, thin, dark haired woman in her mid thirties, ushered Tomas into Peterson's office. "Doctor, this is your new client, Mister Mitchell Harrington."

The office that also served as the counseling chamber was paneled with dark walnut. The desk matched the color of the walls. Various academic degrees and diplomas graced one wall. They were in matching gold frames with black matting. On the opposite wall there was a row of mahogany book selves with a hundred or more books whose binding looked brand new. The entire room was so neat and void of any excess furnishings that Bernardo wondered if the doctor might have an obsessive compulsive disorder.

Peterson stepped out from behind his desk and greeted Tomas by his assumed name. "Mitchell, please have a seat. I'm very happy to meet you." Doctor Peterson drew up a chair opposite Tomas.

"Thank you for seeing me, Sir."

Peterson skipped small talk and gave his new client some ground rules. "The only thing I ask of you, Mitchell, is that you be totally truthful with me. It is the only basis by which we can deal with the reason you have for coming here. Is that possible?"

Tomas looked at the plush beige carpet on the floor and then directly at the doctor. "Well, sir, I have been living a life of so many different personas for such a long time I sometimes don't know which identity is really mine, but I'll try, Sir."

The statement caused Peterson to react as he sat a little straighter. "Just a minute Mr. Harrington, are you saying that you think you have multiple personalities?"

"Not really. What I'm saying is the business in which I've been engaged required me to assume different identities in order to achieve success."

"Just what is the nature of this enterprise that asked you to pass yourself off as different persons?"

Tomas fidgeted in the chair as Peterson made a quick note on a pad of lined yellow paper. It was very difficult for Tomas to sort out in his own mind exactly why he resorted to seeing a psychologist, but he knew he had to open up to someone about his emotional and moral conflicts. He didn't trust anyone, including Pastor Stephner. His only option was a professional counselor who would be bound to guard a client's secrets.

"Sir, will you promise me that anything I say to you will be held in absolute confidence."

Peterson leaned forward as if to emphasize his commitment. "Of course! Your secrets are safe here."

"Another thing, Sir, I saw you write down something. You can't take any notes. There can't be anything in writing."

"Is it that important to you that I not make a record of our conversation? I can assure you that all records are locked away and I alone have the combination to the files."

"Sir, the things I may want to tell you could put you in danger."

The doctor placed the notepad on the table beside his chair. A look of great concern came across his face and his eyes narrowed. "Mitchell, I have the impression that you were in the military. Is that true?"

"Yes, Sir. I was until I received a medical discharge a few years ago."

"That explains why you keep calling me, sir. I would prefer that you call be Marvin. If that isn't comfortable for you, then please just call me, Doctor."

Dr. Marvin Peterson began wondering if the warning of danger was real or something Tomas imagined. Until he could determine the facts, he would consider the warning real; at least real to Tomas. Setting aside that issue for the moment, the doctor needed to get some personal information. "We are about the same age, so that means you have had a few years in the military, but what have you been doing since you left the service?

"Well, Sir; I mean Doctor, I have been serving on the staff of a church for the past nine months, but I'm not really a minister if you mean preaching and conducting worship services. My duties were more along the lines of social activities. I set up programs for young people; mostly young adults, and worked as liaison between the church and community organizations to coordinate social programs. There is another thing I need to clarify before we go any farther. Mitchell

Harrington is an assumed name. It isn't my real name, but I'm not ready to give that to you just yet."

"All right, we will leave it as Mitchell for the time being, but eventually you will have to be more open, or we won't make a great deal of progress. What exactly brings you to me?"

There was a long pause as Tomas tried to determine where to start and just how much he would be willing to reveal to this stranger. He instinctively felt he could trust Peterson, but he also doubted that the doctor would believe everything he had to say.

"Doctor, the information I have is so sensitive politically that I'm almost afraid to share it with you. In fact, I feel you won't want to believe what I have to say."

"Then share something that isn't so sensitive. Tell me about yourself. What are you feeling right now?"

Tomas stood and walked around to the back of his chair. He placed his strong hands on the black leather and his fingers made deep impressions in the padded material. "I feel trapped. I've done some terrible things as a soldier. I mean really horrible things." His voice was soft and in contrast to his very muscular build and square-jawed features.

"Please sit down and tell me about it."

Tomas returned to the chair and sat in a rigid position. "I've been in combat many times and it was kill or be killed. I can live with that, but what has become a burden that is almost too much to bear is the number of souls I have deliberately sent to hell."

That got the doctor's attention. "How do you mean that? How could you be responsible for sending someone to hell."

"I've been a government paid killer: a sniper."

"Isn't that part of war?"

"Yes, but not exactly the way I was ordered to do it. I've taken out bad guys who were non combatants."

"Civilians!" Peterson tried to hide his shock, but his raised voice evoked a response from Tomas.

"Doctor, I don't mean women and children and old men. It was my job to hunt down and terminate certain leftist leaders and directors of worldwide terrorism; enemies of freedom."

"But that is really disturbing you, isn't it? Why do you think that upsets you so much?"

"Some of the people I killed were not shooting at me. They didn't even know I was around. I was an executioner. It also upsets me greatly that I was told lies in order to enlist my cooperation. I thought I was serving the strategic purposes of my country, but in reality I was Shanghaied into a shadowy black opts group not authorized by any of the recognized security agencies. That means every kill I made was illegal."

"You're finding this knowledge hard to live with, aren't you?"

"Of course! I had always thought of myself as a moral person and, as long as I thought what I was being tasked to do was in the interest of national security, I could tell myself what I did was a case of good against evil. Since I got out of the business by changing my identity and going to seminary to serve God through church ministry, I've come to hate the things I did, even though I was sure at the time they needed to be done."

"Okay, Mitchell, I get it. You are remorseful and you need to clear your conscience, but why the secrecy? Can't you report this information to someone in the government you can trust?"

"I don't know who I can trust. If I tell anyone, they are bound to turn me over to be arrested and tried for my part in the operations. I'll pay the price and the people who lied to me will get off. I just know that's how it will turn out."

Thomas revealed to the counselor that he had served at the discretion of a man who represented an official next to the president. He told Doctor Peterson that the man to whom he reported directly passed himself off as a high ranking military officer and everything was arranged so that there was always "plausible deniability" for him and his superiors.

"I'm not saying anything against regular Special Forces people. Some of the greatest people I have ever known were SEALS, Rangers, and Special Forces, but a handful of us were sold the idea that the world's problems could be greatly helped if certain 'bad guys' were not around to lead a global war against democracies. We were idealists and if it made our country's safety dependent upon eliminating tyrants, we were willing to risk our lives for the cause."

"How many people were there who did the kind of missions with which you were involved?"

"I don't know how many, but it was an elite group. Many of us never met. We were hand picked to be used by the shadow organization. I bought into it, but finally couldn't take it any longer. It wasn't just that I had to kill, but some great guys who went with me never came home. Besides that, instead of the world being made better it has just become worse. Every terrorist or tyrant I killed was replaced with another just as bad. I thought I was being patriotic and that's what we were told. We'd being doing our job for the government, or so we thought, and then I found out that the official attitude toward what we did is that we are criminals. If our own legitimate government found out what was being done, we would be punished but the vermin who lied to us would have higher ups to cover for them. I couldn't continue to tell myself that I was doing any good. To have our own leaders disavow us, after all the hell I've seen and experienced, makes me want to do to them what they had us do to other people."

"Mitchell, do you think that will solve anything? Wouldn't that be just as wrong as what you have already done?"

"I suppose it would be, but maybe it would make me feel better!"

Doctor Peterson could not keep a frown from showing a measure of disapproval of Tomas' last remark, but he said nothing.

Bernardo continued to spill out his frustration. "This shadow group won't let me quit! They discovered where I am and what I'm doing. They threaten to expose me so that I can be prosecuted for any number of felonies. I could spend the rest of my life in a federal prison. All the people I care about would find out what I have been."

"Who are the people you refer to as 'they'?"

"The people who gave me my assignments. I'm really sorry, but there is a whole lot more to this than a few dozen assassinated bad guys. I just don't know if I want to put you in the position of knowing too much."

"At the moment, I still don't know who 'they' are. Can you be more specific? Can you name these people?"

"It's better that you don't have names. As far as they're concerned you already know it all."

"Mitchell, you're not making sense. Who are 'they'?"

"People in the government who are connected with the rogue black ops group that arranges murders for hire. More accurately; shadow government people: the government within the government. They have an agenda and anyone who gets in the way or crosses them can just disappear. I know; I worked for them. The organization goes by the name, Abishai."

"That's a strange name."

"You can look it up in the Bible in First Samuel chapter twenty-six, verse eight. It's the name of a friend of David; you know, the David who became king of Israel. This, Abishai was the brother of Joab, another of David's men. David and Abishai went into King Saul's camp at night with the intention of killing the king. The passage quotes Abishai as saying to David, 'God has given your enemy into your hand. Now let me pin him to the earth with one stroke and I will not strike him twice.'"

"I assume the name was adopted because of the efficiency of the killing which Abishai boasted he could do."

"That's what I have been told. Well, it became the name for this private black ops group under contract to the shadow government. I thought I was serving my country and then I discovered they turned me into a mercenary. I should have known something was wrong"

"What information do you have that is so threatening to this shadow government that they would be after you, and why don't they just kill you and be done with it?"

"Because they don't know if I've documented the information and deposited it somewhere. The other way to keep me in line is to force me back into action for them."

"How can they do that if you don't want to get involved again?"

"They have already killed my brother to coerce me to keep me serving them. There are others they have threatened to kill if I don't comply. I just don't know what to do. The worst part is that I know how far this subversion in America goes. It goes right into the Oval Office."

"Come now, Mitchell, how do you know that?"

"A big shot in Al Qaeda bragged in front of me about it. I was a captive and about to be executed. He thought it would be safe to gloat over how they would take over the United States from within without firing a shot. They would do it politically after creating a great economic collapse."

"He must have just wanted to torment you with lies before he killed you."

"Doctor, I have enough experience to know when a man is just bragging to intimidate and when he's doing it because he's confident in his information. That man knew what he was saying was true. He had no idea that I was able to hear him."

"Where is this man now?"

"He doesn't exist any more. I killed him in Indonesia."

"Mitchell, stop and think for a moment. If what he said is true and you escaped with that knowkedge, don't you believe he might have warned others among his fellow terrorists that you just might have that information?"

"He wouldn't have admitted to it once I escaped. It would have exposed him to those above him as being too loose with information. The fact that I found him again on the Celebes Island proves he kept his secret."

"You know that to be a fact?"

"Didn't I just say I took the man's life? That was over four years ago."

"Then why are you so concerned about him saying something since he's dead?"

"It isn't him! It's me! I made the mistake of reporting what he said when I was debriefed. I trusted the wrong people. I was a soldier talking with other soldiers, comrades in arms, brothers, or that's what I believed."

"But Mitchell, this just doesn't fit. You have described what sounds like a radical right wing paramilitary group: this Abashai, but Al Qaeda couldn't be connected with Abishai. They seem to be opposites."

"That puzzled me at first, but what I see is an overall effort to cause as much confusion as possible. I think Al Qaeda wants people to think that these high profile assassinations are official United States military approved murders. At some point Abishai could be sacrificed, but for now the group is part of the convoluted thinking of movements that are willing to give up some low level leftists and Al Qaeda leaders around the world for the sake of the grander plan. With attention diverted to Abishai, the mole in our government can begin to take more power. When congress gets all wrapped up in hearings into these assassinations, the infiltration of our government by Al Qaeda operatives can go on without being hindered. It's an effort to get congress looking in one direction while doing something worse in another direction."

"Mitchell, I have to admit that this sounds to me as a rather fantastic scenario you have described, even if it is real. Who else might have known about an alleged mole high up in our government?"

Mitchell lowered his head. "My brother. I told him and now he's dead! I was told it was an accident, but circumstances surrounding the crash leave too many questions."

"So, you're convinced someone, either an undercover terrorist mole, or an agent in one of our intelligence groups was involved. That sounds a bit unbelievable, don't you agree? Our government wouldn't engage in such things."

Mitchell just sat motionless and looked directly into the eyes of the counselor. "Doctor what do you think I was doing for more than five years and what I'm expected to keep on doing as a private contractor? I was a soldier doing his duty for his country. I took an oath, but slowly I became aware of political enemies and their suppression of any sort of free speech. They use intimidation and censorship. Dissidents will not be tolerated. Their grab for power will become more open as they spread out through the government. I'm being forced to do one more mission in order to save a friend who is being held captive by the same people I've been telling you about."

"How do you know they will kill your friend if you refuse to do their bidding?"

"Because there are others just like me who will do whatever they are told without any hesitation."

"But you have hesitated."

"Yes, but I've had my conscience awakened. I made a pledge to God."

"But you're willing to break that pledge."

"Not willingly! Oh, how my sins haunt me! How will I ever find redemption and release from all the souls I've destroyed?"

"Mitchell, God is the God of grace. He will forgive, but you have to stop and not continue on this path. You'll lose contact with reality."

"Doctor, maybe I have already. I'm sorry, but I have to leave now. I have to save my friend!"

Doctor Peterson urged Tomas to stay, but he just kept walking and closed the door behind him. He left the building and hurriedly went to his car and just sat for several minutes before driving out of the garage. Something inside motivated Tomas to drive by the Doctor's address. He slowed down as he passed the building and then sped up and left the area. He failed to notice the large black vehicle parked across from Peterson's office. Two men got out of the car, crossed the street, and entered the psychologist's building. Fifteen minutes later they left, quickly got into their vehicle, and sped away. Several minutes later a fire alarm sounded and smoke could be seen by people on the street as the heat forced it from beneath the doors.

Bernardo was unaware of the tragedy until later that evening when the television news carried the story of a fire in the officers of a Doctor Marvin Peterson that completely gutted the rooms. Amid the debris were two badly burned bodies of a man and a woman. They were identified as the doctor and his receptionist. Tomas watched in stunned silence. He thought, *Is there no end to what Tagart and his people would do to protect their cause? I have no choice but to take the next mission and when that's done and Bev is safe, I'll deal with the Colonel myself. This has to end.*

CHAPTER NINE

YEMEN: AGAINST HIS WILL

Tomas Bernardo went to the offices of Colonel Tag Tagart to get his final briefing on the next mission, but he also gave the man who had become his enemy a warning. "Tagart, you've done enough damage to the people I care about most in order to get at me and I don't want any more innocent people dieing. I'll do this one mission for your dirty organization and then you have to turn me loose for good."

"And if I don't?"

"It's your funeral, Colonel. I really don't care what happens to me, but you better know I've documented the entire sordid mess. It stays a secret unless you promise that this is the end of our association and you leave everyone else connected with me alone." Tomas was being deceptive. He hadn't put anything on paper or transmitted it by any other means. All the information was still in his head. As long as the Colonel didn't know that, Bernardo had the edge temporarily.

"Okay, Angel! But you had better hold up your end of the deal or you're the one who will pay the price along with the people you're trying to protect. You got that. Mister!?"

Tomas didn't respond to the threat. "Who do I get to brief me on the assignment?"

"We have a man who just came out of Yemen who can orient you as to people and geography. Once you're in country, it's your job to nose around enough to get a line on the target. You had better be at your best, because almost everyone there carries a weapon and they won't hesitate to take you down if they even suspect you're trouble."

A meeting was arranged with a man named Anar Bednam who began to prepare Tomas for his understanding of a country that was a total enigma to him. Bednam was a totally fictitious name, adopted as a reverse spelling of the strait connecting the Red Sea with the Indian Ocean, Bab-el-Mandeb.

"I am told you are called, Tomas, but you have used the name, Angel. What shall I call you?"

"At this point in my life you might as well use my given name. Secrecy is a thing of the past, at least in this country."

"Well, Tomas, secrecy will save your life in Yemen. Finding your man in that country will be like looking for a particular grain of sand in the desert."

"If it's going to be that difficult, why should I bother?"

"Colonel Tagart tells me you have good reason to find Ishmael Omar. He had gone to ground and he will not be using that name, but first things first. Yemen is larger than it looks on a map, but is dwarfed by Saudi Arabia. It has just over nineteen hundred kilometers of coast line and over seventeen hundred kilometers of border with Saudi Arabia and Oman. The border with Oman is less than three hundred miles, so what you have is a country that is long and narrow."

"What about elevations?"

"The topography ranges from coastal plain to an interior of mountains up to twelve thousand feet above sea level: that would be the mountain Jabal an Nabi Shuayb. The coastal area rises quickly to a plateau with rolling hills. The eastern plateau region and the desert in the north are hot and dry with very little vegetation. The northeastern area is known as the Empty Quarter. There is hardly any rain and sometimes the dry spells can be prolonged. As a contrast, the central highlands get enough rain for raising crops."

"Okay; in which part of this uninviting place may I expect Omar to be hiding?"

"I don't think he will be in the eastern region or the mountains. There is so much barren area because only four percent is wooded land. He could find more places to hide where there is a population. The twenty-nine million people are concentrated in cities and towns. What I know about him is that he likes to be where there are ladies and good food; not necessarily in that order."

That possibility didn't seem right to Tomas. "If he knows he's on Tagart's list, wouldn't he be in deep cover?"

"When I said he has gone to ground, I didn't mean he is totally out of where the action is. He will come to a population center from time to time to feed his carnal appetites. Oh, by the by, one thing you'll have to deal with is the extreme change in temperatures. Away from the coast it can go from nearly ninety degrees in the day and drop to freezing at night. Along the western coastal plain the temperature can reach one hundred twenty-nine degrees."

"I'll be sure to pack my travel bag accordingly."

Over the next two weeks Tomas familiarized himself with the Yemen population centers in preparation for leaving to search for the man he was supposed to execute as the price for Beverly's release and his own freedom. There was the lingering thought that there could still be strings attached to his ability to get completely free of Tagart and the information he held over Tomas.

The Colonel had built a wall of protection around himself. There were people in the right places of government who could keep him out of the justice system, but Bernardo was a pawn in the game and had no protection. Never-the-less, he had to go forward with the deal to find Ishmael Omar.

Tomas spoke Arabic and could easily pass for someone from that part of the world. Just to be sure that he had an identity that fit who he was pretending to be, he chose the name, Jabal el-Tihamah. The people who made up the documents began their work to provide Tomas with passports: one for Yemen and another for Morocco in case he needed a back up. He would be carrying currency for both countries. In order to have a means for drawing out his prey, Tomas took the cover of being a buyer for precious and semi-precious metals. Yemen had minor deposits of gold, nickel and copper, as well as lead.

✳   ✳   ✳

From Washington, D. C., Bernardo flew to London. At Heathrow, he changed planes for Morocco, and then took a flight to Aden where he checked into a hotel under his assumed name and began making the rounds of those establishments where he might bump into Omar. They were not the places Tomas wanted to be, but it was necessary. He had a mental picture of Ishmael Omar, but also carried a photo of him that he could show around if that became expedient. Tomas would rather not have anyone know that he was looking for someone in particular.

It could spook the whole search. It could take weeks, even months to uncover Omar.

One of the first things Tomas did was to pick up information for a lead on a hand gun. The black market ran a brisk business in all kinds of weapons. He prowled the ally ways until he spotted a street corner transaction and waited until the seller was free before making his approach. "I'm a gun collector with some money to spend and I understand you're the man to see."

"You say you collect guns? What sort of guns?"

"Small ones that fit in a pocket. Say nine millimeters?"

"Where do you come from, Mister?"

"Jabal. My name is Jabal. I come from Morocco and Yemen. My mother is Yemeni."

"You know, Jabal, if you are lying to me you will not make it out of this ally."

"Is that a way to speak to a paying customer? I assumed you have a few friends to watch your back, so I would be a fool to be deceptive. What is the price?"

"Two hundred American dollars. The price is firm. I don't negotiate. I have nothing for you right today, but you come back here at nine o'clock tonight and you can have your merchandise."

"Sorry, my friend, I don't do business after dark, but I will meet you here at nine o'clock in the morning."

"I like a man who is cautious. I am cautious too. If I am not here at that time, please wait and you will get what you came for. Agreed?"

"You have what I want so I agree. Just make sure the merchandise is in very good condition and with the necessary attachments."

"A box of ammunition is one hundred dollars extra."

"Agreed."

On the next day, after waiting two hours, the transaction was completed. I quick check of the weapon's condition, and Tomas was armed for the next phase of his mission: finding Omar.

One week quickly passed. Tomas was pressing hard to stir up some interest in finding someone who would like to sell minerals and metals. A few contacts were made and a great deal of talking but no serious negotiations. He made sure his offers for the few possibilities that were presented to him were low enough that no one wanted to sell.

Another week passed and all efforts were like hitting a dry well; nothing was produced. For a man noted for women and gluttony, Omar was nowhere to be found in any of the places Tomas canvassed. It was time to begin to ask if anyone had seen him. Tomas gave people the story that he was a buyer for precious metals and had heard that the man in the photo was someone who could steer Tomas to the right sellers.

In the third week, Bernardo got a hit. The proprietor of a little back ally restaurant said he had seen such a person a few times, but not for a month. He also said he didn't think Omar was the type of person who would have contacts in which Tomas was interested. After a generous amount of money changed hands for the information, Tomas chose to stake out the place since he had no other leads. The wait went on for two more dreary weeks until one late afternoon a man resembling Ishmael Omar walked into the joint and ordered something to drink and a large plate of food that Tomas could not identify.

The owner of the restaurant got Bernardo's attention and indicated with a nod that this was the man for whom he had been searching. He slipped into a chair at Omar's table and asked, "May I buy you a cup of coffee?"

Omar stiffened and made a gesture toward his pocket. "I do not drink with strangers!"

Bernardo put one hand on the table palm down over several pieces of currency and kept the other hand in his pants pocket. "But, friend, we are not really strangers. We have a mutual acquaintance."

Tomas noticed Ishmael's eyes flitted between the stack of bills and the man who sat opposite him. His curiosity was peaked by both. "And who is this mutual friend?"

"I didn't say he was a friend. In fact, I would describe him as a mutual enemy if my information is correct." Omar was even more intrigued, but maintained a firm grip on the item concealed in his pocket.

"Is this mutual enemy, as you describe him, a colonel?"

"He is."

"If you are lying to me and he is not really your enemy as well as mine, then one of us will not leave this place alive."

"That would be a terrible shame, because I must be able to go back and report to him that you are dead. If he doesn't get verification of that fact, then he will have members of my family and my friends killed."

Ishmael Omar leaped to his feet with gun his hand, but Tomas remained seated and slowly placed both hands on the table. "I didn't come here to kill you, so sit down and listen to what I have to say. You have the gun. My hands will stay where you can see them."

Omar kept the gun pointed at Tomas as he slipped back into the chair. "Mister, whoever you are, you make no sense."

"Then hear me out and it will become clear. The Colonel wants both of us dead. I know he's lying to me and the only way we both escape the trap is to be smarter than he is."

"Go on."

"Tagart has you on the list because he says you have switched sides. He thinks you might talk to the wrong people and expose names and places. You know too much you're no longer a threat. That means, he has to believe you're dead. He also has to believe that I finished the job."

"And just how do I die and still live?"

"It can be done, but you have to not shoot me."

"So, if I don't shoot you, then what?"

Tomas Bernardo laid out a plan where he and Omar would find a remote house where they would set up a fake bomb making scene. The bomb would be real because it had to be the means of Ishmael's supposed death. To satisfy Tagart that Omar was really dead there had to be a body identified by someone credible enough to be believed. The problem was finding a body and someone corrupt enough to swear falsely.

Having listened to the scheme, Omar took several minutes to mull it over before speaking. With the gun still visible, he finally spoke. "To get someone to say that a dead body is me only takes money and you have already gotten my attention with your money, but there had better be more currency than you were showing. As far as a body is concerned; that means someone has to die."

Tomas shook his head. "No. Someone has to already be dead. We need a freshly buried man."

"You would rob a grave?" Ishmael Omar acted like he was shocked.

Bernardo replied, "You would kill someone?"

"It would be easier!"

"Ishmael, if all I wanted to do is kill someone, I could have killed you and the problem would have been solved, but I don't want to kill anymore, unless someone is trying to kill me. I'm sick of it!"

"You are a very strange person. Do you realize that?"

"Look, we have to find a place out from other houses so that no one is hurt from the explosion. First, we need explosives. After that we have to watch a cemetery for a newly buried man."

"If I am to do this terrible thing, I need to know the name of the criminal I am going to share the punishment with if we are caught."

"Just call me, Angel."

"Angel? More like Devil!"

"Ishmael, I will turn out to be your guardian angel if this plan works."

✳   ✳   ✳

With an agreement that the two men would not try to kill each other and would instead concentrate on dealing with their common enemy, Colonel Tagart, Tomas and Ishmael set about to locate a small house or shed several miles north of Aden. They could not find an abandoned house, but were able to negotiate the rental of a ten foot by twelve foot shed that had been used for animals. The smell was horrific, but since they did not intend to do anything more than blow it to pieces as soon as they could locate a stand-in body for Omar, the odor didn't really matter.

Obtaining the explosives was a simple task. Yemen had all the things that go boom that anyone would ever want, except nukes, but that might not be too far in the future if the Al-Qaeda elements could meet the terms set by Iran. Of course, Iran continued to deny having a functional nuclear devise. The more difficult part of Tomas' plan was finding a fresh grave from which Ishmael could borrow a suitable body. Omar kept telling Tomas that he could more easily find a live substitute, but Bernardo wouldn't go along with it.

Within a week the body of a man who had been killed in a brawl became available. There was no one to claim the corpse so it was wrapped in a shroud and put in an unmarked grave. This was just what the two men needed. As soon as evening became sufficiently dark Tomas stood watch while Ishmael unearthed the body and the conspirators hauled it to the shed miles outside of town.

The explosives were rigged to detonate by way of a cell phone signal;

something Omar had learned how to do from some of his Yemeni friends. The corpse was situated where the explosion would be enough to have killed a living person, but not totally destroy the remains. Ishmael's Identification papers were placed in the pockets of the clothes as a means of confirming that he was the dead man.

The following day Ishmael alerted the bribed official of the time for the event to take place and this person arranged to be conveniently in the area and able to make the identification of the body before others disturbed the scene.

"Ishmael, is your man ready to earn his money?"

"Yes. And what do we do after the blast?"

Tomas gave a slight laugh. "I'm going to be far enough away to observe but remain clear of the area. Will you be with me, or have you other plans?"

"Angel, I would not miss this for the world. It isn't every day a man gets to see himself blown up and still walk away."

Tomas cautioned, "We have to make sure no one is close enough to be hurt when the detonation takes place. First, because I don't want to see any other casualties and also because I am not clear that Tagart didn't send someone to make sure I've done the job."

Bernardo and Omar set the bomb and the body in place. The two men exited through a small window at the rear of the shed so that no one watching the door would see them leaving. At the last minute, Omar decided he would check the bomb one more time and crawled back through the window.

Tomas never knew what happened, but the explosion triggered and the force tossed him a few yards from the shed. He staggered to his feet in a daze with his left arm sending searing pain to his brain. A shard of wood had torn into his upper arm like an arrow. Tomas' shirt was soaked with his blood. When his eyes focused on the scene there was little left of the small structure.

Among shattered pieces of wood there were two bodies. Ishmael had become the instrument of his own death. Soon people would be gathering and Tomas had to leave the area quickly. As he stumbled away from the pile of debris, he jerked the sliver of wood out of his arm and clasped his right hand tightly over the wound. He couldn't afford to return to Ishmael's car. His own two feet had to serve him in his avoidance of the few people who came from distant houses. Their focus was on what was left of the shed and the two bodies. To anyone inspecting the blast, it would look like two terrorists had been accidentally killed when the bomb they were making exploded prematurely.

Tomas had to stop and attend to his wound. He took his belt and twisted it around his upper left arm to control the bleeding. Before he could show himself in town he needed to change his shirt, but where? At a house on the edge of the city he saw clothes drying on a fence. Making sure no one was looking his way; Tomas lifted a man's tunic from the fence, slipped it over his head, and quickly began stuffing the excess fabric into his pants.

An hour after the explosion, Bernardo staggered into his hotel room and dropped onto his bed. He was totally exhausted. Tomas lay on the bed for several minutes and then forced himself to get up and go into the bathroom to attend to his wound. The best he could do was take a bathroom towel and cut it into strips. He wound layers of the towel around his arm and tightly tied smaller strips to hold the makeshift bandage in place. The material served to absorb any residual bleeding until he could obtain proper bandages and a disinfectant.

Tomas Bernardo chose not to leave his room until the next morning. He checked his temporary bandage and found that the blood had not come all the way through, so he wrapped the area with a plastic bag, put on a fresh shirt and left the hotel in search of the supplies he needed to treat his wound. He stayed clear of the areas of town where he had previously been when looking for Omar. Finally, he found a pharmacy. He then visited at a tailor's shop and bought a curved needle and some thread. The proprietor was reluctant to part with the needle until a large enough payment was received. With all that he needed to attend his wound, Tomas returned to his hotel and made repairs to his torn flesh. He took a few painful stitches in his skin and re-bandaged his arm.

Bernardo never intended to take Ishmael's life. He had hoped to find a way where he could satisfy Colonel Tagart's demand without having another soul's blood on his hands. It was time to arrange for a flight out of Aden and back to London by way of Ankara, Turkey. From London, Tomas boarded a flight to Washington, D.C. By the time he arrived back in the States the throbbing pain in his left arm had subsided to a point where it was tolerable, but whenever he brushed against anything it reminded him of how tender the wound still was.

From Washington, Tomas returned to Virginia and arrived at Tagart's office around four in the afternoon and was told by a male receptionist to wait. "Colonel, there is a man in the outer office who says he has completed an assignment you gave him."

"That must be my friend, Angel. Show him in!"

Tomas entered the office and Tagart got up from his chair and greeted Bernardo as if he actually was a friend. When he placed his hand on Tomas' shoulder, the pain caused him to wince and pull back. "What's this?"

"A little souvenir I picked up in Yemen. The job is done!"

"I know! In fact, I thought you were dead too. The report I got was that there were two bodies found where the blast took place."

"There were, but that's not what I want to talk about. When can I see Beverly?

"I'm a man of my word. She's in a safe house thirty minutes from here, but we have to agree on some ground rules first."

"Ground rules! I did my part!"

"Don't get yourself in an uproar. You and she have to understand that you are sworn to silence about this whole deal, including her being detained."

"Or?"

"Or we are back to where we were a few weeks ago and a dossier about your illegal activities finds its way to congress. Are we on the same page?"

"It looks like a stalemate. You get my silence and Beverly goes free, but have you explained the rules to her?"

"She fully understands and knows the consequences."

"Then this is goodbye."

"Not exactly. I'm waiting on forensic verification of what my agent gave me verbally. You can join your girl friend now and when I get the verification you are free to go."

"You keep saying that Bev is my girl friend, but she is just a friend. I'm not close enough to anyone to…. Never mind. There's always a catch with you! Nothing is straight forward! Omar is dead! He went into the shed and did something that caused the explosion.

"So, there's more to this Yemen situation than I thought. I thought you personally iced Omar!"

"Indirectly I did. He was messing with explosives at my suggestion and it triggered. If I had been two feet closer the blast would have killed me."

"Whose idea was it to handle explosives and why?"

"What difference does it make? He's dead! That's what you wanted. That was the deal!"

"Okay, but I know there's more to the story. The car is waiting. The driver will drop you at the safe house and you will remain there until I say you can leave."

"Colonel, some day the seeds you have been planting will be reaped."

"Is that Tomas or the minister doing the talking?"

"That's a biblical principle. You reap what you sow."

"That cuts both ways, Tomas. You have been doing a lot of sowing yourself."

✳   ✳   ✳

Bernardo was driven to the safe house and locked in a room with Beverly. For three days they were sequestered and given fast food meals. When they wanted out of the room to take care of personal needs a guard accompanied them to and from their quarters. Finally, the Colonel came to see them with the information from Yemen for which he had been waiting.

"Angel, you are a clever man, but not clever enough. My contact in Aden informed me that Omar's I.D. was found on a different corpse that was in the rubble of the shed along side Omar. It seems that you were trying to pull a scam on me, son. I'm guessing that you and Ishmael had a deal to fake his death and it backfired. How about it, Tomas?"

"I'm sick of killing. I didn't want to take the life of a man who wanted nothing more than to live free of you and your organization. That's all that I want."

"Well, now what do I do with you two? I can't just let this go. If I would, there would be no discipline and others could get the idea that I don't have things under control. Someone else might get the notion they can do what you did."

"Do what you want with me, but leave my friends and family alone."

"I could do that, but I have to think about this overnight. I'll see you sometime tomorrow. If I were you, I'd practice up on my praying. Maybe you can get some divine help."

Tagart left the room and the door was locked. Guards took turns sitting on a chair in the hallway. Beverly lay on the bed while Tomas took a pillow and stretched out on the floor. Neither of them could sleep as they thought about what might happen the next day.

"Tomas, why did they kidnap me and bring me to Virginia? And how does this affect you?"

"Kid, I didn't want you hurt; that's why I told you to go out west. The story is too long. The short version is I thought I was serving my country, but it ends up I have been used by a group that is like a shadow government. I know too much about them and I did one last job with the promise that you would be set free and I wouldn't be prosecuted for doing their dirty work."

"How can this be?"

"Honey, when I discovered the outfit wasn't legit I hid out for awhile. During that time I thought I found the Lord in a little church in the hills of West Virginia, but I was too messed up in my head to be honest with the preacher and with God."

"Tomas, I heard you went to seminary and studied for the ministry, why did you do that if you weren't sure what you were doing?"

"I just wanted a new life and I foolishly thought a religious profession would get me as far from my past as possible, but they found me and coerced me to do another mission. I have to admit, I don't always think rationally. Most of the time, I revert to my military training and to acts of self-preservation. Sometimes I feel like a bomb ready to explode!"

"What's going to happen to us? What will they do to me?"

"Bev, we have to get out of here."

"How? They have guns and we're locked in here. There are bars on the widow!"

"I'll wait until those two goons have had time to get bored and sleepy and then I'll ask to go to the toilet. If you know how to pray, I could use some help. These guys may not be rocket scientists and that gives me an edge."

Three hours passed and Tomas began banging on the room door. "Hey! I have to use the bathroom!"

"Go to sleep and knock off the racket!"

"Man! Listen, I need to go to the bathroom!" Tomas continued to pound on the door until the guards couldn't take the noise any longer.

"Okay, but you make one false move and I'll blow a hole in your head!" The door opened and the guard pointed an automatic hand gun at Tomas' face. "Hands behind your head and stay four feet in front of me."

The other guard remained in the hall outside of the room while Tomas was escorted to the restroom. Bernardo's mind raced as he devised a plan of attack. He needed both guards close to him to make it work. Inside the restroom, Bernardo check for a sharp edge, but found none. He then took loose his belt and used the tong of the buckle to scratch each wrist until he drew blood. The cuts were not deep enough to be life threatening but the results looked really nasty. By the time he had finished setting the stage for his next move the guard was demanding that Tomas come out. When there was no response, he pushed open the door and found Bernardo on the floor with bloody arms.

The guard yelled for his buddy to assist him. "Jack, get down here! This guy has tried to commit suicide!"

"Why didn't he wait until tomorrow and the Colonel would take care of that!"

"Quit being a wise guy and give me a hand getting him out into the hall! As the two goons took hold of Tomas to drag him into the hall, Bernardo snapped to his feet in such a surprise move that he caught both men completely off guard. With the efficiency of a master black belt assassin they were both unconscious before they could respond to Tomas' attack.

Bernardo quickly grabbed the billfold of each man. He needed the cash until he could get to his bank and access his safety deposit box for his back up identification documents, reserve cash, and credit cards. There was no going back to his apartment. Tomas kicked the room door open, splintering the door jam and trim. He took Beverly by her arm and led her out of the building. They didn't stop walking until he was able to hail a taxi which took them to a twenty-four hour grocery store. There was safety in numbers and the couple had a need to secure some prepared food while they waited out the reminder of the night and on through the morning until the bank opened.

Tomas and Beverly sat on benches just inside the store doors and ate the food and drank their beverages. From time to time store employees would glance their way. They surely wondered why the couple was spending so much time in the store, but no one ventured to question them. When it was the right time, Tomas phoned for a taxi.

They arrived as the bank opened for business and Tomas went directly to the safety deposit box area and gained access to his stored items. He always had his important papers and funds at the bank before each overseas mission. There were other items he placed in the box when it became necessary to keep documents safe rather than at his apartment while Tomas was out of the country.

Bernardo used a grocery bag he had kept from the store and began to fill it with the contents of the box. There was a passport and credit cards in the name of Ricardo Mareno, along with thirty thousand dollars which was denominated in mostly one hundreds and fifties. There was also a stack of twenties. From the bank, the couple took another taxi to the train station and purchased tickets for Fort Lauderdale, Florida. As the miles fled from beneath the wheels of the train, Tomas began to relax. Beverly still had issues. What was she going to do with her life? Where could she go? She had no resources and all her documents were back in Chicago.

Bernardo had an answer for that. He would give her ten thousand dollars. He also knew a man in Miami who could provide all the documents she needed for her new identification. It took a week for those items to be prepared and for Beverly to become Beatrice Cook. Her new life would be in New Orleans. The documents gave her an address to that effect. It was a location often used as transitional for people who needed the services of the man in Miami.

Tomas, now Ricardo Mareno, had a different destination. After cleaning out his Miami money stash he was headed back to Viginia. If he couldn't find Tagart there, he would locate him in Washington, D.C. There was a score to settle and some people to protect. Tomas feared that the Colonel would retaliate against Clarise Bernardo, his sister-in-law and widow of Joaquin, and there was the safety of other family members to consider. They may have turned on him after Joaquin's death, but they were still family and Tomas cared what might happen to them.

Colonel Tagart had sent men to New York to keep an eye on the home of Clarise Bernardo in case Tomas tried to make contact with her. Tomas knew better than try to call her. He was sure her phone would be tapped. The plan was to locate where Tagart had moved his headquarters and stake it out until he could see his enemy and stalk him. When the time was right he would do to the Colonel what he had ordered Tomas to do to others. It would be poetic justice.

Bernardo felt that he was justified in taking out the Colonel. He reasoned it would not be murder. It would be a matter of kill or be killed. The fact that the hit would come from a sniper didn't matter as far as Tomas was concerned. His heart was warped by his experiences. The aborted effort at being religious was an insincere gesture. It was a self-deception. It was a desperate grab at something that might keep him from sinking farther into the depths of his moral collapse. In reality, his heart was divided and that made him unstable in everything he tried to do. He felt lost and he was. He would revert to the one thing he knew how to do best.

CHAPTER TEN

THE MOLE REVEALED

On a cool and slightly breezy morning in March, Tomas was perched on the top of a building across the street from the offices of Colonel Tag Tagart. It had taken a month to track down the man, but he would soon be in the cross hairs of the very person the Colonel had molded into an efficient and lethal weapon. It wasn't yet the right time for action. However, the best way to kill a snake is to cut off its head. Tagart was the head of a snake burrowing its way into the security of the nation and he had to be stopped along with his superiors. No one else could do it. That early morning on the roof top was a time for observation, but the action couldn't be prolonged indefinitely. As long as Tagart was heading up operations, the shadow government had its key operative to orchestrate the eventual emergence of the mole: the man called Saleem Karab.

Today was the first public sighting of the Colonel in a great while. He emerged from his building as the sun began to break through the overcast. He had with him two "blue suits" and three other men who were as large as professional football linemen. They had to be body guards. Tomas recognized one of the blue suits as the interrogator he loved to hate. The other man also looked familiar, but he wasn't sure why for a little while and then, as the group got into a large black SUV, Bernardo's recognition of who the man was came like a punch in the face. It was the president's right hand man; his chief of staff.

Meelaster Rabak had been chosen by President Achan Fenster to run the Whitehouse and be the primary policy maker for the administration. Newspaper articles written by members of the opposition party often portrayed Rabak as the real power in the Oval Office. They also accused him of being hard on Israel, but soft on the Palestinians and the war against Al Qaeda. Seeing Rabak with the Colonel only added more confusion to Tomas' thinking. Why would the man closest to the president be meeting with people whom Tomas knew constituted a fifth column for Middle Eastern bad guys? Chances were that Tomas would never make a clean escape after putting a hit on the Colonel, so he began to reason whether Rabak ought to be eliminated along with Tagart.

This wasn't the day for that. His biggest beef was with Tagart, but if someone got in the way, then that would be collateral damage. Tomas had always worked with a one shot situation. Two or more shots meant more time for his location to be spotted and less time to get away. After the SUV pulled away from in front of the building, he began scouting an escape route over roofs and down to the street a couple of blocks south of the shooter's nest. Bernardo noticed that the building adjacent to the one on which he stood was ten feet shorter. A wire from the taller building to the next one would give him a rapid slide over the ally that separated the two structures and then a dash across the roof of the shorter building to a pre-arranged rope down to the ground would quickly put two blocks between him and the Colonel's body.

Tomas estimated that from the time of the shot, a race across two buildings, and then to the ground would take the average man ninety seconds. He could do it in much less time. People would still be looking around the immediate scene for that length of time. A car stashed on a side street another two blocks farther on would give him enough head start to make it to a safe place to change out of the coveralls and drive out of town on a prearranged route.

He would use the freeway to the outer ring where he would then switch to secondary streets and roads on his way to route 50 through Virginia and into West Virginia. It was a crooked highway and, for the first part, it meandered northwest. Eventually Tomas would be able to do a few route changes near Winchester and hook up with route 220 going south through the Appalachian Mountains. He could not take a chance with airplanes or trains; those would be covered by the authorities.

With the plan for escape outlined, the immediate task was to stake out Tagart's place during the day and wait for the right opportunity to settle the score. Tomas was hardwired to do the job, but it did not come without some feelings of guilt. He knew that the Bible said, "Vengeance is mine, says the Lord." Was he was doing the wrong thing for the right reason? Or were both the deed and the reason wrong? Had he given in to the old, cold blooded philosophy: that the end justifies the means? Beverly would have said, yes. Joaquin would also have told Tomas that he was wrong, but Joaquin was dead and Tagart was the man behind his murder.

The nightly wrestling with his damaged conscience produced a sleep deficit and that was creating a set of unsteady nerves. What he felt he had to do required steady hands. Time was also slipping away and that added some pressure that Tomas had not known before. All of his missions had been without personal feeling for or against the one lined up through the scope, except for the hit in Indonesia which was very personal and face to face, but the issue with Tagart was also deeply personal.

With Meelaster Rabak, the Whitehouse chief of staff, in the picture Tomas' plans now included a person almost at the top of the pecking order for Washington. If Saleem Karab was code for Rabak, then he should be the primary target, but Bernardo wanted the Colonel. His death would cause a stir, but taking out Rabak would create a fire storm and an all out effort to track down the assassin. There wouldn't be a safe place in the world. There was the possibility that someone besides Meelaster was the mole. It wasn't all that clear. Tomas could only think of one other person it might be, but he shook off that thought. It had to be Rabak.

When it came to the Al Qaeda plan for bringing down the United States from within, Rabak might be the bomb, but Tagart was the fuse. He had the network of killers to stir up more hatred of the United States around the world and turn so called friends against America. It was bad enough having a weakling as a president, but to have Al Qaeda's own man in the oval office as the brains behind the president was far more dangerous.

The economy was rapidly becoming critical and the de-funding of the military was emboldening terrorist cells and Iran's leaders to step up actions against American interests throughout the Middle East. The geopolitical climate was also placing Israel in greater danger and pushing her toward decisive action in the face of Arab and Iranian threats.

*   *   *

Tomas Bernardo sat up in bed. His mind was whirling with conflicting thoughts. He had been a tool in creating a worldwide backlash against his own country and it caused him to seethe with anger. He came to a snap decision that before he resorted to a sniper attack he wanted to face the Colonel. It would be when and where Tomas decided.

The private line of Colonel Tagart began ringing. Bernardo let it ring until Tagart had to wake up and answer it. "This better be an absolute emergency!"

"We have to meet!"

"Angel? Where are you?"

"Never mind that. I want to see you and Magdar!" That was the name of the blue suit who had given Tomas a hard time and always seemed to be with Tagart wherever he went.

"Just who the blazes do you think you are demanding anything of me?"

"Your worst nightmare, unless we can make a deal."

"What sort of deal?"

"A better one than the last deal! That didn't turn out so well. By the way, why is Chief of Staff Meelaster Rabak making buddy, buddy with you?" There was a long silence. "Colonel, are you still there?"

"Yes, Angel, I'm listening."

"Have I dialed in on who Saleem Karab is?"

Another long silence while Tagart tried to wrap his mind around how Tomas was able to connect the dots.

"You think you have it all figured out, don't you?"

"What I can't figure out is why you became a traitor to the country that has given you everything."

"Listen, you two bit punk! I picked you up from going nowhere and made something of you. Don't you question what you know nothing about!"

"Calling me names, Colonel, doesn't make you less of a traitor."

"Who do you think you are? You're in this over your head! I have protection and you're out there on a limb with no place to go. You say this country has given me everything? Look, mister, I gave my all to the United States for thirty years and in return I was passed over twice for promotion and then downsized right out on my back side!"

"And what do you have now, Colonel?"

"Money! Power! More money than you'll ever see. You want to mess with me? Forget it, Tomas! You're nobody: a used up mercenary!"

"If you don't have the guts to face me like a man, send Aries Magdar and I'll pass on to him what I want and you can consider it when you're cooler. Or should I just contact the cable news stations, the international press, and the newspapers with information from an unnamed source?"

"Where and when do you want to meet him?"

"Just have him drive to the river at five-thirty in the morning and park. Have him walk south on the boardwalk. If I see that he's not being shadowed, then I'll approach him. If there is any sign of surface or air surveillance, I'm gone and what I know goes public the next day." Bernardo didn't wait for an answer. He switched off the phone.

∗   ∗   ∗

The next morning Magdar began walking south along the Potamac River shortly before six o'clock. He was late. A hint of light was all that was showing to the east and visibility was still limited. He pulled the collar of his jacket up around his neck and glanced from side to side as he walked. There were a few power walkers getting their morning exercise, but no indication that Tomas was in the vicinity. Coming toward Magdar was an old man with a cane. Everyone else was going the same direction with Magdar. When the old man came along side of him, the frail looking gentleman stumbled and sank to one knee. Magdar instinctively reached out to assist him to his feet, but Tomas took him by the arm and shoved the barrel of a gun into the man's ribs.

"Remember me? Don't make any sudden moves or try to signal someone. Just help me to my feet and walk with me toward the drainage underpass."

When the two men reached the railing they stopped face to face. Tomas was still hunched over as part of his disguise. For anyone observing them it looked innocent enough.

"Tell the Colonel that I'm through with his games. Tell him that unless he leaves me and mine alone permanently that he's my next target. That goes for you too. If he so much as looks cross-eyed at people I care about, he will feel the Chameleon's bite when he least expects it. He knows what I'm capable of doing. Have you understood this deal?"

"Buddy, you're the one who doesn't know it yet, but you just bit off more than you can chew."

There followed a heated exchange of words and a threat by Magdar that both Tomas and his family would be wiped out just like Joaquin was if sensitive information ever found it's way to the printed page or to television news. "This comes right from the Colonel."

The admission that Tagart, and possibly Magdar, were directly responsible for his brother's death set off an explosion of wrath from Tomas. A single shot through the heart and Magdar slipped from Bernardo's grasp. That was when he realized that two men were running across the expanse of lawn toward him.

Tomas leaped over the railing and into the culvert for water runoff. Pre-positioned at the bottom of the spillway was a small boat with a big outboard motor. Tomas scrambled into the craft. He started the motor and the boat roared into action, pitching the bow out of the water and sending out a large wake and giant plume from the stern. Six minutes later Tomas ditched the boat on the Alexandria side of the river, hopped onto a small motorized skateboard he had stashed in a large trash container and disappeared into the morning traffic as he dashed and swerved between cars.

There would be one more person to feel the wrath of the Angel. Once Tagart got the news about Magdar there was the possibility that he might hole up for awhile, but the Colonel's pride probably wouldn't let him hide for long. Tomas scooted down an ally where he left the skateboard for a more conventional mode of transportation. He took a Taxi to a mall where he calmly had lunch at the food court. The white wig and beard was sufficient to ward off any consideration by authorities. The coolness by which Tomas met his situation gave evidence of his confidence and training. He could sit in the middle of a public place and feel totally at ease. It also gave evidence that he had no remorse over taking down an enemy.

As the day wore on and Tomas thought that his prolonged presence in the mall might become noticed, he took a bus back to the neighborhood where Tagart had his offices. From the bus stop, Bernardo walked six blocks to the building opposite the Colonel's. He produced black coveralls from his backpack, along with credentials of an electrician and made his way to the twelfth floor and then through an unlocked access to the roof. The Chameleon was back in his nest for the night. The previous night he had gained entrance to the building directly behind his location and rigged a slide cable between structures and a drop line he would use to zip down the side of the building. His escape route was ready, as was the car located blocks away. All that remained was for Tagart to show himself.

Tomas had to be alert to the possibility that the Colonel might be checking high places in the vicinity of his offices. He had trained Tomas to use the high ground for the best advantage on a hit. The sniper had to be like a shadow and next to invisible. He had to know the way out of an area and have every move planned. Time was of the essence. Any delay could prove fatal to the shooter. Tomas would not show himself until he had a target and then only long enough to make the hit, drop the weapon, and make like Bat Man.

The second night on the building faded as morning light began to bath the roof top. Tomas stirred from the shadows of his hiding place and stealthily made his way to the edge to get a view of the front of Tagart's building. The familiar black SUV was just pulling up to the curb: a sure sign that the Colonel was either coming to his office or was about to leave. Bernardo ran back to his nest and grabbed the rifle. Tagart was emerging from the building as Bernardo flopped to his stomach in shooting position behind the low roof edge. The Colonel had been in his office throughout the night and was changing locations. The evidence for that was the brief cases he carried and the roll away trunk being brought out by one of his men who proceeded to push it into the back of the vehicle.

The Colonel tossed his brief cases into the back seat as Tomas made ready for the shot. "This one is for Joaquin." He had Tagart in the crosshairs when the door of the stairway to the roof opened behind Tomas. A maintenance man shouted, "What are you doing up here!?"

Tomas swung the rifle toward the man who ducked back into the stairway. Instantly, he pivoted back toward the street. The round struck the Colonel with such force it slammed him to the sidewalk. There was no time to verify the kill; there was only time to drop the weapon, race across the roof to the opposite edge, snap the ring onto the cable and go airborne. The metal on metal screamed as Bernardo zipped to a landing on the lower building, unsnapped, and raced across that roof to the drop rope while putting on thick leather gloves. He flung the rope over the side and slid rapidly to the ground. The gloves were hot by the time he planted his feet in the ally.

The back streets were mostly deserted as the Angel of Death sprinted the four blocks to a car. There was the chirp of the doors being unlocked, followed by the roar of an engine, and Tomas was on his way. From the shot, across two roofs, and to the car took fifty-five seconds. The scene he left behind was of his old mentor lying mortally wounded on the sidewalk, but not yet dead. Would Bernardo ever know if he had administered the kill shot? He was afraid that the interruption by the maintenance man had made the shot less than perfect.

Tomas hooked up with McArthur Boulevard that ran west parallel to the Clara Barton Parkway. He avoided the 495 Beltway and used side streets to snake his way west and then south to junction with route 50 and then northwest on 50 as he had planned, but elected to turn off onto route 340 at Berryville, Virginia and take it south. It was a secondary highway that had a low percentage for being watched. It was also doubtful that anyone had information on his car. He had stayed alive in circumstances more dangerous than the current problem because he knew how to cover his trail. Somewhere in the Appalachian Mountains he would get off the road and spend a couple of days re-accessing his strategy and inventorying his resources.

At Wyanesboro, Tomas change routes to go west and picked up route 220 in West Virginia. That route took him down the back of the Allegheny Mountains and then into the Appalachians to a dot on the map called Warm Springs. It had been five hours since he left the nation's capitol. He needed to gas up the car and get something to eat. At a little one-stop-fits-all hole in the wall, Bernardo pulled off the road and took a brief survey of the one horse town before going inside.

"Hey there, stranger. You jes passin' through?"

"Yes and no. I plan to pass on through, but I need to rest up for a day or two before moving on."

"Can I git you somthin' ta eat?"

"Yeah. I could use some eats. How about some scrambled eggs, bacon, and toast?"

"Comin' right up. How'd you git yurself way up here?"

"I left Columbus, Ohio and started east, but decided I wanted to see some of the mountains. It sure is pretty country."

"It is if you like mountains and trees. What you drinkin'?"

"Coffee: black."

In a few minutes Tomas had his food and the man behind the counter went on about his business. There were two old gentlemen in the store who looked like they were just killing time. When Bernardo finished eating and paid his check he wanted to know if there was a used car business anywhere near by. One of the men who overheard the question said he was sure Hank down at the filling station always had a few cars he had rebuilt, but the nearest place for a regular car dealership was Covington on route 60. "It's about fifty miles south."

"Is there a motel close here?"

"It ain't what you'd call a motel. There are some cabins ol' lady Jacobs might rent if you was to ask nice and polite. She's a rough ol' bird."

"I'll give Hank a try first and then I'll check with Mrs. Jacobs about a room for the night."

"Son, why in the world would you be lookin' for another car when you got a perfectly good lookin' one out there? You rob a bank or somthin'?"

Tomas laughed and so did the other men. "No, I didn't rob a bank, but I hear a noise and I don't want to get stranded in the mountain with a car going sour."

"Hank's a mechanic and he can fix anythin'."

"Just the same, if it needs parts, he may have to send for them and that could hold me up longer than I want to hang around. I'd just feel a lot more secure with a car I knew was okay."

"Suit yurself, son. It's yur money, or is it the bank's money?"

Everyone burst out laughing again and Tomas waved goodbye. At the filling station, Hank took Tomas out to two vehicles he had restored after they were wrecked. One was a Ford 150 pickup with a camper top and the other was a Toyota Camry. Neither one of them looked as good as the car Tomas had.

"How much for the Pickup?"

"If yur tradin' I'd take yurs and four thousand."

"Let's hear the engine."

Hank started the truck and moved it forward and back to show that the gears were good. "This here pickup is in good shape. I jes had to do some body work on it."

"Well, Hank, I'd like to have a truck. I want to do some camping out in the mountains and a truck with a camper top would fit the bill, but my car is a lot newer than the truck."

"Mister, you got papers on yur car?"

"Yes."

"Then let's make it two thousand. Have we got a deal?"

"Deal. But I need plates to go with the truck."

"That ain't no problem. We'll do the paper work and you'll have yur pickup."

Hank knew he was getting the best part of the deal and didn't mind fudging a little on the documents. Tomas didn't care either as long as he had plates for the vehicle. When he got where he ultimately wanted to be he'd ditch the truck. He wouldn't need it anymore, but he could sleep in it rather than risk motels where his picture might show up on the television. With the truck and a full tank of gas, Bernardo decided to skip staying the night. The more road he could put between himself and Washington the better.

With different wheels Tomas felt more confident to use some of the interstate highways. From Covington, he took I-64 to Beckly and then picked up I-77 south. At the first rest area, Bernardo pulled off and found a parking spot well away from the restrooms and snack machines. It was time to take a nap before the long haul he would have the next day.

An hour later Tomas Bernardo felt refreshed enough to continue south. Around Rocky Gap, Virginia he encountered a seven mile grade of a very steep decline and the pickup was gaining speed which required frequent application of the brakes. In attempting to slow the decent, Tomas pressed the brake peddle harder and it went clear to the floorboard. He was traveling too fast to attempt gearing down and the truck began to shudder from excessive speed.

Tomas blasted the horn to warn other motorist of his out of control approach and drivers blasted their horns in reply to the maniac who flashed past them. The growing darkness only added to the feeling that he was about to crash into someone or miss a turn in the road and plunge thousands of feet over the side of the mountain.

In the distance, and rapidly coming up, was a runaway truck ramp. It provided an elevated roadway covered with piles of sand and gravel to give enough friction to bring a large semi truck and trailer to a safe stop. A pickup truck would stop a great deal faster. It might even be such a sudden deceleration that the driver could be injured. Bernardo took the ramp. He had no other choice and the pickup slammed into the soft material at eighty miles an hour. The low profile of the truck caused the vehicle to hit the sand like it was a soft wall. Metal crumpled and, in spite of the seat belt, Tomas' chest and head hit the steering wheel. He blacked out. Before he regained consciousness a trucker, who had been going in low gears down the seven mile grade, stopped to give assistance.

Bernardo regained consciousness as the trucker was checking him for vital signs. "Say, buddy, how bad are you hurt?"

"I don't know." Tomas felt his arms and legs. His chest was sore but there didn't seem to be any broken ribs. He then felt his forehead and the warm blood running down his face. "Looks like I gashed my head a little."

"You know, buddy, the way things are supposed to be done is I call for an ambulance."

"No! I don't need an ambulance! I'm not hurt that badly and I have to get the Florida by tomorrow afternoon."

"I don't know why you're in such an all fired hurry to risk your neck. You could have a concussion, but I have a first aid kit in the truck. I'll get it and put a patch on you."

The truck driver retrieved his first aid kit and opened it to get some gauze and alcohol to wipe away enough blood to see how badly Tomas was cut. "You're one lucky son-of-a-gun. I'll put a compress on this and you'll be much better."

"Thanks, mister."

"Name's Tanner. George Tanner. And yours?"

For a moment Tomas couldn't think of what name he was now using. He was still dazed from the blow to his head. "Uh, Ricardo. Just call me Richard."

"Well, Richard, if you're up to it, we have to get this pickup backed out of here. It can't be left right in the middle of the ramp in case some other poor sap has to use it to get stopped. I'll get around front and shove while you steer it off to the side."

It was hard gong to dislodge the pickup from the sand that had built up beneath it, but the giant size George Tanner freed the vehicle. With the pickup far enough off the main part of the ramp it was time to decide what to do next.

"Hey, buddy, I'll carry you on down the mountain to Wytheville and you can arrange tomorrow to have a wrecker come back for your pickup. That's the best I can do."

"Friend, you've already done a great deal. Let me give you this fifty for helping me."

"Keep it, friend. Someday another person will give me a hand when I need it. I believe what comes around goes around, don't you?"

"Yeah, I guess I do, but sometimes it needs a little nudge to get all the way around."

"You got me on that one, Richard. As long as you know what you mean it's all that matters."

The two men broke off the exchange of home spun philosophies as the semi rolled on down the mountain. Tomas had a massive headache and really didn't feel like talking. What was on his mind was finding the means for getting the rest of the way to a suburb of Pompano Beach. If he hadn't had the accident he would have been where he needed to go in fourteen hours. He could have gotten there faster, but planned to keep the speed at or below the limit. He didn't need any highway patrol pulling him over. However, Bernardo's plans went bust when the brakes failed.

At Wytheville, George Tanner dropped Tomas at an all night truck stop where he could get some food. A wrecker company had a place on the same property as the truck stop.

"Say, George, I am really in a hurry to get to South Florida. That old pickup isn't worth my being delayed. I'm going to sign over the title to the wrecking company and let them keep the tub of bolts. I've got a deadline on getting to Pompano. Do you think one of your trucker friends would give me a lift to Charlotte, North Carolina and then I can get a flight out of there to Lauderdale. That will put me right next to where I need to go?"

"Let me see what I can do, buddy. You take care of getting rid of your truck and I'll be in the restaurant talking to some of the guys. Not everyone will take a rider. Some companies won't allow it for insurance reasons, but there might be an independent trucker who'd help you."

✳   ✳   ✳

Tanner found a trucker who would take Tomas on to Charlotte for the fifty he had offered George. The deal was made and for the balance of the night Tomas listened to loud country music. He wasn't used to hearing it and it only added to his headache.

When Tomas was delivered to Charlotte, instead of booking a flight, he made his way to a bus station. Buses didn't run as many routes or as often as they once did, but there wouldn't be the checks of passengers like with the airlines or trains. There was no sense risking being identified now that he had gotten half way to his destination. One of the things an assassin had to do was leave cashes of money and documents in various places near major points of entrance or exit from a country. South Florida was one of those points and Tomas had a safe box in a small bank in North Lauderdale as well as the one he had already closed in Miami.

Each mission Tomas completed always brought a bonus from his handlers. He never questioned about the extra funds, after all, he was putting his neck on the line every time he went after a bad guy. There were also expenses that Tagart covered, but Tomas had no problem living cheap and pocketing all he could. Everything was done with cash. There could not be a paper trail. This now worked to his advantage.

Something in the back of Bernardo's mind told him that Colonel Tagart may have survived the shot. There wasn't time back on the roof in Washington to verify the effect of the round. Tomas knew he had hit his target, but it was a hurried shot and not one to the head. If the Colonel was still able to give orders, the net cast for catching Tomas would be a very wide one. Tagart needed to turn all of his operatives loose to track down the Chameleon and kill him.

CHAPTER ELEVEN

EXPOSURE AND AVOIDANCE

Back in Wytheville, Virginia, the office manager of the wrecker company started to file the document for the pickup Tomas left on the mountain and began to suspect some problems with the title to the truck. For one thing, the registration was for one vehicle and the license plates were for another. A check by computer with the Department of Motor vehicles confirmed the discrepancy. A phone call to the previous owner who ran the filling station in Warm Springs raised more questions about the legitimacy of the transaction that put the pickup in Tomas' hands. That led to a call to authorities and a red flag popped up. Could the man who used the name Ricardo Mareno be the fugitive wanted in the Washington, D.C. shootings?

A multi-state alert went out to all local and state police agencies to be on the look out for Tomas Bernardo, a.k.a. Ricardo Mareno. The authorities knew that Tomas was headed south and the first thing they did was alert trains and airports. The last word they had was that he got a ride with a trucker going south on I-77. When the driver was located much farther south on I-26 out of Columbia, South Carolina the driver informed them that he had left a man by the name of Richard back in Charlotte.

The question became, was Tomas still in North Carolina or had he found another means of transportation? If that were true, the fugitive could be almost anywhere. The police needed a break to find him. Television and the internet began carrying photos of Tomas Bernardo, along with some of his aliases. The alert soon expanded to include interstate buses. The instant information age was working.

The express bus carrying Tomas left Charlotte hours before an alert

156

was broadcast. It took route 74 east to I-95 and therefore by passing Colombia. Its first stop would be Savannah, Georgia and then on to Jacksonville, Florida. The next stop was scheduled for Fort Lauderdale. That's where Tomas wanted to go.

At Savannah there was a rest stop for the passengers and everyone left the bus to get something to eat and use the restrooms. That was also where Tomas' plans changed again. While in the cafeteria he saw a bulletin for a wanted killer and his picture. It was time to make another change of appearance. He went for a walk outside of the terminal and slipped between some buildings. He withdrew from his knapsack all that was needed to take on a new face and when he emerged he had aged by forty years.

Tomas needed to throw off those who might connect him with the express bus to Ft, Lauderdale. He purchased a ticket on a bus going to Macon Georgia which was 160 miles west. At Macon the "old man" transferred to a bus going to Naples, Florida.

✳   ✳   ✳

From his hospital bed, Colonel Tagart whispered orders to his lackeys that he wanted Bernardo's head. "Find him. If you can't bring him to me, kill him and bring me his tongue as proof."

A doctor interrupted. "Gentlemen, you have to leave now. The patient needs rest. His heart rate is too fast and he has to calm down."

"Okay, Doc! Colonel, don't worry. We'll turn over every rock."

Once the two agents of Colonel Tagart were out into hallway they checked over the information they had from police reports. Durant and Donaldson had been recruited in the same way as Tomas, but were more into the business of enforcing than the work of assassinations. If they and Tomas were to ever meet face to face, it would be even odds as to who would come out the winner.

"The last bulletin we have is that Bernardo left the express bus at Savannah, Georgia. That's where we have to go and try to pick up his trail."

"We better do more than try. If the Colonel survives, we had better be able to prove we've taken care of his boy."

"I think that's why Tagart hates Bernardo so much. He was his favorite and now he has gone rogue. There is no fury like the Colonel's when he's been crossed."

✳   ✳   ✳

Tomas made the transfer of busses in Macon and was on I-75 headed south. Every additional twist in his circuitous maneuvering added some time to his efforts to avoid capture, but just sitting on a bus was not his way of dealing with an issue. He had always been the hunter and now he was being hunted. Tomas would rather face his enemy and have it done with, but the setting had to be more favorable. He was better suited to deal with an adversary when both were on unfamiliar turf. The advantage turned to Tomas when he was beyond the scope of the police forces of the United States. He needed to get out of the country and he knew where he wanted to go. Getting past screening agents at airports and shipping ports limited his choices.

The bus made a rest stop at Tampa, and Tomas, still staying in the character of an old man, made a quick pit stop and got back on the bus. He had gone long periods without eating on his various missions and he chose to limit his time mingling with the crowd in the cafeteria. The less he was exposed to curious eyes, the better he would be. While Bernardo waited for the other passengers to return to their seats he observed two uniformed officers roaming around the terminal and scanning faces. Trained eyes might spot a flaw in his disguise that others would not. It was best that he stay away from places where people congregate and was relieved when the bus finally pulled back onto to highway and continued south toward Naples.

The intention of the driver was to go as far as Fort Meyers and make one last stop in the town before reaching the terminus for the trip at Naples. From Fort Myers, the bus would travel Route 41. That was the plan, but as the bus approached the exit the driver of a fast moving sports car chose the same exit and cut off the bus.

To avoid a collision with the little red roadster and the blond driving it, the bus driver jammed the brakes and veered right onto the emergency lane and whipped back to the left. The bus driver overcompensated and swung the large vehicle too far back to the right again which ran it off the road. The bus slide sideways down and embankment and the momentum laid the bulky, top heavy bus on its side as several passengers screamed and others ducked down to protect themselves.

Tomas Bernardo was seated on the left side. He held tightly to the seat as the bus tipped over and continued to skid down toward a drainage ditch, stopping just short of the water. It took all his strength to keep from falling on the right side passengers beneath him. Tomas found some footing, drew his large hunting knife from its sheath and used the heavy metal butt to smash a window. He stood on the arm rest of the seat and began assisting passengers who were able to extricate themselves from the tangle of bodies. Tomas shoved several people up through the widow as motorists who had stopped at the accident scene helped lower them back to the ground.

Bernardo's mind came back to the reality of his situation. He was a fugitive. In a short while the place would be swarming with State Patrol and emergency vehicles. He had to get out of the bus and clear from the scene. When he first got on the bus, Tomas had deliberately wedged his knapsack between the seat and the side of the bus. It had money, a handgun and other essential items for survival. With that gripped tightly, he climbed out of the bus and was assisted to the ground.

One of the vehicles that stopped along the northbound lanes of the interstate was a stake bed truck containing construction equipment, including sand, boards, and bags of cement. While everyone was focused on the bus and the passengers, Tomas crossed the interstate, passing slowly between cars and vans until he came to the truck. Making sure he was not being observed, Bernardo crawled up among the materials and wedged himself between bags of mortar mix and the timbers. He made himself as low a profile as possible and waited.

An hour passed while Tomas hid in the back of the truck. The whole accident scene was a bee hive of activity as emergency workers took the wounded and bleeding away to area hospitals. He heard someone get back into the truck. Two doors slammed shut, so he knew there were at least two men in the cab. The motor started and the truck pulled away and continued up I-75. At some point Bernardo had to get out of the truck and find a way back south to put distance between himself and Tagart's men. Tomas was sure the Colonel would do everything possible to find him. If Tagart's men located him, there would be a fight to the death.

At the exit for North Port, the truck left the interstate and took a road leading to Venice, Florida. The driver pulled in at a fast food restaurant and the two men went inside. Tomas was a long way from where he wanted to go, but it was time to find a different mode of transportation to Naples and then across Alligator Ally to Fort Lauderdale. He started walking from the restaurant along the roadside of route 41. The March sun in Florida was a whole lot hotter than the March sun in the mountains. Tomas pulled off his jacket and tied the sleeves together around his waist. He then slung the backpack over his right shoulder and continued walking. The warmth of the sun made Bernardo's disguise very uncomfortable, but he had to keep the old timer's look for awhile longer.

Tomas walked south and stuck out his thumb to hitch a ride. The days were long gone when drivers would give a hiker a ride. The threat of car jackings and the high speeds that vehicles traveled limited the possibility that Tomas would get someone to stop. Vehicle after vehicle flashed right by him. No one was interested in some old geezer. He looked too much like a vagabond. If he were 25, female, and blond, cars would be screeching to a stop to offer a ride.

Bernardo walked about an hour when he heard a car slowing down behind him. He turned around to see a black and tan with red and blue flashing lights roll up beside him. The patrolman didn't get out. He just rolled down the passenger side window. "Hey, Old Timer. Where are you headed?"

"Hi, officer. I'm hoping to get to Naples. Not many people care about stopping for a hiker, but I can't blame them."

"What's waiting for you in Naples?"

"Work and a paycheck I hope. Things haven't been going so well. I lost my job as a school janitor six months ago and I'm getting low on savings." Bernardo added a few more lies to the pile of his deceptions.

"Well, tell you what, I can't give you a job but I can take you as far as Port Charlotte and you can get a bus. It's not safe for you to be out here on the side of the road."

"Young man, that is mighty kind of you and I gratefully accept."

Tomas got into the back seat. The passenger side of the front seat had computer equipment that took up half the space. Tomas' ability to be cool and calm under the most adverse circumstances helped him convince the officer that he was who he appeared to be. After twenty minutes of small talk and a lot of lies the officer dropped Bernardo at the bus station and waited until his passenger went inside before pulling away.

Was it providence that kept Tomas from being discovered or just blind luck? That thought had crossed his mind. He felt there was no reason at all for God to be helping him after all the sins and crimes he had committed. His own estimation of his worth was so low it was a wonder he hadn't just shot himself and gotten out of the rat race, but for reasons he didn't understand he wanted to continue living and he wanted to still expose the conspiracy that involved even the president of the United States and the man closest to him.

Could Tomas risk another bus ride? He didn't think so. Bus stations would also be on notice by now. He had to have his own mode of transportation. A car would be too hard to come by, but a motorcycle might be found for the taking. What difference would it make if he added grand theft to the list of charges that could be leveled against him? He began walking until he came across someone coming toward him. He had a question to ask.

"Pardon me for just a moment, sir."

"Sorry buddy, I don't have any money to spare."

"I don't want any money. I just want to know where the nearest high school is."

The man looked at Tomas for an extra moment and then asked, "And why would a man your age want to know about a high school?"

"I'm looking for a job as a custodian."

"Well, in that case, at the next corner take a left. Go seven blocks east and then four blocks south. You'll find a school, but I think you have to apply at the headquarters of the Board of Education and I'm not sure of that address."

"Thanks so very much. I'm sure someone at the school can direct me to where I need to go. Thanks again!"

When Tomas arrived at the school he found what he expected to see: a few light weight motorcycles chained to posts in the school parking lot. One way to get his own transportation would be for him to wait for school to let out and try to buy one of the bikes by paying a kid more money than he could refuse, but that would raise all kinds of questions. Some parent would call the police and they would be looking for the bike and who bought it, but Tomas needed to get on down the road. He didn't have time to negotiate.

Making sure the coast was clear, Bernardo selected a bike with a rather flimsy looking lock. He took his large hunting knife from its sheath and jammed it between the lock where the chain was attached. A sudden twisting downward motion and the lock snapped open. It only took a matter of a few seconds and Tomas was on his way out to the Interstate and south again.

It was time to rethink what he ought to do next. Rather than risk going all the way on I-75 Tomas left the interstate at Fort Meyers and then took route 80 east to a connection with route 27 south which took him to Fort Lauderdale. The roads were less traveled than I-75 and better for the lower speed at which the commandeered small cycle would move. Spotty rain showers proved to be inconvenient and only temporary.

The biggest problem for Tomas came on route 27 down along the side of the Everglades where the road was two lanes and drivers of large trucks competed with every other motorist for space. A semi-tractor-trailer with a heavy load of sod from a grass farm pulled out onto the highway in front of Tomas and forced him into a sudden change of lanes right into the path of another truck headed north. There was no time to do anything but to continue off the road. Tomas timed the maneuver so that as the oncoming truck was almost upon him he jerked the bike left and then back to the right and gunned the engine. The truck driver blasted the horn as he passed Tomas. The front wheel of the motorcycle came up in the air as the rear tire dug into the ground, biting deeply enough to change the direction and whip the bike back onto the pavement.

After all the death defying missions Tomas had survived, he nearly bought the farm on a motorcycle on a Florida road. The irony of it was not lost on him as he sped along route 27. He roared with laughter over his razor thin escape.

At the juncture with the east end of Alligator Ally, Tomas made the left turn and headed into Fort Lauderdale. He needed to find a quiet place to decompress and consider what he would do next. He had a plan, but making it work was something he had yet to finalize. At University Drive, Bernardo took the left turn and a few blocks later pulled into the parking lot of the Broward Mall. He found a sidewalk newspaper box and bought a paper. Scanning the classifieds, he came to the notices for which he was looking.

One item was: "For Sale by Owner. 24 foot boat with twin outboard motors and trailer: $25,000.00. Must Sell." Someone had gotten too deep into buying big boy's toys. Tomas noted the address and phone number. The next item listed was a 2005 SUV for $15,000.00. The vehicle would be the first purchase. The boat and trailer were next. Before the afternoon was over Bernardo had negotiated possession of the combination for a total of $32,000.00; $8,000 below the asking for all the items. Cash on the spot induced the sellers to lower the prices.

There was just enough time left to take his new possessions and go north to the little bank in North Lauderdale where Tomas emptied out his safety deposit box. With an additional supply of cash, credit cards, and a second 9mm automatic, he was ready to make a major move. He didn't have all the necessary licenses for the vehicle and the boat, but he wasn't going to need them if his plan succeeded.

From the bank, the fugitive headed straight to Hillsboro Inlet. It was the closest point of debarkation for Tomas. It was time to leave the States and set himself up somewhere else. There, he would be able to write his story, document names, dates, and places, and expose the corruption and danger with which he had been involved. He would try to wake up the right people and put a spotlight on the dark secrets of the Fifth Column in the American administration. Unable to break free of his past and unable to find release from his guilt, Tomas' instinct was to run and keep running until he found an answer, or until his past caught up with him.

        ✳   ✳   ✳

Little by little, information was being gathered on Tomas Bernardo's movements since he left Savannah, Georgia. The pursuers were able to reason that he had changed directions on them rather that go straight south on I-95. Bus drivers and ticket sellers were located and questioned. Information was phoned back to Tagart and he supplied the fact that Tomas often used the disguise of an old man. That led to the highway patrolman who had given an old fellow a lift. Even though Tagrat's men didn't have all the information about how their prey managed to keep moving, they assumed the destination was the Florida east coast.

The pursuers also reasoned that Tomas would try to leave the country by private boat because every other means of exit would be covered. Other agents were sent to the many places where a boat might be launched. It was reasonable to also suspect that Bernardo would not go to a marina to obtain a craft. He would either buy or steal what he needed from a private source. The devil's hounds were beginning to narrow the time gap, but Tomas still had the advantage.

The Hillsboro Inlet was not easy to navigate. At the mouth of the inlet the water was often very turbulent and small crafts found it dangerous. The 24 foot boat Tomas had would be able to make it out into the Atlantic without too much trouble. Having fueled the tanks, he slipped the boat off the trailer into the calm water at the launching ramp, secured the lines, and then parked the SUV and the trailer. He wiped down everything he thought he might have touched and boarded the craft and safely went through the churning inlet. Once Tomas was clear of the no wake zone he revved the motors and pointed the bow toward Grand Bahama.

✳   ✳   ✳

Free Port in the Bahamas was the closest point of land east of Hillsboro. If someone was following Bernardo, it would be the logical place they would go to first. The extra gas tanks he had on board gave Tomas the option of heading south to Bimini Island. Once he was far enough out to sea, he changed course. It would be a more dangerous move. There was a lot of open water before he could find a port to refuel, but Tomas was used to taking risks and doing the illogical.

Back at Hillsboro, three men began asking questions of the boaters and fishermen. The answers they got made the men scramble to rent a boat. The one they obtained was larger and more powerful than Bernardo's 24 footer. Soon the chase boat was through the inlet, out to sea, and leaving a huge rooster tail of water behind it. The men who were looking for Tomas were also very persuasive in getting the boat captain to turn his inboard engine at top rpms.

The gray of the gathering evening made it difficult to spot any other craft. Until it was dark enough to see ruining lights Tagart's goons had to just hope they were headed in the right direction. Tomas, however, was moving south at a right angle to his pursuers and adding time as well as distance between them.

With the sun fading rapidly in the west, the dim lights from cities along the Florida coast provided Tomas a way of estimating his location. He would use no running lights and not even a flashlight to check instruments until he was well south of the direct line from Hillsboro to Grand Bahama. The one thing he had to be careful of was a large ship that would not see him.

Bernardo was suffering from exhaustion. He hadn't slept for two days and the monotonous, droning sound of the motors caused him to nod off momentarily every few minutes. Tomas decided to reduce speed, secure the steering to hold a southerly compass, and leaned his head against the instrument dashboard. The hope was that he could doze just enough to take the edge off his drowsiness.

Sleep came quickly and deeper than Tomas had intended. The stress and exertion of the last few days took its toll. An hour passed and although the boat was on its set course, its captain was not aware of the danger looming ahead. Plying its way north was a massive container ship out of Miami. The ship that once was a mere blip on the horizon line between water and sky steadily grew larger and larger. It became a monstrous hulk aimed right at the sleeping Bernardo.

The container ship narrowly missed a direct hit on the small boat and set a wake against the side of Tomas' craft that almost capsized it. The sudden roll of the boat tossed him against the bulkhead of the cabin so hard Bernardo's right shoulder took a very painful blow, but it jolted him fully awake and thankful that he wasn't in the water and stranded miles form shore.

Bernardo was now alert. He switched on the boat's running lights and pushed the throttle forward. He wanted to make Bimini before daylight. Once in port he would refuel at the earliest opportunity and chart his course for Nassau. Bimini was reached without further incident. Bernardo tied up and took time to sleep a little without worrying about being run over by another vessel.

At first light, fishermen began to gather to get an early start. Activity picked up in the port and it was time for Tomas to fill his tanks, including the extra containers, and get back out to sea. The weather was good and the seas offered swells of one to two feet. The next piece of land on his map was Berry Island which he skirted to the west and adjusted to a more southerly direction. Bernardo guided his craft across the Northeast Providence Channel directly to Nassau where he topped off his tanks, took on a supply of food and water, and hurriedly set a course for Great Exuma Island.

Once again, the fleeing assassin took the opportunity to pull into port, but this time he did not go ashore for supplies. Tomas would make do with what he had. Up to this point, he had followed nearly direct lines between the places he stopped, but now he decided to take a more evasive course as he zigzagged his way between the many small islands of the Bahamas in the general direction of the Turks and Caicos. He had to make one more port at Albert Town on the Crooked Island. From there, he was sure he could make the Turks and Caicos without any problem.

✳   ✳   ✳

When Tagart's men did not locate a craft headed into Grand Bahama, it seemed clear that if Thomas Bernardo, a.k.a. Angel, had altered course, it had to be southerly. The larger craft would eat up the difference in time between it and Bernardo's boat. The men ordered the captain to make a change in course to the south. The boat's captain said he couldn't make the voyage and needed to go back to Hillsboro, Florida. When he could not be persuaded with money, threats were employed to get him to change his mind. When that failed to silence his objections, the defenseless man was tossed into the Atlantic without a raft or other flotation devise. One of the goons wanted to shoot the hapless man, but the other two argued that the sharks would get him before anyone would find him.

The pursuers made Bimini an hour after Tomas had left. The dock attendant for the gas pumps indicated that a boat the men were looking for had taken on gas and supplies, but he didn't know where it was headed after it left the port. The goons had to guess and unfortunately guessed that Nassau would be the logical destination. They began to gain time and reduced the distance between themselves and Tomas. However, they had no clue as to where he might go after Nassau. That made the advantage swing back to Bernardo. There were many islands and a great deal of water to navigate. He knew where he was going, but Tagart's men didn't.

The only thing the killers knew to do was head for the largest ports where supplies were available. The next one was Great Exuma. There they discovered that the object of their search had gassed up and left 45 minutes ahead of them. They were gaining time, but still could only guess where Tomas would be going. It was a game of chess on the water and the end of the game would not a checkmate, but death for someone.

After leaving Albert Town, Tomas made a swing around the north tip of Crooked Island, sailed East of Plana Cays and Mayaguana Island, crossed the waters of the Caicos Passage, and continued east past the largest island of the Turks and Caicos. Beyond the Turks Island Passage, Tomas put into port at Cockburn Town to fuel the boat's tanks and add supplies to his stores. He intended to head for Puerto Rico. He purchased another container to take on an extra supply of gasoline. He would need it if he had to make a run through the long open water from Cockburn Town to Arecibo on the north side of the island of Puerto Rico. Anyone following him would expect Bernardo to hug the coast of Hispaniola.

*   *   *

Tagart's men left Great Exuma and charted a course for Great Inagua Island. It seemed to them to be the next largest port of call, but after reaching Matthew Town and finding that Tomas had not put in there, they had to decided where next to search. It didn't seem that he would have had enough fuel to make it all the way to Haiti or to the Dominican Republic. So they set a course for the Turks and Caicos. That decision put them on the southwest side of the islands about the time Tomas was leaving Cockburn Town on a southeastern direction. Because the larger boat did not have to refuel as often and could make much better time than Tomas' craft, the distance between them had been narrowed to ten miles.

The chasers discovered at Cockburn Town that they were closing the gap. They powered out of port and began a zigzag pattern to try to locate Bernardo who was feeling that time was running out for him. His sixth sense told him that rather than give whoever might be on his trail the advantage in an open water race, he should alter course and head south southwest for land. That land mass would be Hispaniola. Tomas reasoned that Tagart would expect him to head for Puerto Rico, the homeland of his mother. Since the Dominican Republic was Spanish speaking, that would be the next place they might assume he would go if he could not make it to Puerto Rico. Therefore, Tomas would aim for the north coast of Haiti instead.

The logical mind of Tomas Bernardo began to race through his options. He could put in at Cap Haitien, the largest city in the north, but that would be exactly where his enemies would expect him to go and they very well could catch up with him before he could make the port. A less obvious landing would be Port-de-Paix west of Cap Haitien. However, a direct line to a landing would not be wise. Tomas chose to go farther west around the Island de la Tortue which was directly off from Port-de-Paix.

As Bernardo's craft made the east tip of de la Tortue he saw a fast moving boat aiming directly for him. It was still a few miles out, but eating up the distance with the bow high out of the water which indicated it was being pushed by a powerful inboard engine. Tomas turned to the right and put the small island between himself and the approaching boat. Soon he was out of their line of sight and able to skirt along the south coast of the island to the farthest west point. There he would wait to see what his adversaries decided to do.

Tagart's men veered off from their course for Cap Haitien when they spotted what they were after and cruised toward Port-de-Paix. They knew that Tomas could not outrun them as they drew closer to land, but there was no sign of a fast boat near the port. In fact, there were only a few small dugout boats used by fishermen.

The man who seemed to be the decision maker shouted "Take her around that island!"

Tomas waited around the point. He knew there was no chance of trying to play tag with the bigger boat. He only had his 9mm hand guns and hunting knife for weapons. That meant he was also out gunned. How he wished he had his sniper rifle. This fight was going to up close and personal.

The larger craft came slowly cruising toward the point as Bernardo motored out on the water away from the island, but still out of sight. He then looped the boat around to build maximum speed so that when the big boat came into view Tomas would meet it at full throttle. Surprise and a ramming attack became his weapons. By the time the men in the other boat realized what was happening they could not speed up quickly enough to avoid a collision.

Seconds before the two boats met, Tomas dove into the water with the backpack he had covered in plastic tied to a flotation ring. One man from the other boat managed to leap into the water just as the boats exploded in flames because of the extra gasoline aboard Tomas' craft. A giant plume of flame and black smoke shot skyward and fragments were flung into the air and then began splashing back into the water.

Bernardo's Special Forces training gave him the deadly advantage over the lone survivor of Tagart's men.

Before Tomas could get to the man, his adversary fired two shots. One round splashed the water near Bernardo; the other struck his right shoulder and he went below the surface. He came up behind the man and they struggled. There was another aimless shot followed by the slicing of a large bladed knife: the water turned red.

✳   ✳   ✳

Three days passed before the coastguard cutter that had been dispatched to search for a stolen speed boat arrived off the coast of Haiti. A passing fishing boat out of Hillsboro, Florida had accidentally come across the captain of the stolen craft. He was trying to stay afloat and was near the end of his strength but able to give the description of his craft. That triggered a wide search. He also told them that the three men on board were trying to chase down another boat with one man on board.

Currents had moved the debris from the two burned out boats away from the location of the explosion, but there were still two bodies tangled in the pieces that were clinging together. Identification found on one of the bodies contained the phone number of a Colonel Tag Tagart of Washington, D.C. The Coastguard notified Colonel Tagart of what was found and he inquired of the number of bodies. When the report was given to him that only two bodies were found and neither of them could be identified as Tomas Bernardo, the Colonel cursed and slammed down the phone. "Get Bernardo! I don't care how long it takes or where you have to go!" Two more of his men snapped to action and the hunt for Angel was still active.

The monitors at the hospital ICU nursing station for room 504 began setting off alarms for code blue. The crash cart team raced to Tagart's bedside and began resuscitation efforts. Paddles were used to shock the heart. After the third attempt, the Colonel's heart began to beat, but it was erratic. The doctor in charge demanded, "What brought this on?"

"He was on the phone and shouting at someone."

"Take out the phone and sedate him! I want this man isolated! One more episode like this one and we might not be able to rescue him again."

The orders had already been given to scour the Islands. The order was, "Find and terminate Bernardo!"

Chapter Twelve

BETWEEN THE PEN AND THE SWORD

On the first day of May a sunburned man inquired of an official at the Cap Haitien, Haiti city hall about the purchase of an empty house located on the side of the mountain above the city. The city official asked, "How do you know about this place, seeing that you are just coming into our city?"

"I came over the mountain and stopped there to ask for some food and water, but saw right away that no one was living there. Who do I see about buying the property?"

"Monsieur, you don't appear to be a rich man, but I will inquire for you. It may take a long time."

"Would it take less time if this would help you?" Tomas pulled a small bundle of currency from his pocket.

"Qui, Monsieur. The property is owned by missionaries who had to leave the country because of serious illness. There are people who know them well and have contact with them. Perhaps they will negotiate a purchase for you."

Tomas thought, *It seems like money talks in every country.* The official already had the information that was needed and was probably going to ask for a large sum of money to accommodate the stranger, but Bernardo had been in enough places around the globe that he anticipated the situation. "While I wait for news, where can a rent a room?"

"La Beck Hotel. I will give you directions."

"Many thanks. If I purchase the house, would you also help me find a maid and a watchman? Also, I'd like a large, mean looking dog. Make sure the maid is young; preferably single and not ugly or mean. Can you handle that?"

"Qui: for a price. The boy will look ugly and the dog will be mean, but the girl will not look ugly or be mean. Is that what you want?"

"Yes. That's exactly what I want. I want a maid, not grandmother."

"Monsieur, for one thousand American dollars I can arrange for what you want. Will you need anything else?"

The sunburned man answered, "Yes, I need a lap top computer and a printer."

"Monsieur, that will he hard to find, but for another two thousand dollars I can get that for you also. Are you going to write a book?"

"Something like that. It's said that 'the pen in mightier than the sword,' but if the pen doesn't do it, I still have the sword." The official looked surprised and didn't know how to respond. Tomas went on to say, "You supply what I want and I'll pay. And, Mon Ami, if someone ever asks about me, you know nothing. We never met. In that way, we will both live to see many sunrises and sunsets. Do you understand?"

"Qui, Monsieur." There was a brief moment of reflection upon the seriousness of Tomas' words. "Qui, Monsieur!"

Tomas Bernardo reached into his backpack and handed Louis Pierre some more money. "This will help you get started on my requests."

Three weeks passed before Louis Pierre was able to get back to Tomas that he had made contact with the owners of the house through other missionaries and they were willing to sell. Louis could have found the information earlier, but he was going by Haitian time. Nothing happens quickly for Haitians, except death.

"Monsieur, you may meet with representatives of the house owners tomorrow in my office."

"What time?"

"Ten in the morning. They will be punctual. They are Americans."

Tomas was pleased to know that there were a few people who paid attention to time. Perhaps he would eventually relax enough to adopt the easier approach to life that the Islanders had, but he was still governed by the clock.

The next day Bernardo was early for the meeting and happy to see the representatives of the sellers arrive on time with the papers. With the documents signed and funds paid, he could take possession of the house. The city official, Louis Pierre, informed Tomas that his maid and watchman would meet him at the house the next day. It would take a little longer to find the particular dog he requested.

Tomas thanked everyone for their cooperation, tucked the documents in his backpack, and got on his newly acquired motor bike. He had already vacated his quarters at the Beck. From the center of town, he rode up the hill and made the sharp left hand curve at the Mont Joli Hotel, went past the tennis courts, and took the ever rising road as it snaked up the side of the mountain where he could look down on the rusty metal roofs of color-varied painted houses. A quarter of a mile after a sweeping right turn where the unpaved road leveled off, Bernardo turned right and down a long rutted driveway into his new property.

He dismounted his bike and just stood for several minutes surveying his domain. It was so different from anything he had ever known. There were no other houses within his line of sight. From the edge of his yard, the land dropped precipitously down to the city, but from where he stood Tomas saw only the higher part of the mountain behind him and the bay of Cap Haitien in front of him. He had only known city life since his birth, except for his military excursions into remote corners of the world. He certainly had experienced many mountains and third world countries when on a mission, but this was home. The very word sounded strange to him.

Inside the house, Tomas found everything in good condition and clean. He had entered through the kitchen door on the west side and, as he walked through to the main part of the house, he found the east wall was composed of a several windows on three sides which not only gave a panoramic view, but also provided good ventilation. That was important in a climate where summer weather lasted a major part of the year.

The mountain was well wooded and covered with vegetation. A great part of Haiti was denuded because of the cutting of trees for charcoal and so Bernardo felt blessed to have so much greenery around him. For a few moments he forgot how he got into the country and why he was here. He knew it was a place that few would consider a paradise because of the poverty and disease, but for Tomas it came as close to it as anything he had experienced. He also knew that one day someone would come looking for him and he had to be on guard.

Just as promised, the next morning a girl who looked to be a teenager, but was actually older, knocked on the door and said, "Monsieur, I have been sent to be your house maid."

"Yes, please come in. Would you please sit over here so I can ask you some questions?"

The rather timid girl of a creamy brown complexion cautiously sat in a wicker chair while Tomas sat on the couch. She glanced around the living area as Bernardo began to try to find out as much as he could about this pretty Haitian girl.

"What is your name?"

"Geraline, Monsieur."

"A pretty name. And how old are you?"

"Twenty, Monsieur."

"I think you are going to have to know me by something other than Monsieur. Please call me Michael." Geraline nodded that she would. "Are you married?" Geraline looked down and indicated by moving her head from side to side that she was not married. "Then, do you have a boyfriend?" Again she indicated that she had no boy friend. It seemed surprising to Tomas that such an attractive girl would not have several young men courting her.

"You may not want me to work for you Monsieur Michael. The houngan has told everyone I am cursed. The magistrate told me I had to come to see you anyway."

"Geraline, I don't believe in witchdoctors and curses. All I want from you is for you to take care of my house. I'll cook my own meals and you can cook anything you want for yourself."

"Monsieur Michael, where will I stay?"

"Do you have a home?"

"I have been sent away from my home. My family is afraid."

"There are three bedrooms in this house. Choose whichever one you want. There is only one bathroom, so we'll have to share it and the kitchen. I don't suppose you can go to town when we need supplies."

"People in the city don't know about the curse I have. I could go buy food for you."

"If you're not from the city, how is it that you speak English so well?"

"Before the curse, when I was younger, I went to a missionary school and learned your language."

Tomas stood up and walked over to Geraline who was still seated. "Look, Geraline, forget about this curse. There is no such thing. There is no black magic, or witchcraft, or curses allowed on my property. Try to remember that. I want this to be a happy place. I want you to feel happy. I'll pay you five dollars a day for your service."

"Oh, no Monsieur Michael! That is too much money! Servants do not get that much. You have given me a home and food. I do not deserve more than that."

"Look, kid. I don't believe in slavery. If that's too much, then you'll take three dollars a day."

"Please forgive me, Monsieur Michael, but I can not take more than a dollar a day. I don't need more than that."

"I don't understand, but we'll talk about this later. Do you have any clothes with you?"

"No."

"Then I want you to get some clothes. Anyone who works for me will be dressed properly. Get some shoes, too. Take this money and go to town right now and buy two changes of clothes, including whatever you wear under your dresses." The girl hung her head and blushed. "Get some perfume and something to make your hair look nice and don't argue with me. Get going and come back as soon as you can. One more thing; this is very important. Don't talk to anyone about me! You don't need to know why. Just don't say anything to anyone about me."

Geraline took the money and left, but there was a very curious look on her face. She could tell by Tomas' tone of voice he meant exactly what he said. She didn't want to risk losing her new home by disobeying him.

As the girl walked up the lane to the road a large and mean looking man passed her on his way to the house. He turned his head away from Geraline and stepped several feet off the pathway as she continued her long walk to town. Jona Baptiste watched her until she was out of sight and then turned toward the house. Tomas had observed the two Haitian's and noted how the man behaved. Bernardo met him before he reached the house.

"Are you the man Louis Pierre sent?"

"Qui, Monsieur."

"Do you know the girl who just left here?"

"I know of her, but the magistrate said you would protect me."

"I'm telling you just like I told her, there are no curses allowed on this land and in my house. Let's get some things settled right now. If you work for me, I'm the boss. You can call me Boss rather Monsieur. You will live in my house and eat my food and I'll pay you three dollars a day. Is that Okay?"

"I cannot sleep in the same house as that girl."

"I don't know where else you can sleep if you work for me."

"What is in that shed?"

"I don't know. I haven't had a chance to look into it."

"I will make that my place."

The two men walked over to the shed and pulled the door open. It was empty, except for a few boxes. Tomas opened one box and found that it contained dozens of New Testaments of the Bible. They were all new and were written in Haitian Creole.

"If you want to make this into your sleeping quarters, that's up to you, but the offer of a room in the house is still open. Now, as to your duties: you are to watch for anyone approaching my property and when you see anyone coming onto the property you come and tell me immediately. I don't want anyone near my house that I don't know about before they get close. Will you be able to keep a close watch for me?"

"Qui, Boss Man."

"Okay, good! One more thing, in a few days I'll have a large dog here. The dog will be useful to help guard the property, especially at night. It'll bark if someone comes onto the property."

"Why you do this Boss? You think maybe there be problems?"

"Let's just say I like my privacy. Do you want the job?"

"Qui. I want it. I have to go bring my things and make a place in the shed to sleep."

"What is your name?"

"I am called Jona Baptiste."

"All right, Jona. You go get what you need and if you need to get a cot for the shed, I'll pay for it."

"I have a cot, Boss Man."

"Before you go, you have to promise me that you will not speak about me to anyone. You can tell your family you have a job, but you are not to describe me and how I look to anyone. Do you understand this?"

"Qui, Boss."

Tomas stood and watched Jona walk back up to the road that winds its way down the side of the mountain. He wondered if hiring Jona might be a mistake, but he needed someone as mean looking as him to cause people to think twice before venturing onto the property, whether it was a person wanting to rob the house or somebody Tagart might send to look for him. Tomas had to assume that the wreckage of the boats in the vicinity of the Haitian coast would be found and reported. Once Tagart learned of it through his various "eyes and ears" in the government he would make it his search area. Only the Colonel would be interested in sending people to see if Bernardo could be found alive.

   *   *   *

As the late afternoon sun dropped behind the mountain and cast a long shadow over Tomas' hillside retreat, Geraline came back from town with a load of clothes and food staples balanced on her head. She walked along with a light and easy stride as one who had found a purpose for living. Not long after she hung her new clothes on a hook in her room and then stored the groceries on kitchen shelves, Jona arrived with a mattress and some bedding on his back. He went into the shed and made a nest for himself. Soon, he was knocking on the kitchen door. When Geraline opened it, Jona step backward to put some distance between the two of them.

"I'm hungry. You got some bread?"

"Are you sure you want me to hand it to you?"

"Boss Man says no curse allowed on his land. I am hungry."

Geraline cut off a large chunk from a loaf of bread and handed it to Jona who took it very carefully. She also poured a tin cup full of water and set that on the table. "If you want to drink, you come in and get it."

"This all I get?"

"Monsieur Michael says he will fix your food later. He's out front looking down at the bay. I think he is lonely. He just stares out over the water like he was looking for a boat."

"I be sittin' out back on a bench watchin' the road. When Boss eats, tell me so I can eat."

It was almost dark when Tomas came inside and washed his hands before cooking some eggs and bacon to go with the bread. Geraline had eaten and was bathing the dust of the road and the humidity off her body. When she was finished, she put on one of the two new dresses she had purchased. They were simple, straight line garments with a flowered print. The reds, blues, greens and, yellows all mixed together and were typically Caribbean. Her slim form made her look years younger and child-like.

Bernardo turned when he heard Geraline enter the kitchen. "Wow! You look very nice young lady." The girl looked down in embarrassment. She wasn't used to being complimented or spoken to in a tone that was accepting of her as a person. "Turn around so I can see how you look." She made a complete 360 and waited for her employer's approval. "Yes Mam; that will do nicely."

Tomas turned back to his cooking and Geraline stood for a moment basking in a new found feeling of pride in herself and some affection for a man who was still a stranger to her. She turned and went to her room, hung up the new dress and put back on her old garment. When she came back to the kitchen, Tomas was surprised that she had changed.

"Geraline, I want you to wear your new dress and throw that old one away! This is your new life, so I want you to look like it."

A bright smile filled her face and her gleaming white teeth seemed to light up the grayness of the room. Oil lamps cast some illumination, but not even broad daylight could compete with her smile and the glow in Geraline's heart.

Tomas called for Jona to come in and share in the meal. "Don't get used to this, Jona. Starting tomorrow, you'll eat what Geraline fixes for you. I cook for myself when I feel like eating. I want one of us to be watching the property while the other one eats. The dog is supposed to be brought up the mountain tomorrow. I want him chained to the back of the house so that when anyone comes by way of the road the animal will let us know. The dog will hear someone before we can see who it is."

"Hey, Boss. You expect a visitor?"

"Maybe. Just maybe."

✳   ✳   ✳

Life settled into a quiet routine. The odd "family" made up of a Puerto

Rican-Italian former Special Forces sniper, a young Haitian woman shunned by her relatives as cursed, and a scary looking middle aged Haitian man formed a strange combination. Jona played the role of a peculiar uncle. Tomas was the father figure to Geraline, but she secretly hoped for more than that in spite of the age difference. The three had become friends over the last three months, even though the type of friendship was hard to define. Tomas was still the employer and what he said was law, but the application of his rule was soft and kindly.

For a man who had taken the lives of so many other human beings, Bernardo wanted to be more than a killer; more than a fugitive who wouldn't mind having his revenge on Colonel Tagart for deceiving him into thinking his assassination work was a patriotic duty. Tomas' brief foray into a religious venture moved his heart toward what was right, but his conversion to godliness was grossly incomplete.

Tomas began to leave his property on random occasions to help select food from the market. He was always in the company of his maid, who for public appearances, always walked a few paces behind him, but at home there were no formalities. Tomas had begun to think of the young woman as he would a daughter.

He never would have a child of his own and he believed he would never have a wife. What woman would want a man who could not be what a husband should be? He knew how to love in his heart, but it could never be expressed. To keep himself from obsessing over his inabilities he consciously suppressed any desires he might have had before he suffered his devastating wound. A wife and children were for other men, yet he longed for a close friendship. He didn't feel it could be Geraline, but not because she was Haitian. That didn't matter to him. She was fourteen years younger and deserved to find a man her own age who could be to her what a woman would desire in a husband. Tomas resolved to try to protect Geraline from public speculation that there was anything between them other than that of an employer and a house keeper.

The relationship between Geraline and Jona was that of indifference. She saw nothing attractive in him and he still wondered about the possibility that she might be as untouchable as the country people believed her to be. As time passed, the deliberate efforts of Jona to keep a distance between them became somewhat relaxed.

Early on a Sunday morning, after the breakfast dishes were washed and put away, Geraline approached Tomas with a request. "Monsieur Michael, would you allow me to go away for part of today?"

"You have some place you want to go, or someone you want to visit?"

"I have no one to visit, but I would like to go to church."

On one of Gerlaine's solo trips to town for supplies she was noticed by a young girl she had been with in the mission school. It had been a dozen years since they had known each other, but Katia recognized Geraline and approached her. They talked for a few minutes and it was during that encounter that the other girl asked Geraline about attending the Sunday afternoon gathering for worship at a church in town. It was an English speaking group of Christians from various denominational backgrounds. Some of them were missionaries and the rest were English speaking Haitians. Geraline told the girl she couldn't attend because of her work, but the desire to be part of the group grew in her heart. She explained this to Tomas.

"Sure, you go ahead and enjoy yourself. Jona and I can hold the fort here."

"What do you mean, 'hold the fort'? This house is not a fort."

Tomas laughed. It wasn't often that he felt like laughing at anything. "It's just an expression. It just means we will be fine. You go. You need to be around other people."

Over the following few Sundays, Geraline attended the church services and it seemed to add to her light heartedness, but there was something she wished would happen. She wanted Tomas to go with her one Sunday, but was fearful to ask since he stayed so close to the house on the side of the mountain. At last, she mustered up the courage to ask him to go with her.

"Monsieur Michael, it would make me so happy if you would take me to church today. I would feel so much better to have you with me."

"I'm sorry, Geraline, but I don't think that's a good idea."

"Why is it not a good idea? I think it is a very good idea."

Tomas resisted and would not relent. When Geraline left by herself he could tell how disappointed she was. He wished to please her, but the idea of going out among strangers in a close setting like a church gathering was something he found almost fearful.

Here was a man who faced death many times and could fight like a tiger and remain inwardly calm during and after a battle. He could stand physical torture, but the thought of opening himself up to a group of people he did not know and in a land where he was the intruder left him with deep concerns.

Geraline persisted politely. Each Sunday she would ask and each time, Tomas would say that he couldn't. One Saturday evening as they were getting ready to retire for the night, Geraline made her usual request, but she added, "If you wish me to be like a daughter to you, will you be like a father to me and go with me to church tomorrow?"

The comment hit Tomas in his heart. "Would it make you happy if I went just once?"

"Oh Monsieur, it would make me very, very happy."

"Go to bed. I'll think about it."

"Will you pray about it?"

The mention of prayer brought a hesitation. "I said, I'd think about it. You do the praying."

Geraline did just that: she prayed that her employer would go with her to the Sunday afternoon church service and, more than that, she prayed that he would be a real father, since it was clear that Tomas would never be more than that to her.

In the morning, while Bernardo and Geraline ate breakfast, the young lady kept looking at Tomas between spoonfuls of cereal. He noticed, but said nothing. She wanted to ask him again about going with her, but was timid to do so. She didn't want to anger him.

The morning passed, as many days did, with Tomas standing at the edge of the cliff and looking out to sea. Geraline, who was more of a woman than a girl, busied herself with household chores. Soon, it was lunch time and the same thing happened as they ate: she looked directly at him after each bite of chicken and he pretended not to notice. It was frustrating to Geraline, but she kept quiet, even though she felt like bursting into tears.

Tomas finished his meal and left his plate and utensils on the table as he exited the kitchen for his room. Twenty minutes later he emerged dressed in clothes that for him represented the best he had to wear. He walked to the archway between the living space and the kitchen and stood there looking at Geraline. "Come on girl! We don't want to be late for church!"

Geraline screamed a little girl scream of delight as she ran and hugged Tomas. Her head came up only to his shoulder as she placed a cheek against his chest. "Thank you, Monsieur Michael, Thank you!" The broad smile revealed the beautiful sparkle in her deep black eyes. Her joy lit up the room and she quickly ran to change into her best dress. Geraline turned to look back at Tomas and he saw tears of joy rolling down her soft round cheeks.

"Hey, kid, I think it's about time to stop with the Monsieur Michael stuff and make it, Papa Michael, if that's all right with you."

Geraline giggled and wiped the tears away with the backs of her hands. "Yes, Papa Michael, I like that!" She ran back and hugged him again as hard as she could. It was the first real sign of mutual affection that had passed between them and now she could call him by a name that meant so much more to her than any other.

How could Tomas ever tell her that Michael was not his given name and that he had lived by several names in the awful business which had ruined his life. For the first time since the death of his brother, Tomas felt really close to someone and it was the last person he would have imagined it could be. He now had more reason to live, because he felt a responsibility for someone other than himself.

✳   ✳   ✳

Geraline led the way into the church where she was greeted by people who were a mixture of skin colors and accents. Haiti had people whose ancestry represented the French and Spanish who once ruled the country, decedents from African tribes who had been sold into slavery and brought to Hispaniola, Whites who traveled to Haiti on business and married into the population, and missionaries who were mainly from the United States. And then, there was Tomas who also was of mixed nationality. All of these diverse peoples gathered to worship the same God: the God of the Bible.

After Geraline introduced Tomas to the group as Monsieur Michael, so as not to overstep the privacy of her new relationship with the man she would call Papa in private, it was time for the service to begin with singing and then scripture reading and prayer. That was followed by a short sermon by a Haitian pastor who spoke very good English. Pastor

Dumournay spoke about the Prodigal Son from one of Jesus' parables. He emphasized the forgiveness of the father toward a son who had left home and wasted his life, but repented and returned to be fully restored to the love his father had for him. Tomas thought, *I wonder if this was set up for me, but it couldn't be. No one here knows anything about me and my past.*

When the service was over, Pastor Dumournay approached Tomas and shook his hand. "I am so glad you came today. Next Sunday one of the missionaries will be speaking. You will want to come again and hear that message. While I was preaching, I saw something in your face that makes me want to know if there is something you would like to ask me."

"No, Pastor. I can't think of anything, but I did understand everything you said and I want to believe that the heavenly Father is as forgiving as the father in the parable."

"Oh yes, my son, God is infinitely able to forgive when a son repents and comes home."

With that, Tomas signaled Geraline that it was time to leave. As they began to walk toward the Mont Joli Hotel and the road leading up the mountain, she looked up at him and asked, "Papa Michael, you look sad. You should be happy. I am happy, because I am with you."

"I'm not sad and I'm very happy to be with you. I'm just thinking about something the pastor said to me."

"What was that Papa?"

"Maybe I'll tell you later, but right now I want to get home and relax." Tomas took Geraline by the hand and led her at a faster walk. She felt warm all over and it wasn't the sunshine. She and her "Papa" were going *home*.

After the sunshine, clouds began to roll in from the east with the trade winds. It looked like there might be some rain later in the day. The long dry spell left a parched earth in need of the moisture. Tomas was also in need of some divine refreshing for his parched soul. He tried to nap, but the pastor's words kept repeating in his mind, *"God is infinitely able to forgive when a son repents and comes home."* Bernardo also recalled the little country church in McRoss, West Virginia where he went to the front of the sanctuary and asked God to change him. Many godless things happened after that, in spite of the years in seminary.

His head had accepted things that his heart hadn't. He still felt lost and without redemption.

It was useless to try to rest. Tomas got up and went out into the expansive yard that overlooked the bay. He stood there silently for a long time letting the light raindrops fall on him and wishing he could just erase his past, but knowing that the images of people and events were a permanent part of his memory. Maybe God could forgive him, but Tomas did not think it was possible for him to forgive himself.

A tug at his sleeve brought Tomas out of his far off thoughts. "Papa Michael, you are getting wet. It is almost time for supper. I would like to make something for you to eat."

"Thanks, sweetheart, but I really don't feel like eating now. I'll get something later. You go ahead and eat." Geraline just stood beside Tomas and looked with him out to sea. She would like to know why he did that so often, but did not ask.

Tomas looked down at the frail, petite girl beside him. He was nearly thirty-five years of age and she was twenty, he looked older than he was and she looked like she was sixteen. He wondered why this particular young woman was sent his way. He was beginning to believe it was because she needed a father's love. She needed protection and a chance to grow and develop in a healthy way, but then he had the awful thought of what might happen to her if Tagart's men found him.

"Papa Michael, I wish I could help you find what you are looking for." With that, Geraline turned and walked back to the house. She shouted back to him, "Papa, come in out of the rain!" Tomas remained at the edge of the cliff for a few more minutes and then decided he would go inside, but he didn't mind getting damp from the gentle rain.

The top of the mountain was covered by the low hanging clouds with a promise of more rain during the night. The gray late afternoon induced more thinking about his life and how it was immersed in the shadows of what he had become. How he wished he could feel clean inside. He wondered if he had a future. When Tomas was on a missions and hunting a target to hit, he never thought much about the future. It was the *now* with which he was concerned. His goal was fixated on the job and being as precise as he could be. Everything was different in his current situation. There was nothing left for him back in the States. He was a fugitive. Now he was the target.

CHAPTER THIRTEEN

STRANGERS IN TOWN

After months of seclusion on his mountainside retreat where Tomas enjoyed his privacy and his assembled "family," he began in earnest to put together a document declaring the information that the president of the United States was party to a conspiracy that included a mole who was a sleeper agent for Al Qaeda. Tomas had felt the freedom to leave his mountain retreat and even attend church services with his maid; a Haitian young lady whom he had unexpectedly begun to look upon as a daughter. Geraline attached herself to him and settled for thinking of Tomas as her father when she realized he would not return her romantic aspirations.

Bernardo felt he had found a home as well as a safe retreat where he could avoid the outside world and all the trouble it held for him. It was a dream he hoped would prove to be a reality, but as long as he held information that Colonel Tagart wanted destroyed there would be no lasting peace. Tomas wanted to believe that personal peace was still possible, but the nightmares of his past sins persisted.

Tomas began awakening some nights with his body soaked with perspiration and each time it was his loud moaning that brought out if his troubled sleep. It took Geraline's consolation to calm him down and lull him back to sleep. Her affectionate care for him during his bouts with ghosts from the past eventually led to a deepening bond between the beautiful Haitian girl and the troubled soul she called Papa, but it could never lead to anything intimate.

Perhaps writing down the entire story from the very beginning would bring some relief to his mind and so he began to fill his lap top computer with information that perhaps no one would believe. He skipped meals to keep on writing. Geraline begged him to take food, but he became obsessed with completing the documentation.

When he could feel satisfied that he had told everything he remembered, Bernardo planned to take it to the Dominican Republic and mail copies of the disk to various news agencies and magazines in the United States and Great Brittan. Perhaps the English newspapers would print what the Americans wouldn't. It would take weeks to put it all together. Until then, he had little time for food or sleep.

Geraline told Pastor Dumournay about her fears for her Papa's health, even though she had been warned not to talk to anyone about him. That brought the old Haitian pastor to the house to speak with Tomas whom he knew only as Michael. Dumournay found him standing where he often was in the morning; looking out over the bay.

"Michael, good morning. Are you enjoying our very beautiful scenery?"

"Pastor! Yes, I think this is a wonderful place to watch the water. Sometimes I see men going out in their little open boats to fish the deep water."

Dumournay agreed. "They have to go out very early and very far since the bay is so full of silt. You must get up early also."

"I like the mornings. I think best at this time of day."

"And what to you think about, if it isn't too personal for me to ask?"

Tomas paused before answering. He first looked at the ground and then at the pastor. "Please don't be offended, but it is too personal."

Dumournay placed a hand on Tomas' shoulder. "I take no offense at all. If you ever care to tell me your thoughts, I am a good listener and I am not judgmental."

"What brings you up on the mountain, Pastor?"

"You. Geraline loves you very much and she is concerned that you are not taking good care of yourself. She said that you won't listen to her."

"She shouldn't have done that!"

"Michael, please don't be angry at her."

"I'm not, Pastor. I could never be angry at her, but she knows I have a project that has to be finished soon. I come out here in the morning to think through what I need to write and then I spend the rest of the day carefully putting it together. It's a slow process."

Pastor Dumournay frowned. "I take it that this is very important."

"Yes, it is, but I am not at liberty to talk about it. Has she told you anything else?"

"No, but you can. It may help you."

Tomas was very apologetic. "Pastor, I'll walk you back to the road and then I have to get to work. I hope you don't mind."

"Not at all, Michael. Some things cannot keep and I am sure your project is one of them."

The two men said their farewells and Tomas returned to the house and to his lap top. The day seemed to go by quickly. Geraline made a sandwich and set it on the table beside the computer, along with a beverage. Tomas glanced at it and continued to type. Evening came and Bernardo slipped his computer into its case and slid it under his bed. He hadn't shaved for days and felt it was time to cut the beard and take a shower. Once he was refreshed, Tomas told Geraline he was going to bed and that she should make sure all the doors were locked.

Sleep came from exhaustion and it was not restful. About one o'clock in the morning Tomas began to twitch violently and make sounds as though he were quarreling with someone. Soon, that was followed by loud cries like that of a wounded animal. The noise awakened Geraline and she rushed into Tomas' room to find him sitting upright in a cold sweat, but still asleep with his eyes open.

"Papa! What is wrong?"

She got onto the bed and held Tomas to try to stop his shaking. When he awoke he wasn't sure where he was and who had hold of him. His natural reaction was to fight. With very little effort he was able to throw Geraline onto the floor. She screamed and the sound brought Tomas fully awake and aware of what he had just done.

"Geraline! Are you all right? Oh, please forgive me! I didn't know what I was doing!" He got out of bed and lifted her in his arms. He then sat her in a chair next to the bed and knelt before her on the floor. "Why were you in my room?"

"Papa Michael, you were having another bad dream and making loud sounds like you were in trouble. I had to try to help you. I am fine now. Let me go get some water and a wash cloth to wipe your face." She didn't wait for an answer. Geraline got up and pushed past Tomas. She was back quickly and used the damp cloth to wipe away the perspiration from his face and arms. She started to wipe his chest, but Tomas took the cloth from her.

Tomas said sharply, "I'm all right now! Thank you for coming to my rescue. You can go back to bed."

Reluctantly, the young woman turned away and went to her room where she muffled her crying with a pillow. She felt she had been rejected and didn't understand why her loving care was not warmly received. Tomas could not explain why he didn't allow her to do any more for him.

Over the next several nights the bad dreams persisted and each time Geraline came to help bring Tomas out of his nightmare. She didn't try to do anything more than awaken him for fear that her efforts would be rejected again. On the morning after the most recent episode, Geraline suggested that Tomas go see one of the missionary doctors. He strongly dismissed her suggestion as unnecessary.

"But Papa, you have lost weight and you don't look well!"

"Honey, I will be just fine as soon as I finish the document and take it to be mailed."

"Papa, I love you and I am afraid of what is happening to you. What will become of me if you become too ill and maybe die?"

Tomas finally realized what his obsession was doing to Geraline. He put his arms around her and tried to comfort her, even as she had tried to do for him when he was trapped in his nightmare. "Please don't be afraid. If it makes you feel better I'll eat something right now. What do we have?"

"Papa, you sit down and I will take care of you like a good daughter should."

     ✳   ✳   ✳

Life for the odd family in the house on the mountain improved. Tomas began to take nourishment on a schedule and he cut back the time he spent at the computer. The father-daughter relationship grew tender and he began to wonder what might become of her if something did happen to him. He was sure Colonel Tagart had not given up the search and would have other authorities around the Bahamas and the Caribbean on alert for anyone matching Tomas' description. Would the girl find someone to marry, or would the fact that she was branded as having a curse upon her make that impossible?

On the other hand, while Geraline was happy to have such a close relationship with Tomas as his "adopted" daughter, she still harbored stronger feelings for him: feelings that could not be fulfilled. She had no interest in finding a male friend, nor anything beyond that.

Bernardo spent most of his time in the next two weeks editing the document to make sure his account of events, since he was recruited by Tagart, were accurate in every detail. The next step was to print out the information for a hard copy and then download the complete document onto disks for distribution. The hard copy proved to be more than fifty pages. It would be hidden in the house and the disks would be mailed.

Tomas and Geraline began to go to town more often once he had gotten to the editing stage of his expose. He felt he owed her a little more time away from the house and she insisted that he go with her when she had to do shopping. She no longer walked a few paces behind him. She didn't care what people might think and Tomas wanted to show to others the equality that had developed in their relationship since he first arrived in Cap Haitien. The townspeople were getting used to seeing them together and it was no longer a curiosity.

In the Haitian culture there was a definite cast system revolving around skin color and associations. The lighter the skin color, the higher the social status. When a light skinned person and a darker skinned person married, or were closely associated with each other in some arrangement, the status of the darker skinned person was elevated. It was a form of racism an outsider would not expect to find in a society dominated by black skin.

On a hot, sunny afternoon in June, Pastor Dumournay made another of his visits to the mountain to see Tomas. He had noticed the closeness of the man and Geraline and wanted to clarify the condition of the relationship. A few people had made some remarks about how comfortable the employee and employer were with each other at the church gatherings.

"Pastor, you sure picked a hot day to hike up the mountain. Something must be very important for you to endure the heat."

"Yes, Michael, it is, but first I need to sit for a moment and catch my breath. Could I have a drink of water, please?"

"Of course. I'll get it right away." Tomas excused himself and went into the house and returned with the water. "I'm sorry that the water isn't cold. I haven't been running the generator and so the refrigerator is just for storage. There isn't anything perishable in it right now."

The pastor drank the water slowly. It was as though he didn't want to get to the purpose of his visit. Finally he turned to Tomas and the expression on his face indicated it was a serious issue he was about to address. "Is Geraline here?"

"No. She went down the mountain to buy some cloth. She wants to sew a shirt for me."

"She is a very lovely young woman, isn't she?"

"Yes, Pastor, she is a very lovely girl."

"It is curious, that I called her a young woman and you called her a girl. Is that how you see her?"

"I see her both ways. Because of her small size I sometimes think of her as being younger than she is."

The pastor shifted his weight in the wicker chair before asking the next question. "Do you love her?"

Tomas stood up and glanced out to the east where the silver flashes where were glinting off the braking water. He turned back to Dumournay. "I'm beginning to see where you're going with this. Do I love Geraline? Yes, of course I do, but not in the way you imply."

"The two of you seem very close for being unequal in status."

"Oh, Pastor, I don't see inequality. I just see two people who each have a role to play, but who are more than employer and employee. Geraline has become like a daughter to me. When we aren't around other people, she calls me Papa Michael."

"How old are you, Michael?"

"I just turned thirty-five last week."

"And how old is Geraline?"

"I think she is about twenty now."

"Under normal circumstances, could you have a daughter who was only fifteen years younger than you?"

Tomas was becoming very uncomfortable with the direction of the conversation which he thought was too much like an inquisition. "No, but these are not normal circumstances for either of us. She is an outcast from her family and many others who believe in the curse the houngan placed on her and, in some ways, I'm also an outcast. We have many things in common, but physical intimacy is not one of them."

"I am very glad to hear you say that, but I am aware that Geraline loves you more than as a father. Do you know that?"

"I admit I have sensed it and I've done what I can to gently discourage it. I don't want a wife and I certainly don't want a physical relationship with Geraline. I can't tell her why, but you need to know that it has to do with wounds I received in combat in Afghanistan that have altered my life. I can't be a husband, especially for a woman who might want to have children."

"Oh, I see. I am beginning to understand and I am very sorry. It must be frustrating for you."

"Actually, Pastor, it isn't. I have reconciled myself to the fact and it allows me to look at life with a calm acceptance, but I don't want others to know about this. It is my secret and it has to stay that way. I wouldn't have told you except for the questions that have come up about us."

"I can reassure people without making any reference to your personal matters. Please be careful of Geraline's feelings. She may think you are rejecting her as a woman. She wants more than you can give."

"I know...I know that and it does bother me, but I do love her...as a daughter."

Pastor Dumournay got up from the chair and gave Tomas a hug. "You have a good heart, young man. It is time for me to go back down the mountain."

As Tomas always did, he walked the pastor to the road and they said their goodbyes. On the way back to the house Tomas thought of what Dumournay said about him having a good heart. If the man only knew what Tomas had been doing for the past several years, he would not have made the statement. The burden of the duplicity of Tomas Bernardo's life was getting heavier and harder to bear. He could not see any way out for himself.

When Tomas reached the patio in front of the house he fell to his knees and began praying. Desperation drove him to do what he had not been able to do before. He begged God to forgive him for his many sins. He had confessed his sins in the past, but never asked for forgiveness. This time he prayed with fervency. He had not expected forgiveness. Now, he had come to the point of realizing he needed forgiveness. He could not restore the lives he had taken and he could not snatch back those souls he sent to hell, but he wished he could. He begged God that Geraline would never find out the truth of who he was. Tomas prayed over and over the same desires until he could say no more. He sat back on the concrete porch with his back against a post and tried to recover his composure.

Geraline came around the corner of the house and saw Tomas and immediately sensed that there was something very wrong. "Papa Michael, are you hurt?" There was pain, but it was in his heart and mind and it showed on his face.

"No, sweetheart, I'm just very tired, but I'm okay."

"I saw pastor Dumournay on my way home. Why was he here?"

"Just visiting."

"You wouldn't fib to me, would you?"

"Geraline, you're too suspicious. What have you brought home for supper?"

Father and daughter went inside and began planning for the meal. When Geraline had first come up the mountain to be the maid, Tomas set the rule that they would each prepare their own food, but now they worked side by side. Tomas liked sharing the chore, but his mind could not get away from the subject the pastor presented to him. How could he show the young woman the affection he had for her without raising her hopes for a stronger bond? He enjoyed things the way they were and feared the embarrassment that would come if he had to tell her the whole truth. The longer they shared the same house, the more difficult it would be. She was less a girl and more a woman every day.

*　　　　　　*　　　　　　*

It was on a Monday when two strangers arrived by a charter flight at the airport outside of Cap Haitien and began asking around for an American who may have arrived within the past six months. They gave several of the names which Tomas had used, but no one had heard of anyone by any of them. Someone in the market place said he knew of a man who had been seen around the city during that time period, but no one knew him because he kept pretty much to himself except for a Haitian girl who was with him occasionally. Further inquiries by the strangers did not reveal where this man might be found.

Geraline was in town one day when the two men were making their inquiries and she overheard the nature of the questions. She hurriedly left the city and used a round about way to arrive at the house on the mountain. She informed her Papa Michael of the men and wondered if he was the one about whom they were inquiring. This led Tomas to quickly take the disks containing the expose' and prepare them to be mailed. He had planned to mail them from the Dominican Republic but with people already looking for him in Haiti there was no advantage to the plan.

Tomas gave Jona money for the mailing and entrusted the packages to him. "Get these to the airport and send them on the next flight by the missionary airline. If they want to know who is sending it, just point to the return name on the envelope and say nothing more. The name on the packages was Rev. Mitchell Harrington. If they refuse to take them, bring them back to me immediately." With that done, Tomas prepared to protect Geraline. He would stay at home until he knew that the disks had gotten on the plane and then he planned to make his stand far away from the house.

"Papa, are those men looking for you?"

"They might be. Just trust me that they are bad men. If anyone comes toward the house the dog will alert us. When that happens, I want you to go to the woods and wait until they leave. They must not find you. I'll make sure they follow me."

"But Papa, why are they looking for you?"

"I can't explain it now. Someday I'll tell you the whole story."

Jona returned with the news that the packages were accepted for the next flight."

"Did you see two strangers in town?"

"I saw two white men who were renting motorcycles."

"That confirms it! Jona, you go back to town and stay there. If those men are looking for me, they will hurt, maybe kill, anyone who gets between them and me. Don't argue with me! Here, take this money and find a place to stay for a few days. If you come back here after that and you don't find me here, take Geraline to Pastor Domournay."

"Okay, Boss Man. Hope you be safe."

     *   *   *

The day Jona left the mountain and made his way down to the city, Tagart's men were seen asking directions to the house on the mountain.

Someone pointed in the direction of the Mont Joli Hotel. The two strangers revved their cycles and sped up the road, making the bend at the tennis courts and then the turn beyond to the mountain road. The dog heard them coming and so did Tomas. He gave Geraline a strong embrace and kissed her cheek. She in turn put her arms around his neck and kissed his lips. She didn't want to let him go, but it had to be.

"Go right now to the woods! Hurry! You haven't any time to waste!"

Tomas got on his motorcycle, raced up the driveway and waited at the edge of the road. The two cyclists were not expecting what happened next. As they slowed down to look toward the house overlooking the sea, Bernardo gunned his bike and shot up beside the first man, kicking him over into the second rider. The agents both went down as Tomas sped for town. Tagart's men untangled themselves and went after him.

At the bottom of the hill, Bernardo turned left for two blocks and then left again onto Spanish Street. He whipped beyond the Brise d' Mer Hotel and then made a tight right turn along the Bay Front; a seldom used street. He knew his way around better than the men chasing him who could not anticipate what he would do next. Tomas raced by the docks and on to the main route going east out of the city.

Getting through the congested conglomeration of people, animals, trucks, cars and motorcycles produced a number of near accidents. It was just as difficult for the two men who were after him. They were some eight hundred yards behind and desperately trying to close the gap. The leading chase bike sideswiped a cyclist coming toward him and they both sprawled on the roadway. The second chase bike swung around and continued after Tomas.

Bernardo flashed by the airport entrance and on toward Milot. He looked back and could see his enemy. The partner had recovered and was a quarter of a mile back of the closest man. Tomas slapped at his hip pocket to make sure his weapon was still there. It was. No doubt Tagart's men were well armed. At the road to the little hamlet of Milot, Tomas slid the bike around the right turn so that he would not lose much momentum, gunned the engine, and quickly passed through on the one main street and then on to the entrance to the trail leading up the mountain upon which there stood a huge fortress: the Citadel.

The ticket taker at the gate leaped out of the way and began yelling at Tomas as he sped toward the Sans Souci Palace ruins. He spun his rear tire at the turn toward the other side of the ruins and then regained momentum on the straight section of road until he came to the sharp left where the terrain rose steeply. The mountain trail consisted of uneven rocks and huge flat stones.

Behind Bernardo were the two men and they were coming hard. They had each nearly run over the ticket taker as they raced after Tomas. The climb up the trail bounced the cycles from side to side. It was worse than riding a wild horse. A shot rang out, but the exaggerated movements of the cycles made hitting Tomas next n to impossible. More shots sent projectiles whining off rocks. The chase and the weapons fire continued. Tomas arrived at the half way point where he turned around and returned fire, hitting the front tire of the first cycle. It stopped the man who quickly ditched the bike and ran for cover.

The second cyclist roared toward Bernardo until he hit a large rock and was dumped over the handlebars. Tomas took the chance given to him to turn his machine around and continue up the mountain. He shot over a rise in the road and down a slope. On the other side of the dip the terrain again rose sharply. Tagart's men were on foot, but the advantage to Bernardo was short lived. At the 3,000 foot level his bike coughed to a stop. He was out of gas. One of the bullets fired at him had punctured the gas tank.

Tomas knew where he was going. He wanted his pursuers to meet him at the top of the mountain and settle things there. He wanted them as far away from Geraline and Jona as he could get them. If there was to be any killing, he wanted it done where they would not see it. Like a mother leopard, he wanted to lead them away from his cub. Whatever happened to him, his "daughter" had to be kept safe.

The last five hundred yards of the trail was especially steep, but there wasn't time to stop and catch his breath. Tomas got up onto the flat ground and moved as fast as he was able across the open area to the first entrance to the fortress. He made his way up a flight of stone steps and into the great open concrete court surrounded on all sides by a three story structure made of cement and blocks. At the first flight of narrow steps, Bernardo took them to an upper level and waited behind a large pillar of solid concrete. The pillar was a support for the next level.

Fifteen minutes later Tagart's men came into the fortress and made their way along the walls on opposite sides of the open area. They scanned the upper stories and did not see Tomas. While one watched, the other man went in and out of several doorways to the side rooms.

"He must be up there somewhere." The man pointed to the flat roof.

"Let's get up there, but be careful that he doesn't jump you."

At the same time Tagart's men began to ascend the steps, Tomas slipped from his hiding place and went up to the next level and then onto the flat roof. He waited at the top of the steps. The men were half way to the roof when Bernardo got the drop on them. He leveled his weapon at the first man.

"My best advice to you is to toss your guns down to the floor below. I'm sick of killing, but if I have to take you out, I will."

The thugs hesitated. "Tagart wants you to come with us."

"Toss the weapons now!" The men complied and their pieces clattered against the concrete two stories below.

The first man asked, "Now what?"

"That's a good question. I think it's up to you."

"The Colonel says all is forgiven and he wants you back for a job."

"You really don't expect me to buy that. Come on up here, but don't make any sudden moves."

The killers stepped out onto the expansive flat roof and slowly separated. Each man moved to flank Tomas where they could rush him and one of them might take him down.

"Look Angel, you know how it goes. If we don't come back with you, we have to answer to the Colonel. Make it easy and cooperate."

"If you keep coming toward me, one or both of you will spill blood right where you stand."

Tomas was not the instinctive assassin he once was and his months of inactivity also left him weakened. God and Geraline had changed him. In years past, the two men would already be dead. Now, if he could muster up the strength, he would use his hand to hand fighting ability and try to subdue his adversaries without deliberately taking their lives.

To the surprise of Tagart's men, Tomas tossed his weapon over the side of the fortress. The moment they realized what he had done, they rushed him. He sidestepped one and did a throat chop on the other that sent him to his knees. The one man still standing made another move to strike Tomas, but caught a fist flush on the nose that broke the bones.

The first man recovered from his chocking and tackled Tomas, who rolled over and then back on his feet like a cat, but he had no more room to back away. He was at the very edge of the roof. Both men rushed forward at the same time. Tomas grabbed one of them and his momentum carried him and Tagart's man over the edge. They dropped together until their bodies struck the severe slope of the terrain some thirty feet below and that caused each man to roll and bounce violently another forty feet into the bottom of a rocky ravine where their bodies came to rest.

The second attacker had barely managed to keep from going over and joining the other bodies in a seventy foot fall. He stood for a moment and stared at the forms sprawled in the ravine and then ran across the roof that encircled the open space and descended the steps on the opposite side from where Tomas went off the roof. Workers and visitors were beginning to gather to discover the cause of the brief fight. They stood and looked at the two figures below them.

✳   ✳   ✳

Going down the mountain was much easier and quicker than the hike to the top for Tagart's man. At the point on the trail where he had been tossed from his motorcycle, Jack Cruse stopped and set his bike upright. He was able to kick start the motor. Dirt and stones flew as the man and his cycle bumped over rocks until reaching the road that skirted the palace ruins. There, he stopped long enough to try his satellite cell phone.

"Give me the Colonel, now!"

"Colonel, Jack here. Your Chameleon bit off more than he could chew. He's toast, but so is Frank."

"I want proof!"

"Can't provide it, Colonel! The body is at the bottom of a ravine. He took a header with Frank and I saw the bodies. I can give you details when I get back. Right now I have to make a run for it and get out of this country."

With that, Jack stuffed the phone in his pocket and raced for the airport. On the way he made another call. This one was to the pilot of the private jet. "Get the engines warmed. I'm ten minutes out and we have to get airborne as soon as I get there."

"What about customs?"

"Forget customs! Just let these back water people try to stop us. They don't have an Air Force! Break out the M-sixteen, just in case."

✳　　　　　✳　　　　　✳

Back at the house above Cap Haitien, Geraline sat on the side of Tomas' bed and hugged his pillow tightly against her body. The beautiful, petite Haitian girl whose features reflected a hint of European ancestry cried a prayer into the pillow over and over, "Please, dear Jesus, let my Papa come home to me! Let my Papa come home!"

At the Citadel, a group of onlookers were fascinated with what had happened. As they began to turn away from looking at the bodies in the ravine someone asked, "Who were they?"

Another answered, "I don't know. I have seen the one man in Cap Haitien. It is rumored that he lived in a house above the city. I have seen him many times with a young woman. I think she was his servant, but I never learned his name."

Suddenly a Citadel worker shouted, "Hey! Look down there! One man still moves!"

Chapter Fourteen

REDEMPTION

With great difficulty, rescuers made their way down the side of the mountain to the place where Tomas and the body of his attacker lay among the rocks. They found a spark of life in Bernardo, but the other man's head had hit one of the large boulders and he was dead. He was left where his body came to rest after violently rolling and thrashing down the side of the promontory upon which the fortress was built. Tomas' attacker had absorbed most of the force of the collision with the extreme slope of the ground.

As gently as it could be done, men carried Tomas in a makeshift stretcher out of the ravine. It was easy to see that he had multiple broken bones, contusions, abrasions, and possibly internal injuries. Once his fractured body was off the mountain, he was transported to the Northern Haiti Hospital. It was the best medical facility available.

Bernardo was innervated and given drugs to try to deal with the shock his body had endured during the fall from the wall. Both of his legs were fractured below the knees, his pelvis was also fractured, and his right forearm had a compound break. In addition to those injuries, Tomas had suffered a serve concussion and a dislocated right shoulder. His internal injuries included a ruptured spleen and a punctured lung from fractured ribs. The prognosis was not promising and the doctors considered having Tomas flown to the United States for treatment, but they believed the risk in moving him was too great.

The spleen was removed and the lung re-inflated before the medical staff proceeded to set the broken bones and place his arm and legs in casts. Weeks went by so slowly and Geraline was allowed to stay on a cot in the corner of Tomas' room so that she could be near him at all times.

She attended to his every need and helped him pass the long hours while he healed. Her presence was a major factor in his recovery.

Weeks later, when Bernardo was able to get out of bed and began to hobble around the room, his strength slowly returned but he was never going to be the robust macho man he was before the fall. Rehabilitation made him mobile but far from agile. The day finally came when Tomas was released to return to his home. He was taken by a SUV up the mountain road and assisted into his house. The broken bones had knitted, but he was far from recovered. Tomas' movements were painful and slow and Geraline was always by his side to help with anything he required. It was difficult for Tomas to have to rely upon anyone. He had always been self-sufficient. Geraline's Papa Michael was a shadow of the man who first employed her as a maid. She was just happy to have him alive and in her care.

Tomas Bernardo continued to chaff and fret because of his inabilities. He was becoming more depressed with each passing day in spite of every effort by Geraline to ease his physical and mental suffering. Weeks went by with Tomas feeling useless, but one morning there was a change. During the night Tomas came to the conclusion that his many brushes with death, including the fall from the Citadel, had shortened his life expectancy and he had to do something immediately to see to it that Geraline would have what she needed to live a decent life when he was gone.

Tomas had Jona make preparations to transport him to the Dominican Republic. At an international bank he used the pen numbers of his overseas accounts to transfer assets from the United States deposited under aliases. It was necessary to make several limited transfers over a period of months and that required several trips to the Dominican Republic to clear out the various accounts where he had stashed the money he gained from his missions as a mercenary.

The next step in Bernardo's plan was to adopt Geraline and make her his legal heir. There was a fly in that ointment. It was the beautiful Geraline. "Michael, I have loved being thought of as your daughter, but you know I love you in a different way. If you want to make me your heir, I want it to be as Madam Bernardo."

"Where did you come up with that name?" Tomas was shocked. He had not told anyone his real name.

"You did a lot of talking in your nightmares "

"Geraline, you don't want to be saddled with a broken down man like me. Furthermore, you know nothing about what I did before I came to Haiti."

"Oh, but I do. When you were in the hospital I found the printed copy of the document you sent to the United States. You are not the man I saw in those pages. That man is dead. I don't care how many names you had or what you were required to do then. This is now and I am no longer the little maid you employed. That girl no longer exists. I am a woman and my love for you is enough to make up for the past."

"But, I can't give you a family. I can't even walk around without these canes. You deserve much better!"

"Tomas Bernardo, I will be the judge of who and what I deserve. If we want children there are more orphans out there than we could ever afford to bring to this house. Surely there would be one or more who could use a loving home."

Tomas was taken back. The little maid had turned into an assertive woman and it pleased him. He would no longer go by any aliases. He was again Tomas Bernardo, the name he was given by his parents.

Pastor Dumournay was contacted and he made his way up the mountain to perform a wedding, but before he officiated there were some things he wanted clarified. "I know that Geraline has loved you for a long time. I also know that you both have learned a great deal about each other over the past two years, but Michael, I mean Tomas, do you love Geraline with the love a husband should have for his wife?"

"Yes, Pastor, I do. I tried to deny it, but I have faced the truth at last."

"Geraline, this man is not the one you fell in love with when you first came into his employment. He is broken and battered. Does that matter to you even a little?"

"No, Pastor. My love is stronger than ever now that I know he will never reject me as a woman."

"Then, my children, I am ready to have you exchange your vows."

The ceremony was brief and to the point. A ring was given by Tomas to his wife and they kissed. It was something new for them, since they had seldom shown any physical affection before the wedding. One embrace and kiss was not enough.

"Children, save that for after I leave. The service is not over until you both jump over the broomstick."

"Pastor, if it is all the same to you, I'll just step over the broomstick. My jumping days are over."

The room was filled with laughter as Jona and two couples from the church witnessed the wedding and gave a loud round of applause when Pastor Dumournay pronounced Tomas and Geraline husband and wife. Following a prayer by the pastor, he and the guest left the mountain.

*　　　　　*　　　　　*

With the funds in the Dominican Republic transferred to new accounts in Gerline's name along with the title to the house, Tomas began to relax and his health improved slightly. He wanted something to do, but could not decided what it should be. Geraline came up with the answer. "You will write a book. It will be titled, 'Out of the Darkness and Into the Light': the story of a chameleon that became a papillon."

"And what is a papillon?"

"A butterfly."

"Me, a butterfly?"

"Yes, my husband. Whatever you were before, you are now gentle and kind. You are my papillon. Jesus has transformed you."

"If I'm gentle, it is also because of you. I like your idea of the book. It will keep my mind occupied. But then, you need to be doing something and I have an idea. We'll have teachers come to the house to instruct you in the subjects of English Grammar, along with computer skills and business management."

Arrangements were made so that Tomas and Geraline became absorbed in their respective projects. At the end of six months Michael had roughed out his story and set it aside to help Geraline with her studies. She progressed rapidly and was very adaptable. The time came after another six months that she was ready for a new challenge.

"Tomas, would you be willing to consider adopting a child?"

"It's odd, but that has been on my mind lately, but we have to make sure that the child is truly an orphan and not one the parents have just abandoned. They could come back someday and make a claim for the child or demand money for us to keep it."

"Pastor Dumournay can help us with that."

Weeks passed before the pastor was able to bring a little three year old girl for the couple to consider. There was an immediate attachment. The adoption process began while the Bernardos acted as foster parents. The child's name was Petit Fleur; meaning little flower, but Geraline chose to call her the biblical name, Ruth. She was soon answering to Little Ruth.

In a few months another mouth was added to the Bernardo household. His name was Jean and with his arrival an idea was born. "Geraline we need to add some rooms to the house along with another bathroom."

"My husband, I think we should add many rooms and two more bathrooms."

"Why?"

"Because God has told me that we should not be selfish. There are more children who need a home."

"But the expense!"

"God will provide. We have a good sum of money and if it is properly managed and we begin to use part of the land to have a large garden and some goats, we can take on more children. We can have a better room for Jona and turn his shed into a chicken house."

"That would mean a great deal of work for you. I'm not able to do much."

"There are people who will work for food and a little pay. I was once a homeless child and you were an outcast. We are the right people to do this."

Tomas greatly surprised. "My love, you have become quite a woman and a fine manager. I believe in you. We can do this with God's help."

"There are missionary groups in the north of Haiti who can advise us, but what shall we call our home?"

Tomas thought for a moment; "I believe it should be 'The House of New Life,' because we have each found a new beginning here."

"Yes, that will be the name, The House of New Life."

           *   *   *

A congressional sub-committee called for an investigation of the allegations found in a document delivered to a Senator by a news organization. At the center of the probe was a man named Tag Tagart. He was summoned to a meeting of the committee and questioned about the allegations contained in the transcript.

"Mr. Tagart, you have been referred to in this document as Colonel Tagart, but our investigators have discovered that you left the military twenty years ago with the rank of major. How do you account for the change in rank, seeing that you have not been in the active or inactive reserves since you resigned?"

"Senator, on advise of counsel, I respectfully decline to answer the question."

"Mr. Tagart, are you invoking the fifth amendment over being asked whether you go by Colonel Tagart?"

"Sir, I respectfully decline to answer."

"You have been accused in this document of having headed up a clandestine and independent assassination squad. Don't you think you should respond to that?"

"Senator, my council advises me not to answer on the ground that it might incriminate me."

"Well, Mister, it seems to me that your refusal to answer is self-incrimination!"

The man sitting to the right of Tagart slid the microphone over in front of himself. "Senator, on behalf of my client, I object to your characterization that my client's silence indicates admitting to some sort of guilt. Until you have a witness we can face and some sort of evidence instead of anonymous allegations, he has nothing to say to your committee."

Senator Tormain leaned closer to his own microphone. "I remind you, counselor, that this is not a court of law. It is an inquiry and Mr. Tagart, or whoever he really is, has taken an oath to tell the truth! He will either answer the questions of this committee or he will be in contempt of Congress!"

"Senator Tormain, there is still the fifth amendment and my client has the right not to speak."

"Mister Tagart, by your silence you lead me to believe that these accusations are factual; that you are a traitor to your country and that you have either committed murder or have caused others to commit murder in the name of this country which you do not legally represent in any fashion!"

Being accused by the senator of traitorous actions in front of the committee and the news organizations covering the hearings pushed

Tagart's button and he boiled over with rage. Ignoring his attorney's orders for him to sit down and keep quiet, Tagart sounded off. "You pompous bag of wind, I served this country in combat in places you wouldn't even stick your toe! I've bled for this nation and what did I get in return? I got passed over for promotion twice while other less qualified men got the rank because they probably knew some fat bellied pig like you!" Tagart didn't stop with those commits but became vulgar in his verbal assault of the senator.

Before Tormain could respond, and as the chairman of the committee began banging his gavel for order, Tagart grabbed his chest, reeled backward into his chair and then slumped forward with his face on the table. The attorney felt for a pulse. "Senators, I believe this man has just died!"

✳   ✳   ✳

Back on the mountain at Cap Haitien, now that the addition of a wing on Tomas' and Geraline's house containing sleeping rooms for a dozen children was completed, it was time to select those who were most in need of a safe place to live and be loved. With the help of volunteer construction teams from the United States, the work on the house had gone rather quickly. A faith based missionary group near Cap Haitien had made the arrangements for the workers and housed them at the mission's compound.

Geraline had become a very efficient business manager and a loving mother to the children, four of whom she and Tomas had adopted. The people who helped build the addition to the house returned to see how it was being used and were so pleased that they gave generously to the budget of The House of New Life. They also began to raise funds from people they knew in the States who had an interest in Haitian orphans. The ministry was on a sound financial footing, but a cloud began to appear on the horizon.

Tomas was beginning to lose his battle with his many health issues. His book was complete, but he decided it should not be published. He felt it needed more editing and he was not strong enough to work on it any longer. One rainy Sunday morning, Geraline went into the bedroom to awaken her husband and found that his spirit had left the body.

✳   ✳   ✳

There was a huge gathering of people around the grave located at the place Tomas used to stand and look out over the water. People had only known the man as Michael. They knew nothing of who he was before he arrived in Haiti and bought the house on the mountain. He could no longer look out over the water. Those days were over. Just the same, it seemed appropriate for his body to be laid in that place overlooking the bay.

When everyone left, Geraline and Pastor Dumournay stood beside the grave and wondered what it would be like on that great resurrection morning that the Apostle Paul described when the bodies of believers who had died before the return of Jesus were raised and glorified along with the believers who would be alive at that glorious moment.

"Pastor Dumouray, Tomas came to me as a chameleon, but he left this earth a papillon. It shows how a man can be transformed when he surrenders himself to our Lord. God also used Tomas to change me."

"Geraline, what is this chameleon of which you speak?"

"Someday I will explain it. Perhaps I will let you read about it in Tomas' own words. I am so glad the man I married was the butterfly and not the chameleon."

"Yes my child, your Tomas had indeed become a new creature in Christ."

"Pastor, I hope I will be standing right here when it happens that I will join Tomas and be given a new resurrection body and be lifted up as we meet Jesus together in the air. Oh, how I pray that the day will be soon. Until then, I have these little one's to love."

✳   ✳   ✳